HE WAS DORSAI

of the Dorsai, his mother a Kenwick, his father a Graeme, names so very old their origin was buried in the prehistory of the Mother Planet. His courage was unquestioned, his world unblemished. He had headed his class. His very blood and bones were the heritage of a long line of great professional soldiers. No blot of dishonor had ever marred that roll of warriors, no home had ever been burnt, its inhabitants scattered and hiding their family shame under new names, because of some failure on the part of one of the family's sons. And yet, they doubted.

For he was somehow . . . different.

DORSAI! is Gordon R. Dickson's classic science fiction novel—the culmination of his projection of a genetically created line of super-soldiers. Donal Graeme was indeed different—and the story of how that difference was determined and resolved is one not easily forgotten.

DORSAI!

GORDON R. DICKSON

DAW BOOKS, INC.
DONALD A. WOLLHEIM, PUBLISHER

1301 Avenue of the Americas
New York, N. Y.   10019

FIRST PRINTING, FEBRUARY 1976

3 4 5 6 7 8 9

CADET

~~~~~~

The boy was odd.

This much he knew for himself. This much he had heard his seniors—his mother, his father, his uncles, the officers at the Academy—mention to each other, nodding their heads confidentially, not once but many times during his short eighteen years of life, leading up to this day. Now, apart, wandering the empty rec fields in the long, amber twilight before returning to his home and the graduation supper awaiting him there, he admitted to the oddness—whether truly in himself, or only in what others thought of him.

"An odd boy," he had overheard the Commandant at the Academy saying once to the Mathematics Officer, "you never know which way he'll jump."

Back at home right now, the family would be waiting his return—unsure of which way he would jump. They would be half expecting him to refuse his Outgoing. Why? He had never given them any cause to doubt. He was Dorsai of the Dorsai, his mother a Kenwick, his father a Graeme, names so very old their origin was buried in the prehistory of the Mother Planet. His courage was unquestioned, his word unblemished. He had headed his class. His very blood and bones were the heritage of a long line of great professional soldiers. No blot of dishonor had ever marred that roll of warriors, no home had ever been burnt, its inhabitants scattered and hiding their family shame under new names, because of some failure on the part of one of the family's sons. And yet, they doubted.

He came to the fence that marked off the high hurdles from the jump pits, and leaned on it with both elbows, the tunic of a Senior Cadet pulled tight across his shoulders. In what way was he odd, he wondered into the wide glow of the sunset? How was he different?

He put himself apart from him in his mind's eye, and considered himself. A slim young man of eighteen years—tall, but not tall by Dorsai standards, strong, but not strong by Dorsai standards. His face was the face of his father, sharp and angular, straight-nosed; but without his father's massiveness of bones. His coloring was the dark coloring of the Dorsai, hair straight and black and a little coarse. Only his eyes— those indeterminate eyes that were no definite color but went from gray to green to blue with his shifting moods—were not to be found elsewhere on his family trees. But surely eyes alone could not account for a reputation of oddness?

There was, of course, his temper. He had inherited, in full measure, those cold, sudden, utterly murderous Dorsai rages which had made his people such that no sane man cared to cross one of them without good reason. But that was a common trait; and if the Dorsai thought of Donal Graeme as odd, it could not be for that alone.

Was it, he wondered now, gazing into the sunset, that even in his rages he was a little too calculating —a little too controlled and remote? And as he thought that thought, all his strangeness, all his oddness came on him with a rush, together with that weird sense of disembodiment that had afflicted him, now and again, ever since his birth.

It came always at moments like this, riding the shoulders of fatigue and some great emotion. He remembered it as a very young boy in the Academy chapel at evening service, half-faint with hunger after the long day of hard military exercises and harder lesson. The sunset, as now, came slanting in through the high windows on the bare, highly polished walls and the solidographs of famous battles inset in them. He stood among the rows of his classmates between the hard, low benches, the ranked male voices, from the youngest cadet to the deep man-voices of the officers in the rear, riding the deep, solemn notes of the Recessional—that which was known as the Dorsai Hymn now, wherever man had gone, and which a man named Kipling had written the words of, eight centuries before.

> . . . Far called, our navies melt away,
> On dune and headland sinks the fire.
> Lo! All our pomp of yesterday,
> Is one with Nineveh, and Tyre . . .

As he had remembered it being sung at the burial service when his youngest uncle's ashes had been brought back from the slagged battlefield of Donneswort, on Freiland, third planet circling the star of Arcturus.

> . . . For heathen heart that puts her trust
> In reeking tube and iron shard,
> All valiant dust, that builds on dust,
> And guarding, calls not thee to guard . . .

And he had sung with the rest, feeling then, as now, the final words in the innermost recesses of his heart.

> . . . For frantic boast and foolish word—
> *Thy Mercy on Thy People, Lord!*

A chill shiver ran down his back. The enchantment was complete. Far and wide about him the red and dying light flooded the level land. In the farther sky the black dot of a hawk circled. But here by the fence and the high hurdles, he stood removed and detached, enclosed by some clear, transparent wall that set him apart from all the universe, alone, untouchable and enraptured. The inhabited worlds and their suns sank and dwindled in his mind's eye; and he felt the siren, deadly pull of that ocean of some great, hidden purpose that promised him at once fulfillment and a final dissolution. He stood on its brink and its waves lapped at his feet; and, as always, he strove to lift his foot and step forward into its depths and be lost forever, but some small part of him cried out against the self-destruction and held him back.

Then suddenly—as suddenly as it had come—the spell was broken. He turned toward home.

As he came to the front entrance, he found his father waiting for him, in the half-shadow leaning with his wide shoulders spread above the slim metal shaft of his cane.

"Be welcome to this house," said his father and straightened up. "You'd better get out of that uniform and into some man's clothes. Dinner will be ready in half an hour."

MAN

The men of the household of Eachan Khan Graeme sat around the long, shimmering slab of the dining board in the long and shadowy room, at their drinking after the women and children had retired. They were not all present, nor—short of a minor miracle—was it ever likely that they would be, in this life. Of sixteen adult males, nine were off at the wars among the stars, one was undergoing reconstructive surgery at the hospital in Foralie, and the eldest, Donal's grand-uncle, Kamal, was quietly dying in his own room at the back of the household with an oxygen tube up his nose and the faint scent of the bay lilac to remind him of his Maran wife, now forty years dead. Sitting at the table were five—of which, since three o'clock this afternoon—Donal was one.

Those others who were present to welcome him to his adulthood were Eachan, his father; Mor, his elder brother, who was home on leave from the Friendlies; and his twin uncles Ian and Kensie, who had been next in age above that James who had died at Don-neswort. They sat grouped around the high end of the table, Eachan at its head, with his two sons on his right and his two younger twin brothers on his left.

"They had good officers when I was there," Eachan was saying. He leaned over to fill Donal's glass, and Donal took it up automatically, listening with both ears.

9

"Freilanders all," said Ian, the grimmer of the two dark twins. "They run to stiffness of organization without combat to shake them up. Kensie says Mara or Kultis, and I say why not?"

"They have full companies of Dorsai there, I hear," said Mor, at Donal's right. The deep voice of Eachan answered from his left.

"They're show guards. I know of those. Why make a cake of nothing but icing? The Bond of Kultis likes to think of having an unmatched bodyguard; but they'd be farmed out to the troops fast enough in case of real trouble between the stairs."

"And meanwhile," put in Kensie, with a sudden smile that split his dark face, "no action. Peacetime soldiering goes sour. The outfits split up into little cliques, the cake-fighters move in and an actual man —a Dorsai—becomes an ornament."

"Good," said Eachan, nodding. Donal swallowed absently from his glass and the unaccustomed whiskey burned fiercely at the back of his nose and throat. Little pricklings of sweat popped out on his forehead; but he ignored them, concentrating on what was being said. This talk was all for his benefit, he knew. He was a man now, and could no longer be told what to do. The choice was his, about where he would go to take service, and they were helping him with what knowledge they had, of the eight systems and their ways.

". . . I was never great for garrison duty myself," Eachan was continuing. "A mercenary's job is to train, maintain and fight; but when all's said and done, the fighting's the thing. Not that everyone's of my mind. There are Dorsai and Dorsai—and not all Dorsai are Graemes."

"The Friendlies, now—" said Mor, and stopped with a glance at his father, afraid that he had interrupted.

"Go on," said Eachan, nodding.

"I was just about to point out," said Mor, "there's plenty of action on Association—and Harmony, too, I hear. The sects will always be fighting against each other. And there's bodyguard work—"

"Catch us being personal gunmen," said Ian, who—being closer in age to Mor than Mor's father—did not feel the need to be quite so polite. "That's no job for a soldier."

"I didn't mean to suggest it," said Mor, turning to his uncle. "But the psalm-singers rate it high among themselves, and that takes some of their best talent. It leaves the field posts open for mercenaries."

"True enough," said Kensie, equably. "And if they had less fanatics and more officers, those two worlds would be putting strong forces out between the stars. But a priest-soldier is only troublesome when he's more soldier than priest."

"I'll back that," said Mor. "This last skirmish I was in on Association, an elder came down the line after we'd taken one little town and wanted five of my men for hangmen."

"What did you do?" asked Kensie.

"Referred him to my Commandant—and then got to the old man first and told him that if he could find five men in my force who actually wanted such a job, he could transfer them out the next day."

Ian nodded.

"Nothing spoils a man for battle like playing butcher," he said.

"The old man got that," said Mor. "They got their hangmen, I heard—but not from me."

"The lusts are vampires," said Eachan, heavily, from the head of the table. "Soldiering is a pure art. A man with a taste for blood, money or women was one I never trusted."

"The women are fine on Mara and Kultis," grinned Mor. "I hear."

"I'll not deny it," said Kensie, merrily. "But you've got to come home, some day."

"God grant that you all may," said Eachan, somberly. "I am a Dorsai and a Graeme, but if this little world of ours had something else to trade for the contracts of out-world professionals besides the blood of our best fighting men, I'd be more pleased."

"Would *you* have stayed home, Eachan," said Mor, "when you were young and had two good legs?"

"No, Mor," said Eachan, heavily. "But there are other arts, beside the art of war—even for a Dorsai." He looked at his eldest son. "When our forefathers settled this world less than a hundred and fifty years ago, it wasn't with the intention of providing gun-fodder for the other eight systems. They only wanted a world where no man could bend the destinies of another man against that second man's will."

"And that we have," said Ian, bleakly.

"And that we have," echoed Eachan. "The Dorsai is a free world where any man can do as he likes as long as he respects the rights of his neighbor. Not all the other eight systems combined would like to try their luck with this one world. But the price—the price—" He shook his head and refilled his glass.

"Now those are heavy words for a son who's just going out," said Kensie. "There's a lot of good in life just the way she is now. Besides, it's economic pressures we're under today, not military. Who'd want the Dorsai, anyway, besides us? We're all nut here, and very little kernel. Take one of the rich new worlds— like Ceta under Tau Ceti—or one of the richer, older worlds like Freiland, or Newton—or even old Venus herself. They've got cause to worry. They're the ones that are at each other's throats for the best scientists, the best technicians, the top artists and doctors. And the more work for us and the better life for us, because of it."

"Eachan's right though, Kensie," growled Ian. "They still dream of squeezing our free people up into one lump and then negotiating with that lump for the force to get the whip hand over all the other worlds." He leaned forward across the table toward Eachan and in the muted light of the dining room Donal saw the sudden white flash of the seared scar that coiled up his forearm like a snake and was lost in the loose sleeve of his short, undress tunic. "That's the danger we'll never be free of."

"As long as the cantons remain independent of the Council," said Eachan, "and the families remain independent of the cantons, there'll be no success for them, Ian." He nodded at all about the table. "That's my end of the job here at home. You can go out to the wars with easy consciences. I promise you your children will grow up free in this house—free of any man's will—or the house will no longer stand."

"I trust you," said Ian. His eyes were gleaming pale as the scar in the dimness and he was very close to that Dorsai violence of emotion that was at once so cold and so deadly. "I have two boys now under this roof. But remember no men are perfect—even the Dorsai. There was Mahub Van Ghent only five years back, who dreamed about a little kingdom among the Dorsai in the Midland South—only five years ago, Eachan!"

"He was on the other side of the world," said Eachan. "And he's dead now, at the hand of one of the Benali, his closest neighbor. His home is burnt and no man acknowledges himself a Van Ghent any more. What more do you want?"

"He should have been stopped sooner."

"Each man has a right to his own destiny," said

Eachan, softly. "Until he crosses the line into another man's. His family has suffered enough."

"Yes," said Ian. He was calming down. He poured himself another drink. "That's true—that's true. They're not to blame."

"About the Exotics—" said Mor, gently.

"Oh, yes," answered Kensie, as if the twin brother that was so much a part of himself had never gotten excited at all. "Mara and Kultis—interesting worlds. Don't mistake them if you ever go there, Mor—or you either, Donal. They're sharp enough, for all their art and robes and trappings. They won't fight themselves, but they know how to hire good men. There's things being done on Mara and Kultis—and not only in the arts. Meet one of their psychologists, one time."

"They're honest," said Eachan.

"That, too," said Kensie. "But what catches at me is the fact they're going some place, in their own way. If I had to pick one of the other worlds to be born on—"

"I would always be a soldier," said Mor.

"You think so now," said Kensie, and drank. "You think so now. But it's a wild civilization, this year of our Lord, 2403, with its personality split a dozen different ways by a dozen different cultures. Less than five hundred years ago the average man never dreamed of getting his feet off the ground. And the farther we go the faster. And the faster the farther."

"It's the Venus group forcing that, isn't it?" asked Donal, his youthful reticence all burnt away in the hot fumes of the whiskey.

"Don't you think it," said Kensie. "Science is only one road to the future. Old Venus, Old Mars—Cassida, Newton—maybe they've had their day. Project Blaine's a rich and powerful old man, but he doesn't know all the new tricks they're dreaming up on Mara and Kultis, or the Friendlies—or Ceta, for that matter. Make it a point to take two good looks at things when you get out among the stars, you two young ones, because nine times out of ten that first glance will leave you fooled."

"Listen to him, boys," said Eachan from the top of the table. "Your uncle Kensie's a man and a half above the shoulders. I just wish I had as good advice to give you. Tell them, Kensie."

"Nothing stands still," said Kensie—and with those three words, the whiskey seemed to go to Donal's head in a rush, the table and the dark harsh-boned faces before him seemed to swim in the dimness of the dining room, and Kensie's voice came roaring at him as if from a great distance. "Everything changes, and that's what you must bear in mind. What was true yesterday about something may not be true today. So remember that and take no man's word about something without reservation, even mine. We have multiplied like the biblical locusts and spread out among the stars, splitting into different groups with different ways. Now, while we still seem to be rushing forward to where I have no idea, at a terrific rate, increasing all the time, I have this feeling—as if we are all poised, hanging on the brink of something, something great and different and maybe terrible. It's a time to walk cautious, it is indeed."

"I'll be the greatest general that ever was!" cried Donal, and was startled as the rest to hear the words leap, stumbling and thick-tongued, but loud, from within him. "They'll see—I'll show them what a Dorsai can be!"

He was aware of them looking at him, though all their faces were blurred, except—by some trick of vision—that of Kensie, diagonally across the table from him. Kensie was considering him with somber, reading eyes. Donal was conscious of his father's hand on his shoulder.

"Time to turn in," said his father.

"You'll see—"said Donal, thickly. But they were all rising, picking up their glasses and turning to his father, who held his own glass up.

"May we all meet again," said his father. And they drank, standing. The remains of the whiskey in his glass flowed tasteless as water down Donal's tongue and throat—and for a second everything cleared and he saw these tall men standing around him. Big, even for Dorsai, they were; even his brother Mor topping him by half a head, so that he stood like a half-grown boy among them. But at that same instant of vision he was suddenly wrung with a terrible tenderness and pity for them, as if he was the grown one, and they the children to be protected. He opened his mouth to say, for once in his life, how much he loved them, and how always he would be there to take care of them—and then the fog closed down again; and he was only aware of Mor leading him stumblingly to his room.

Later, he opened his eyes in the darkness to become aware of a dim figure drawing the curtains of his room against the bright new light of the double moon, just risen. It was his mother; and with a sudden, reflexive action he rolled off his bed and lurched to her and put his hands on her shoulders.

"Mother—" he said.

She looked up at him with a pale face softened by the moonlight.

"Donal," she said tenderly, putting her arms around him. "You'll catch cold, Donal."

"Mother—" he said, thickly. "If you ever need me . . . to take care of you—"

"Oh, my boy," she said, holding his hard young

body tightly to her, "take care of yourself; my boy . . .
my boy—."

MERCENARY

~~~~~~

Donal shrugged his shoulders in the tight civilian
half-jacket and considered its fit as reflected in the
mirror of his tiny, boxlike cabin. The mirror gave him
back the image of someone almost a stranger. So
much difference had three short weeks brought
about in him, already. Not that he was so different,
but his own appraisal of himself had changed; so that
it was not merely the Spanish-style jacket, the skin-
tight under-tunic, and the narrow trousers that disappeared into boots as black as all the rest of the
costume, that made him unfamiliar to himself—but
the body within. Association with the men of other
worlds had done this to his point of view. Their relative shortness had made him tall, their softness had
made him hard, their untrained bodies had made his
balanced and sure. Outbound from the Dorsai to
Arcturus and surrounded by other Dorsai passengers,
he had not noticed the gradual change. Only in the
vast terminal on Newton, surrounded by their noisy
thousands, had it come on him, all at once. And now,
transhipped and outbound for the Friendlies, facing
his first dinner on board a luxury-class liner where
there would probably be no others from his world, he
gazed at himself in the mirror and felt himself as
suddenly come of age.

He went out through the door of his cabin, letting it latch quietly behind him, and turned right in the tightly narrow, metal-walled corridor faintly stale with the smell of dust from the carpet underfoot. He walked down its silence toward the main lounge and pushed through a heavy sealing door that sucked shut behind him, into the corridor of the next section.

He stepped into the intersection of the little cross corridor that led right and left to the washrooms of the section ahead—and almost strode directly into a slim, tall girl in an ankle-length, blue dress of severe and conservative cut, who stood by the water fountain at the point of the intersection. She moved hastily back out of his way with a little intake of breath, backing into the corridor to the women's washroom. They stared at each other, halted, for a second.

"Forgive me," said Donal, and took two steps onward—but between these and a third, some sudden swift prompting made him change his mind without warning; and he turned back.

"If you don't mind—" he said.

"Oh, excuse me." She moved back again from the water fountain. He bent to drink; and when he raised his head from the fountain, he looked her full in the face again and recognized what had brought him back. The girl was frightened; and that strange, dark ocean of feeling that lay at the back of his oddness had stirred to the gust of her palpable fear.

He saw her now, clearly and at once, at close range. She was older than he had thought at first—at least in her early twenties. But there was a clear-eyed immaturity about her—a hint that her full beauty would come later in life, and much later than that of the usual woman. Now, she was not yet beautiful; merely wholesome-looking. Her hair was a light brown, verging into chestnut, her eyes wide-spaced and so clearly green that, opening as she felt the full interest of his close gaze, they drove all the other color about her from his mind. Her nose was slim and straight, her mouth a little wide, her chin firm; and the whole of her face so perfectly in balance, the left side with the right, that it approached the artificiality of some sculptor's creation.

"Yes?" she said, on a little gasping intake of breath —and he saw, suddenly, that she was shrinking from him and his close survey of her.

He frowned at her. His thoughts were galloping ahead with the situation, so that when he spoke, it was unconsciously in the middle of the conversation he had in mind, rather than at the beginning.

"Tell me about it," said Donal.

"You?" she said. Her hand went to her throat above the high collar of her dress. Then, before he could speak again, it fell to her side and some of the tightness leaked out of her. "Oh," she said. "I see."

"See what?" said Donal, a little sharply; for unconsciously he had fallen into the tone he would have used to a junior cadet these last few years, if he had discovered one of them in some difficulty. "You'll have to tell me what your trouble is, if I'm going to be any help to you."

"Tell you—?" she looked desperately around her, as if expecting someone to come upon them at any moment. "How do I know you're what you say you are?"

For the first time Donal check-reined the horses of his galloping estimate of the situation; and, looking back, discovered a possible misconception on her part.

"I didn't say I was anybody," he answered. "And in fact—I'm not. I just happened to be passing by and saw you seemed upset about something. I offered to help."

"Help?" Her eyes widened again and her face suddenly paled. "Oh, no—" she murmured, and tried to go around him. "Please let me go. Pleasel"

He stood his ground.

"You were ready to accept help from someone like me, if he could only provide proofs of identity, a second ago," said Donal. "You might as well tell me the rest of it."

That stopped her efforts to escape. She stiffened, facing him.

"I haven't told you anything."

"Only," said Donal, ironically, "that you were waiting here for someone. That you did not know that someone by sight, but expected him to be a man. And that you were not sure of his bona fides, but very much afraid of missing him." He heard the hard edge in his own voice and forced it to be more gentle. "Also that you're very frightened and not very experienced at what you're doing. Logic could take it further."

But she had herself under control now.

"Will you move out of the way and let me by?" she said evenly.

"Logic might make it that what you're engaged in is something illegal," he replied.

She sagged under the impact of his last word as if it had been a blow; and, turning her face blindly to the wall, she leaned against it.

"What are you?" she said brokenly. "Did they send you to trap me?"

"I tell you," said Donal, with just a hint of exasperation, "I'm nothing but a passer-by who thought maybe I could help."

"Oh, I don't believe you!" she said, twisting her face away from him. "If you're really nobody . . . if nobody sent you . . . you'll let me go. And forget you ever saw me."

"Small sense in that," said Donal. "You need help

evidently. I'm equipped to give it. I'm a professional soldier. A Dorsai."

"Oh," she said. The tension drained from her. She stood straighter and met his eyes with a look in which he thought he read some contempt. "One of those."

"Yes," he said. Then frowned. "What do you mean *one of those?*"

"I understand," she answered. "You're a mercenary."

"I prefer the term professional soldier," he said—a little stiffly in his turn.

"The point is," she said, "you're for hire."

He felt himself growing cold and angry. He inclined his head to her and stepped back, leaving her way clear. "My mistake," he said, and turned to leave her.

"No, wait a minute," she said. "Now that I know what you really are, there's no reason why I can't use you."

"None at all, of course," said Donal.

She reached in through a slit in her tight gown and produced a small, thick folding of some printed matter, which she pushed into his hand.

"You see this is destroyed," she said. "I'll pay you— whatever the usual rates are." Her eyes widened suddenly as she saw him unfold what he held and start to read it. "What are you doing? You aren't supposed to read that! How dare you!"

She grabbed for the sheet, but he pushed her back absently with one hand. His gaze was busily running down the form she had given him, his own eyes widening at the sight of the facsimile portrait on it, which was that of the girl herself.

"Anea Marlivana," he said. "Select of Kultis."

"Well, what if I am?" she blazed. "What about it?"

"Only," said Donal, "that I expected your genes to imply intelligence."

Her mouth fell open.

"What do you mean by that?"

"Only that you're one of the worst fools I've had the bad fortune to meet." He put the sheet into his pocket. "I'll take care of it."

"You will?" Her face lit up. A second later it was twisted in wrath. "Oh, I don't like you!" she cried. "I don't like you at all!"

He looked at her a little sadly.

"You will," he said, "if you live long enough." He turned about and pushed open the door through which he had come just a few minutes ago.

"But wait a minute—" her voice leaped after him. "Where will I see you after you've got rid of it? How much do I have to pay—"

He let the door, sucking to behind him, be the period to that question of hers—and his answer to it.

He went back through the section he had just traversed to his own cabin. There, with the door locked, he considered the sheet she had given him, a little more closely. It was nothing more—and nothing less —than a five-year employment contract, a social contract, for her services as companion in the entourage of William, Prince, and Chairman of the Board of that very commercial planet Ceta which was the only habitable world circling the sun Tau Ceti. And a very liberal social contract it was, requiring no more than that she accompany William wherever he wished to go and supply her presence at such public and polite social functions as he might require. It was not the liberalness of the contract that surprised him so much —a Select of Kultis would hardly be contracted to perform any but the most delicately moral and ethical of duties—but the fact that she had asked him to destroy it. Theft of contract from her employer was bad enough, breach of contract infinitely worse—calling for complete rehabilitation—but destruction of contract required the death penalty wherever any kind of government operated. The girl, he thought, must be insane.

But—and here the fine finger of irony intruded into the situation—being the Select of Kultis she could not possibly be insane, any more than an ape could be an elephant. On the extreme contrary, being the product of a number of the most carefully culled forebearers on that planet where careful genetic culling and wizardry of psychological techniques was commonplace, she must be eminently sane. True, she had impressed Donal on first acquaintance as possessing nothing much out of the ordinary except a suicidal foolishness. But this was one instance where you had to go by the record books. And the record books implied that if anything about this business was abnormal, it was the situation itself, and not the girl involved in it.

Thoughtfully, Donal fingered the contract. Anea had clearly had no conception at all of what she was requesting when she so blithely required him to destroy it. The single sheet he held, and even the words and signatures upon it, were all integral parts of a single giant molecule which in itself was well-nigh indestructible and could not be in any way altered or tampered with short of outright destruction. As for destruction itself—Donal was quite sure that there was nothing aboard this ship that could in any way burn, shred, dissolve, or in any other fashion obliterate it. And the mere possession of it by anyone but William, its rightful owner, was as good as an order of sentence.

A soft chime quivered on the air of his cabin, announcing the serving of a meal in the main lounge. It chimed twice more to indicate that this was the third of the four meals interspersed throughout the ship "day." Contract in hand, Donal half-turned toward the little orifice of the disposal slot that led down to the central incinerator. The incinerator, of course, was not capable of disposing of the contract —but it might be that it could lie unnoticed there until the ship had reached its destination and its passengers had dispersed. Later, it would be difficult for William to discover how it had reached the incinerator in the first place.

Then he shook his head, and replaced the contract in his pocket. His motives for doing so were not entirely clear to himself. It was that oddness of his at work again, he thought. Also, he told himself that it seemed a sloppy way of handling the situation this girl had got him into. Quite typically, he had already forgotten that his participation in the matter was all of his own contriving.

He straightened his half-jacket and went out of his cabin and down the long corridor through various sections to the main lounge. A slight crowding of likewise dinner-bound passengers in the narrow entrance to the lounge delayed him momentarily; and, in that moment, looking over the heads of those before him, he caught sight of the long captain's table at the far end of the lounge and of the girl, Anea Marlivana, amongst those seated at it.

The others seated with her appeared to consist of a strikingly handsome young officer of field rank—a Freilander, by the look of him—a rather untidy, large young man almost as big as the Freilander, but possessing just the opposite of the other's military bearing; in fact, he appeared to half-slouch in his seat as if he were drunk. And a spare, pleasant-looking man in early middle age with iron-gray hair. The fifth person at the table was quite obviously a Dorsai—a massive, older man in the uniform of a Freiland marshal. The sight of this last individual moved Donal to sudden action. He pushed abruptly through the little knot of people barring the entrance and strode openly across the room to the high table. He extended his fist across it to the Dorsai marshal.

"How do you do, sir," he said. "I was supposed to look you up before the ship lifted; but I didn't have time. I've got a letter for you from my father, Eachan Khan Graeme. I'm his second son, Donal."

Blue Dorsai eyes as cold as river water lifted under thick gray brows to consider him. For part of a second the situation trembled on the balance-point of Dorsai pride with the older man's curiosity weighed against the bare-faced impudence of Donal's claim to acquaintance. Then the marshal took Donal's fist in a hard grip.

"So he remembered Hendrik Galt, did he?" the marshal smiled. "I haven't heard from Eachan for years."

Donal felt a slight, cold shiver of excitement course down his spine. Of all people, he had chosen one of the ranking Dorsai soldiers of his day to bluff acquaintance with. Hendrik Galt, First Marshal of Freiland.

"He sends you his regards, sir," said Donal, "and . . . but perhaps I can bring you the letter after dinner and you can read it for yourself."

"To be sure," said the marshal. "I'm in Stateroom Nineteen."

Donal was still standing. The occasion could hardly be prolonged further. But rescue came—as something in Donal had more than half-expected it would— from farther down the table.

"Perhaps," said the gray-haired man in a soft and pleasant voice, "your young friend would enjoy eating with us before you take him back to your stateroom, Hendrik?"

"I'd be honored," said Donal, with glib promptness. He pulled out the empty float before him and sat

down upon it, nodding courteously to the rest of the
company at the table as he did so. The eyes of the
girl met him from the table's far end. They were as
hard and still as emeralds caught in the rock.

MERCENARY II

"Anea Marlivana," said Hendrik Galt, introducing
Donal around the table. "And the gentleman who was
pleased to invite you—William of Ceta, Prince and
Chairman of the Board."

"Greatly honored," murmured Donal, inclining his
head toward them.

". . . The Unit Commandant, here, my adjutant
. . . Hugh Killien—"

Donal and the Commandant Freilander nodded to
each other.

". . . And ArDell Montor, of Newton." The loose-
limbed young man slumping in his float, lifted a
careless, half-drunken hand in a slight wave of ac-
knowledgment. His eyes—so dark as to appear almost
black under the light eyebrows that matched his rather heavy, blond hair, cleared for a disconcerting fraction of a second to stare sharply at Donal, then faded
back to indifference. "ArDell," said Galt, humorless-
ly, "set a new high score for the competitive exams
on Newton. His field was social dynamics."

"Indeed," muttered the Newtonian, with something
between a snort and a laugh. "Indeed, was. Was, indeed." He lifted a heavy tumbler from the table be-

fore him and buried his nose in its light golden contents.

"ArDell—" said the gray-haired William, gently reproving. ArDell lifted his drink-pale face and stared at the older man, snorted again, on laughter, and lifted the tumbler again to his lips.

"Are you enlisted somewhere at the moment, Graeme?" asked the Freilander, turning to Donal.

"I've a tentative contract for the Friendlies," said Donal. "I thought I'd pick between the Sects when I got there and had a chance to look over the opportunities for action."

"Very Dorsai of you," said William, smiling, from the far end of the table, next to Anea. "Always the urge to battle."

"You over-compliment me, sir," said Donal. "It merely happens that promotion comes more quickly on a battlefield than in a garrison, under ordinary conditions."

"You're too modest," said William.

"Yes, indeed," put in Anea, suddenly. "Far too modest."

William turned about to gaze quizzically at the girl.

"Now, Anea," he said. "You mustn't let your Exotic contempt for violence breed a wholly unjustified contempt for this fine young man. I'm sure both Hendrik and Hugh agree with him."

"Oh, they would—of course," said Anea, flashing a look at the other two men. "Of course, they would!"

"Well," said William, laughing, "we must make allowances for a Select, of course. As for myself, I must admit to being male enough, and unreconstructed enough, to like the thought of action, myself. I . . . ah, here comes the food."

Brimming soup plates were rising above the surface of the table in front of everybody but Donal.

"You'd better get your order in now," said William.

And, while Donal pressed the communicator key before him and attended to this necessary duty, the rest of them lifted their spoons and began their meal.

". . . Donal's father was a classmate of yours, was he, Hendrik?" inquired William, as the fish course was being served.

"Merely a close friend," said the marshal, dryly.

"Ah," said William, delicately lifting a portion of the white, delicate flesh on a fork. "I envy you Dorsai for things like that. Your professions allow you to keep friendship and emotional connections unrelated to your work. In the Commercial area"—he gestured with a slim, tanned hand—"a convention of general friendliness obscures the deeper feelings."

"Maybe it's what the man is to begin with," answered the marshal. "Not all Dorsai are soldiers, Prince, and not all Cetans are entrepreneurs."

"I recognize that," said William. His eyes strayed to Donal. "What would you say, Donal? Are you a simple mercenary soldier, only, or do you find yourself complicated by other desires?"

The question was as blunt as it was obliquely put. Donal concluded that ingenuousness overlaid with a touch of venality was perhaps the most proper response.

"Naturally, I'd like to be famous," he said—and laughed a trifle self-consciously, "and rich."

He caught the hint of a darkening cloud on the brow of Galt. But he could not be concerned with that now. He had other fish to fry. There would, he hoped, be a chance to clear up the marshal's contempt for him at some later time. For the present he must seem self-seeking enough to arouse William's interest.

"Very interesting," said William, pleasantly. "How

do you plan to go about becoming these pleasant things?"

"I was hoping," said Donal, "maybe to learn something of the worlds by being out among them—something I might be able to use to my own advantage, as well as others."

"Good Lord, is *that* all?" said the Freilander, and laughed in a way that invited the rest of the table to join in with him.

William, however, did not laugh—although Anea joined her own clear amusement to that of the commandment, and ArDell's snorted chuckle.

"No need to be unkind, Hugh," he said. "I like Donal's attitude. I had the same sort of notion myself once—when I was younger." He smiled in a kindly fashion on Donal. "You must come talk to me, too," he said, "after you've had your chat with Hendrik. I like young men with ambition."

ArDell snorted with laughter again. William turned to look sadly at him.

"You should try to eat, ArDell," he said. "We'll be making a phase shift in four hours or so; and if you don't have something solid on your stomach—"

"My stomach?" said the young man, drunkenly. "And what if my stomach should reach universal dimensions, out of phase? What if *I* should reach universal dimensions; and be everywhere and never come back to point position again?" He grinned at Williams. "What a waste of good food."

Anea had paled to a sickly color.

"If you'll excuse me—" she murmured, rising hastily.

"I don't blame you a bit!" said William sharply. "ArDell, that was in inexcusable bad taste. Hugh, help Anea to her stateroom."

"I don't want him!" flared Anea. "He's just like all the rest of you—"

But the Freilander was already on his feet, looking almost like a recruiting poster in his trim uniform and coming around the table to take her arm. She jerked away from him, turned, and went unsteadily out of the lounge, Hugh following closely behind her. They passed through the doorway into the corridor, but as they turned to move out of sight, Donal saw her turn to the tall soldier and lean into the protection of his arm, just before they disappeared.

William was continuing to speak calm and acid words of disapprobation to ArDell, who made no retort, but gazed drunkenly and steadily back at him out of his black, unmoving eyes. During the rest of the meal the talk turned to military affairs, in particular field strategy, in which triologue—ArDell pointedly excluded—Donal was able to win back some of the personal credit which his earlier remark about fame and riches had cost him—in the marshal's eyes.

". . . Remember," William said, as they parted in the corridor outside the lounge, after the meal. "Come in and see me after you've finished with Hendrik, Donal. I'll be glad to help you if I can." And with a smile, and a nod, he turned away.

Donal and Galt went off down the narrow corridor that forced them to walk one behind the other. Following the thick shoulders of the older man, Donal was surprised to hear him ask: "Well, what do you think of them?"

"Sir?" said Donal. Hesitating, he chose what he took to be the safest subject. "I'm a little surprised about the girl."

"Anea?" said Galt, stopping before a door marked with the number nineteen.

"I thought a Select of Kultis would be—" Donal

stopped, honestly at a loss, "more . . . more in control of herself."

"She's very healthy, very normal, very intelligent—but those are only potentialities," retorted the marshal, almost gruffly. "What did you expect?"

He threw open the door, ushered them both in, and closed the door firmly behind them. When he turned around, there was a harder, more formal note to his voice.

"All right now," he said, sharply, "what's all this about a letter?"

Donal took a deep breath. He had tried hard to read Galt's character during the course of the dinner —and he staked everything now in the honesty of his answer, on what he thought he had seen there.

"No letter, sir," he said. "To the best of my knowledge, my father never met you in his life."

"Thought as much," said Galt. "All right—what's it all about, then?" He crossed to a desk on the other side of the room, took something from a drawer, and when he turned about Donal was astonished to find him filling an antique pipe with tobacco.

"That Anea, sir," he said. "I never met such a fool in my life." And he told, fully and completely, the story of the episode in the corridor. Galt half-sat on the edge of the desk, the pipe in his mouth now, and alight, puffing little clouds of white smoke which the ventilating system whisked away the second they were formed.

"I see," he said, when Donal had finished. "I'm inclined to agree with you. She is a fool. And just what sort of insane idiot do you consider yourself?"

"I, sir?" Donal was honestly astonished.

"I mean you, boy," said Galt, taking the pipe out of his mouth. "Here you are, still damp from school, and sticking your nose into a situation a full planetary government'd hesitate at." He stared in frank amazement at Donal. "Just what did you think—what did you figure . . . hell, boy, what did you *plan* to get out of it?"

"Why, nothing," said Donal. "I was only interested in seeing a ridiculous and possibly dangerous situation smoothed out as neatly as possible. I admit I hadn't any notion of the part William played in the matter —he's apparently an absolute devil."

The pipe rattled in Galt's suddenly unclenched jaws and he had to grab it quickly with one thick hand to keep it from falling. He took it from his lips and stared in amazement at Donal.

"Who told you that?" he demanded.

"No one," said Donal. "It's obvious, isn't it?" Galt laid his pipe down on the table and stood up.

"Not to ninety-nine per cent of the civilized worlds, it isn't," he retorted. "What made it so obvious to you?"

"Certainly," said Donal, "any man can be judged by the character and actions of the people with which he surrounds himself. And this William has an entourage of thwarted and ruined people."

The marshal stiffened.

"You mean me?" he demanded.

"Naturally not," said Donal. "After all—you're a Dorsai." The stiffness went out of Galt. He grinned a little sourly and, reaching back for his pipe, retrieved and relit it.

"Your faith in our common origin is . . . quite refreshing," he said. "Go on. On this piece of evidence you read William's character, do you?"

"Oh, not just that," said Donal. "Stop and think of the fact that a Select of Kultis finds herself at odds with him. And the good instincts of a Select are inbred. Also, he seems to be an almost frighteningly brilliant sort of man, in that he can dominate personalities like Anea, and this fellow Montor, from

Newton—who must be a rather high-level mind himself to have rated as he did on his tests."

"And someone that brilliant must be a devil?" queried Galt, dryly.

"Not at all," explained Donal, patiently. "But having such intellectual capabilities, a man must show proportionately greater inclinations toward either good or evil than lesser people. If he tends toward evil, he may mask it in himself—he may even mask its effect on the people with which he surrounds himself. But he has no way of producing the reflections of good which would ordinarily be reflected from his lieutenants and initiates—and which, if he was truly good—he would have no reason to try and hide. And by that lack, you can read him."

Galt took the pipe from his mouth and gave a long, slow whistle. He stared at Donal.

"You weren't brought up on one of the Exotics, by any chance, were you?" he asked.

"No, sir," said Donal. "My father's mother was a Maran, though. And my mother's mother was Maran."

"This," Galt paused and tamped thoughtfully in the bowl of his pipe—it had gone out—with one thick forefinger, "business of reading character—did you get this from your mother, or your grandmother—or is it your own idea?"

"Why, I imagine I must have heard it somewhere," replied Donal. "But surely it stands to reason—anyone would arrive at it as a conclusion, with a few minutes thought."

"Possibly the majority of us don't think," said Galt, with the same dryness. "Sit down, Donal. And I'll join you."

They took a couple of armchair floats facing each other. Galt put his pipe away.

"Now, listen to me," he said, in a low and sober

voice. "You're one of the oddest young fish I can remember meeting. I don't know quite what to do with
you. If you were my son, I'd pack you up in quaran-
tine and ship you home for ten more years seasoning
before I let you out among the stars—all right—" he
interrupted himself abruptly, raising a silencing hand
as Donal's mouth opened. "I know you're a man now
and couldn't be shipped anywhere against your will.
But the way you strike me now is that you've got perhaps one chance in a thousand of becoming something remarkable, and about nine hundred and ninety-nine chances of being quietly put out of the way
before the year's out. Look, boy, what do you know
about the worlds, outside the Dorsai?"

"Well," said Donal. "There are fourteen planetary
governments not counting the anarchic setups on
Dunnin's World and Coby—"

"Governments, my rear echelon!" interrupted Galt,
rudely. "Forget your civics lessons! Governments in
this twenty-fifth century are mere machinery. It's the
men who control them who count. Project Blaine, on
Venus; Sven Holman, on Earth; Eldest Bright on
Harmony, the very planet we're headed for—and
Sayona the Bond on Kultis, for the Exotics."

"General Kamal—" began Donal.

"Is nothing!" said Galt, sharply. "How can the Elec-
tor of the Dorsai be anything when every little canton
hangs to its independence with tooth and nail? No,
I'm talking about the men who pull the strings between the stars. The ones I mentioned, and others."
He took a deep breath. "Now, how do you suppose
our Merchant Prince and Chairman of the Board on
Ceta ranks with those I mentioned?"

"You'd say he's their equal?"

"At least," said Galt. "At least. Don't be led astray
by the fact that you see him traveling like this, on a
commercial ship, with only the girl and Montor with

him. Chances are he owns the ship, the crew and officers—and half the passengers."

"And you and the commandant?" asked Donal, perhaps more bluntly than was necessary. Galt's features started to harden; and then he relaxed.

"A fair question," he rumbled. "I'm trying to get you to question most of the things you've taken for granted. I suppose it's natural you'd include myself. No—to answer your question—I am First Marshal of Freiland, still a Dorsai, and with my professional services for hire, and nothing more. We've just hired out five light divisions to the First Dissident Church, on Harmony, and I'm coming along to observe that they operate as contracted for. It's a complicated deal—like they are all—involving a batch of contract credits belonging to Ceta. Therefore William."

"And the commandant?" persisted Donal.

"What about him?" replied Galt. "He's a Freilander, a professional, and a good one. He'll take over one of the three-Force commands for a short test period when we get to Harmony, for demonstration purposes."

"Have you had him with you long?"

"Oh, about two standard years," said Galt.

"And he's good, professionally?"

"He's damn good," said Galt. "Why do you think he's my adjutant? What're you driving at, anyway?"

"A doubt," said Donal, "and a suspicion." He hesitated for a second. "Neither of which I'm ready to voice yet."

Galt laughed.

"Save that Maran character-sniffing of yours for civilians," he said. "You'll be seeing a snake under every brush. Take my word for it, Hugh's a good, honest soldier—a bit flashy, perhaps—but that's all."

"I'm hardly in a position to argue with you," murmured Donal, stepping aside gracefully. "You were about to say something about William, when I interrupted you?"

"Oh yes," said Galt. He frowned. "It adds up to this —and I'll make it short and clear. The girl's none of your business; and William's deadly medicine. Leave them both alone. And if I can help you to the kind of post you're after—"

"Thank you very much," said Donal. "But I believe William will be offering me something."

Galt blinked and stared.

"Hell's breeches, boy!" he exploded after half a second. "What gives you that idea?"

Donal smiled a little sadly.

Another one of my suspicions," he said. "Based on what you call that Maran character-sniffing of mine, no doubt." He stood up. "I appreciate your trying to warn me, sir." He extended his fist. "If I could talk to you again, sometime?"

Galt stood up himself, taking the proffered fist, mechanically.

"Any time," he said. "Damned if I understand you."

Donal peered at him, suddenly struck by a thought.

"Tell me, sir," he asked. "Would you say I was—odd?"

"Odd!" Galt almost exploded on the word. "Odd as—" his imagination failed him. "What makes you ask that?"

"I just wondered," said Donal. "I've been called that so often. Maybe they were right."

He withdrew his fist from the marshal's grasp. And on that note, he took his leave.

MERCENARY III

Returning again up the corridor toward the bow of the ship, Donal allowed himself to wonder, a little wistfully, about this incubus of his own strange difference from other people. He had thought to leave it behind with his cadet uniform. Instead, it seemed, it continued to ride with him, still perched on his shoulders. Always it had been this way. What seemed so plain, and simple and straightforward to himself, had always stuck others as veiled, torturous, and involved. Always he had been like a stranger passing through a town, the ways of whose people were different, and who looked on him with a lack of understanding amounting to suspicion. Their language failed on the doorstep of his motives and could not enter the lonely mansion of his mind. They said "enemy" and "friend"; they said "strong" and "weak" —"them" and "us". They set up a thousand arbitrary classifications and distinctions which he could not comprehend, convinced as he was that all people were only people—and there was very little to choose between them. Only, you dealt with them as individuals, one by one; and always remembering to be patient. And if you did this successfully, then the larger, group things all came out right.

Turning again into the entrance of the lounge, he discovered—as he had half-expected to—the young Newtonian ArDell Montor, slumped in a float by one end of the bar that had made its appearance as soon as the dinner tables had been taken up into the walls. A couple of other small, drinking groups sparsely completed the inhabitants of the lounge—but none of these were having anything to do with Montor. Donal walked directly to him; and Montor, without moving, listed the gaze of his dark eyes to watch Donal approach.

"Join you?" said Donal.

"Honored," replied the other—not so much thickly, as slowly, from the drink inside him. "Thought I might like to talk to you." His fingers crept out over the buttons on the bar-pad next to him. "Drink?"

"Dorsai whiskey," said Donal. Montor pressed. A second later a small transparent goblet, full, rose to the bartop. Donal took it and sipped cautiously. The drinking the night he had attained his majority had acquainted him with the manner in which alcohol affected him; and he had made a private determination never to find himself drunk again. It is a typical matter of record with him, that he never did. Raising his eyes from the glass, he found the Newtonian staring steadily at him with his eyes unnaturally clear, lost, and penetrating.

"You're younger than I," said ArDell. "Even if I don't look it. How old do you think I am?"

Donal looked him over curiously. Montor's face, for all its lines of weariness and dissipation, was the scarcely mature visage of a late adolescent—a situation to which his shock of uncombed hair and the loose-limbed way he sprawled in his float, contributed.

"A quarter of a standard century," said Donal.

"Thirty-three years absolute," said ArDell. "I was a school-child, a monk, until I was twenty-nine. Do you think I drink too much?"

"I think there's no doubt about it," answered Donal.

"I agree with you," said ArDell, with one of his sudden snorts of laughter. "I agree with you. There's no doubt about it—one of the few things in this God-abandoned universe about which there is no doubt. But that's not what I was hoping to talk to you about."

"What was that?" Donal tasted his glass of whiskey again.

"Courage," said ArDell, looking at him with an empty, penetrating glance. "Have you got courage?"

"It's a necessary item for a soldier," said Donal. "Why do you ask?"

"And no doubts? No doubts?" ArDell swirled the golden drink in his tall tumbler and took a swallow from it. "No secret fears that when the moment comes your legs will weaken, your heart will pound, you'll turn and run?"

"I will not, of course, turn and run," said Donal. "After all, I'm a Dorsai. As for how I'll feel—all I can say is, I've never felt the way you describe. And even if I did—"

Above their heads a single mellow chime sounded, interrupting.

"Phase shift in one standard hour and twenty minutes," announced a voice. "Phase shift in one standard hour and twenty minutes. Passengers are advised to take their medication now and accomplish the shift while asleep, for their greatest convenience."

"Have you swallowed a pill yet?" asked ArDell.

"Not yet," said Donal.

"But you will?"

"Of course." Donal examined him with interest. "Why not?"

"Doesn't taking medication to avoid the discomfort of a phase shift strike you as a form of cowardice?" asked ArDell. "Doesn't it?"

"That's foolish," said Donal. "Like saying it's cowardly to wear clothes to keep you warm and comfortable, or to eat, to keep from starving. One is a matter of convenience; the other is a matter of"—he thought for a second—"duty."

"Courage is doing your duty?"

". . . In spite of what you personally might want. Yes," said Donal.

"Yes," said ArDell, thoughtfully. "Yes." He replaced his empty glass on the bar and pressed for a refill. "I *thought* you had courage," he said, musingly, watching the glass sink, fill, and begin to re-emerge.

"I am a Dorsai," said Donal.

"Oh, spare me the glories of careful breeding!" said ArDell, harshly, picking up his now-full glass. As he turned back to face Donal, Donal saw the man's face was tortured. "There's more to courage than that. If it was only in your genes—" he broke off suddenly, and leaned toward Donal. "Listen to me," he almost whispered. "I'm a coward."

"Are you sure?" said Donal, levelly. "How do you know?"

"I'm frightened sick," whispered ArDell. "Sick-frightened of the universe. What do you know about the mathematics of social dynamics?"

"It's a predicative system of mathematics, isn't it?" said Donal. "My education didn't lie in that direction."

"No, no!" said ArDell, almost fretfully. "I'm talking about the statistics of social analysis, and their extrapolation along lines of population increase and development." He lowered his voice even further. "They approach a parallel with the statistics of random chance!"

"I'm sorry," said Donal. "That means nothing to me."

ArDell gripped Donal's arm suddenly with one surprisingly strong hand.

"Don't you understand?" he murmured. "Random chance provides for every possibility—including dissolution. It must come, because the chance is there. As our social statistics grow into larger figures, we, too, entertain the possibility. In the end, it must come. We must destroy ourselves. There is no other alternative. And all because the universe is too big a suit of clothes for us to wear. It gives us room to grow too much, too fast. We will reach a statistically critical mass—and then," he snapped his fingers, "the end!"

"Well, that's a problem for the future," said Donal. But then, because he could not help reacting to the way the other man was feeling, he added, more gently, "Why does it bother you, so much?"

"Why, don't you see?" said ArDell. "If it's all to go —just like that—as if it never has been, then what was the use of it all? What's to show for our existence? I don't mean things we built—they decay fast enough. Or knowledge. That's just a copying down from an open book into our own language. It has to be those things that the universe didn't have to begin with and that we brought to it. Things like love, and kindness —and courage."

"If that's the way you feel," said Donal, gently withdrawing his arm from the other's grasp, "why drink this way?"

"Because I *am* a coward," said ArDell. "I feel it out there, all the time, this enormousness that is the universe. Drinking helps me shut it out—that God-awful knowledge of what it can do to us. That's why I drink. To take the courage I need out of a bottle, to do the little things like passing through phase shift without medication."

"Why," said Donal, almost tempted to smile. "What good would that do?"

"It's facing it, in a little way," ArDell fixed him with his dark and pleading eyes. "It's saying, in one little instance—go ahead, rip me to the smallest shreds you can manage, spread me over your widest limits. I can take it."

Donal shook his head.

"You don't understand," said ArDell, sinking back in his float. "If I could work, I wouldn't need the alcohol. But I'm walled away from work nowadays. It's not that way with you. You've got your job to do; and you've got courage—the real kind. I thought maybe I could . . . well, never mind. Courage wouldn't be transferable, anyway."

"Are you going to Harmony?" asked Donal.

"Whither my Prince goes, there go I," said ArDell, and snorted his laugh again. "You should read my contract, sometime." He turned back to the bar. "Another whiskey?"

"No," said Donal, standing up. "If you'll excuse me—"

"I'll see you again," muttered ArDell, keying for another drink. "I'll be seeing you."

"Yes," said Donal. "Until then."

"Until then," ArDell lifted his newly filled glass from the bar. The chime sounded again overhead, and the voice reminded them that only seventy-odd minutes remained before shift-time. Donal went out.

Half an hour later, after he had gone back to his own room for one more careful rereading and study of Anea's contract, Donal pressed the button on the door of the stateroom of William, Prince and Chairman of the Board, on Ceta. He waited.

"Yes?" said the voice of William, over his head.

"Donal Graeme, sir," said Donal. "If you aren't busy—"

"Oh, of course—Donal. Come in!" The door swung open before him and Donal entered.

William was sitting on a plain float before a small

deskboard holding a pile of papers and a tiny portable secretary. A single light glowed directly above him and the deskboard, silvering his gray hair. Donal hesitated, hearing the door click to behind him.

"Find a seat somewhere," said William, without looking up from his papers. His fingers flickered over the keys of the secretary. "I have some things to do."

Donal turned about in the gloom outside the pool of light, found an armchair float and sat down in it. William continued for some minutes, scanning through his papers, and making notes on the secretary.

After a while he shoved the remaining papers aside and the deskboard, released, drifted with its burden to over against a farther wall. The single overhead light faded and a general illumination flooded the cabin.

Donal blinked at the sudden light. William smiled.

"And now," he said, "what's the nature of your business with me?"

Donal blinked, stared, and blinked again.

"Sir?" he said.

"I think we can avoid wasting time by ignoring pretenses," said William, still in his pleasant voice. "You pushed yourself on us at the table because you wanted to meet someone there. It was hardly the marshal —your Dorsai manners could have found a better way than that. It was certainly not Hugh, and most unlikely to be ArDell. That leaves Anea; and she's pretty enough, and you're both young enough to do something that foolish . . . but, I think not, under the conditions." William folded his lean fingers together, and smiled. "That leaves me."

"Sir, I—" Donal started to stand up, with the stiffness of outraged dignity.

"No, no," said William, gesturing him back. "Now it'd be foolish to leave, after going to all this trouble to get here, wouldn't it?" His voice sharpened. "Sit down!"

Donal sat.

"Why did you want to see me?" asked William.

Donal squared his shoulders.

"All right," he said. "If you want me to put it bluntly . . . I think I might be useful to you."

"By which," said William, "you think you might be useful to yourself, by tapping the till, as it were, of my position and authority—go on."

"It so happened," said Donal, "that I came into possession of something belonging to you."

William extended his hand, without a word. After a second's hesitation, Donal extracted Anea's contract from his pocket and passed it over. William took it, unfolded it, and glanced over it. He laid it carelessly down on a little table beside him.

"She wanted me to get rid of it for her," said Donal. "She wanted to hire me to dispose of it for her. Evidently she didn't know how hard it is to destroy a sheet of the material contracts are made on."

"But you took the job," said William.

"I made no promises," said Donal, painfully.

"But from the start, you intended to bring it straight to me."

"I believe," said Donal, "it's your property."

"Oh, of course," said William. He smiled at Donal for a long moment. "You realize, of course," he said, finally, "that I needn't believe a word of what you've said. I only need to assume that you stole it yourself and later got cold feet about disposing of it—and dreamed up this cock-and-bull story in an attempt to sell it back to me. The captain of this ship would be glad to put you under arrest at my word and hold you for trial as soon as we reach Harmony."

A slight, cold, galvanic shiver ran down Donal's spine.

"A Select of Kultis won't lie under oath," he said. "She—"

"I see no reason to involve Anea in this," said William. "It could all be handled very conveniently without her. My statement against yours."

Donal said nothing. William smiled again.

"You see," said William, "the point I'm laboring to bring home to you. You happen not only to be venal, but a fool."

"*Sir!*" the word shot from Donal's lips. William waved a disinterested hand.

"Save your Dorsai rages for someone who'll be impressed by them. I know as well as you do, you've no intention of attacking me. Possibly, if you were a different sort of Dorsai—but you're not. You are as I say, both venal and a fool. Accept these statements for the obvious facts they are; and we can get down to business."

He looked at Donal. Donal said nothing.

"Very well, then," went on William. "You came to me, hoping I could find you of some use. As it happens, I can. Anea is, of course, just a foolish young girl—but for her benefit, as well as my own, being her employer, we'll have to see she doesn't get into serious trouble. Now, she has confided in you once. She may again. If she does so—by no means discourage her. And to keep you available for such confidences," William smiled again, quite good humoredly, this time, "I believe I can find you a commission as Force-Leader, under Commandant Hugh Killien, when we touch down on Harmony. There is no reason why a military career shouldn't go hand in hand with whatever other uses I can find for you."

"Thank you, sir," said Donal.

"Not at all—" A chime sounded from some hidden wall speaker. "Ab—phase shift in five minutes." William picked up a small silver box from a table near his feet, and sprung it open. "Have you taken your medication, yet? Help yourself."

He extended to Donal.

"Thank you, sir," said Donal carefully. "I have."

"Then," said William, helping himself to a white tablet, and replacing the box. "I believe that is all."

"I believe so, sir," said Donal.

Donal inclined his head and went out. Stopping outside the stateroom door only long enough to take one of his own phase shift sedatives, he headed back toward his own stateroom. On the way, he stopped by the ship's library to check out an information spool on the First Dissident Church, of Harmony; and this delayed him sufficiently so that he was passing down one of the long sectional corridors when the phase shift occurred.

He had been prudently asleep during those previous shifts he had gone through while outbound from Dorsai; and, of course, he had learned years ago what to expect. In addition, he was fully medicated; and the shift itself was over before it was really begun. In fact, it took place in no time, in no conceivable interval at all. Yet it *had* happened; and some inextinguishable recognizing part of him *knew* and remembered that he had been torn apart, down to the most fractional elements of his being, and spread to the wide universe and caught and collected and reassembled some arbitrary point light-years from his destruction. And it was this memory, not the shift itself, that made him falter, for one short step, before he took up again his steady march back to his stateroom. And the memory would stay with him.

He continued on down the corridor; but he was far from having run his gauntlet for the day. As he reached the end of one section, Anea stepped out from the cross-bar corridor there that was the exact duplicate of the one, several sections down, where he had first met her. Her green eyes were afire.

"You've been seeing him!" she snapped, barring his way.

"Seeing . . . oh, William," he said.

"Don't deny it."

"Why should I?" Donal looked at her almost with wonder. "Surely, it's nothing to make a secret about?"

She stared at him.

"Oh!" she cried. "You just don't care for anything, do you? What did you do . . . about what I gave you?"

"I gave it back to its owner, of course," said Donal. "There was no other sensible thing I could do."

She turned suddenly so white that he almost reached out to catch her, certain she was about to faint. But she did no such womanish thing. Her eyes, as she stared at him, were shocked to enormity.

"Oh!" she breathed. "You . . . you traitor. You *cheat!*" and before he could make a move or say a word to stop her, she had whirled about and was running off down the corridor back in the direction from which he had come.

With a certain wry unhappiness—for, in spite of his rather low opinion of her common sense, he had really expected her to listen to his explanation—he took up his solitary walk to his stateroom. He traveled the rest of the way without meeting anyone. The corridors, in the aftermath of the phase shift were deserted by prudent passengers.

Only, passing a certain stateroom, he heard sounds of sickness from within; and, looking up, recognized the number on its door as one he had looked up just now on his recent trip to the library.

It was the stateroom of ArDell Montor; and that would be the man himself inside it now, unmedicated and racked by the passing of the phase shift, fighting his own long battle with the universe.

FORCE-LEADER

"All right, gentlemen," said Hugh Killien.

He stood, confident and impressive in his chameleon battle-dress, with the fingertips of his right hand resting on the gently domed surface of the mapviewer before him.

"If you'll gather around the viewer, here—" he said. The five Force-Leaders moved in until all six men stood thickly clustered around the meter-square area of the viewer. The illumination from the blackout shell enclosing them beat down and met the internal upward illumination of the viewer, so that Donal, glancing around at his fellow-officers, was irresistibly reminded of men caught between wrath and wrath, in some small package section of that hell their First Dissident Church Liaison-Elder had been so eloquent about, only a few hours since at the before-battle service.

". . . Our position is here," Hugh was saying. "As your commandant I make you the customary assurance that it is a perfectly tenable position and that the contemplated advance in no way violates the Mercenaries Code. Now—" he went on more briskly, "as you can see, we occupy an area five kilometers in front and three kilometers in depth, between these two ridges. Second Command of Battle Unit 176 to our right, Fourth Command of Battles to out left.

"The contemplated action calls for the Second and Fourth Commands to hold fast in full strength on both our flanks, while we move forward at sixty per cent of strength and capture a small town called Faith Will Succour, which is *here*—"

His index finger stabbed down and rested upon the domed image of the map.

". . . At approximately four kilometers of distance from our present position. We will use three of our five Forces, Skuak's, White's and Graeme's; and each Force will make its separate way to the objective. You will each have your individual maps. There are woods for the first twelve hundred meters. After that, you will have to cross the river, which is about forty meters in width, but which Intelligence assures us is fordable at the present time with a maximum depth of a hundred and twenty centimeters. On the other side it will be woods again, thinning out gradually right up to the edge of the town. We leave in twenty minutes. It'll be dawn in an hour and I want all three Forces across that river before full daylight. Any questions?"

"What about enemy activity in the area?" asked Skuak. He was a short, stocky Cassidan, who looked Mongoloid, but was actually Eskimo in ancestry. "What kind of opposition can we expect?"

"Intelligence says nothing but patrols. Possibly a small Force holding the town, itself. Nothing more." Hugh looked around the circle of faces. "This should be bread and butter. Any more questions?"

"Yes," said Donal. He had been studying the map. "What sort of military incompetent decided to send us out at only sixty per cent of strength?"

The atmosphere in the shell froze suddenly and

sharply. Donal looked up to find Hugh Killien's eyes on his across the viewer.

"As it happened," said the commandant, a slight edge to his words, "it was *my* suggestion to Staff, Graeme. Perhaps you've forgotten—I'm sure none of the other Force-Leaders have—but this is a demonstration campaign to show the First Dissident Church we're worthy of our hire."

"That hardly includes gambling the lives of four hundred and fifty men," retorted Donal, unmoved.

"Graeme," said Hugh, "you're junior officer here; and I'm commandant. You ought to know I don't have to explain tactics to you. But just to set your mind at rest, Intelligence has given a clear green on enemy activity in the area."

"Still," persisted Donal, "why take unnecessary chances?"

Hugh sighed in exasperation.

"I certainly shouldn't have to give you lessons in strategy," he said bitingly. "I think you abuse the right the Code gives you to question Staff decisions. But to put an end to this—there's a good reason why we'll be using the minimum number of men. Our main thrust at the enemy is to come through this area. If we moved forward in strength, the United Orthodox forces would immediately begin to strengthen defenses. But doing it this way, it should appear we're merely moving to take up a natural vacuum along the front. Once we have the town tied down, the Second and Fourth Commands can filter in to reinforce us and we are in position to mount a full-scale attack at the plains below. Does that answer you?"

"Only partially," said Donal. "I—"

"Give me patience!" snapped the Freilander. "I have five campaigns to my credit, Force-Leader. I'd hardly stick my own neck in a noose. But I'll be taking over White's Force and leaving him in command back here in the Area. You, I and Skuak will make the assay. *Now*, are you satisfied?"

There was, of course, no reply to be made to that. Donal bowed his head in submission and the meeting broke up. Walking back to his Force area, however, alongside Skuak, Donal remained unreconstructed enough to put an extra question to the Cassidan.

"Do *you* think I'm starting at shadows?" asked Donal.

"Huh!" grunted Skuak. "It's his responsibility. He ought to know what he's doing." And, on that note, they parted; each to marshal his own men.

Back in his own Force area, Donal found that his Groupmen had already assembled his command. They stood under arms, drawn up in three lines of fifty men each, with a senior and junior Groupman at the head of each line. The ranking senior Groupman, a tall, thin Cetan veteran named Morphy, accompanied him as he made his rounds of the ranks, inspecting the men.

They were a good unit, Donal thought, as he paced down between the rows. Well-trained men, battle-seasoned, although in no sense elite troops, since they had been picked at random by the Elders of the First Dissident Church—William having stipulated only his choice of officers for the demonstration Battle Unit. Each man carried a handgun and knife in addition to his regular armament; but they were infantry, spring-rifle men. Weapon for weapon, any thug in the back alley of a large city had more, and more modern firepower; but the trick with modern warfare was not to outgun the enemy, but carry weapons he could not gimmick. Chemical and radiation armament was too easily put out of action from a distance. Therefore, the spring-rifle with its five thousand-sliver magazine and its tiny, compact, non-metallic mechanism which could put a sliver in a man-sized target at a thousand meters time after time with unvarying accuracy.

Yet, thought Donal, pacing between the silent men in the faint darkness of pre-dawn, even the spring-rifle would be gimmickable one of these days. Eventually, the infantryman would be back to the knife and short sword. And the emphasis would weigh yet again more heavily on the skill of the individual soldier. For sooner or later, no matter what fantastic long-range weapons you mounted, the ground itself had to be taken—and for that there had never been anything but the man in the ranks.

Donal finished his inspection and went back to stand in front of them.

"Rest, men," he said. "But hold your ranks. All Groupmen over here with me."

He walked off out of earshot of the men in ranks and the Groupmen followed him. They squatted in a circle and he passed on to them the orders of the Staff he had just received from Hugh, handing out maps to each of them.

"Any questions?" he asked, as Hugh had asked his Force-Leaders.

There were none. They waited for him to go on. He, in turn looked slowly around the circle, assessing these men on whom his command would depend.

He had had a chance to get to know them in the three weeks previous to this early morning. The six who faced him represented, in miniature, the varying reactions his appointment as Force-Leader had produced in the Force as a whole. Of the hundred and fifty men under him, a few were doubtful of him because of his youth and lack of battle experience. A larger number were unequivocably glad to have him over them because of the Dorsai reputation. A few, a very few, were of that class of men who bristle automatically, as man to man, whenever they find themselves in contact with another individual who is touted as better than they. The instinctive giant-killers. Of his type was the Senior Groupman of the Third Group, an ex-Coby miner named Lee. Even squatting now in this circle, on the brink of action, he met Donal's eye with a faint air of challenge, his brush of dark hair stiffly upright in the gloom, his bony jaw set. Such men were troublemakers unless they had responsibility to hold them down. Donal revised his original intention to travel, himself, with the Third Group.

"We'll split up into patrol-sized units of twenty-five men each," he said. "There'll be a Senior or Junior Groupman to each unit. You'll move separately as units, and if you encounter an enemy patrol, you'll fight as a unit. I don't want any unit going to the rescue of another. Is that clear?"

They nodded. It was clear.

"Morphy," said Donal, turning to the thin Senior Groupman. "I want you to go with the Junior unit of Lee's Group, which will have the rearguard position. Lee will take his own half-group directly in front of you. Chassen"—he looked at the Senior Groupman of the Second Group—"you and Zolta will take positions third and fourth from the rear. I want you personally in fourth position. Suki, as Junior of the First Group, you'll be ahead of Chassen and right behind me. I'll take the upper half of the First Group in advance position."

"Force," said Lee. "How about communications?"

"Hand-signal. Voice. And that's all. And I don't want any of you closing up to make communication easier. Twenty-meter mimimum interval between units." Donal looked around the circle again. "Our job here is to penetrate to the little town as quickly and quietly as we can. Fight only if you're forced into it; and break away as quickly as you can."

"The word is it's supposed to be a Sunday walk," commented Lee.

"I don't operate by back-camp rumor," said Donal flatly, his eyes seeking out the ex-miner. "We'll take all precautions. You Groupmen will be responsible for seeing that your men are fully equipped with everything, including medication."

Lee yawned. It was not a gesture of insolence—not quite.

"All right," said Donal. "Back to your Groups."

The meeting broke up.

A few minutes later the almost inaudible peep of a whistle was carried from Force to Force; and they began to move out. Dawn was not yet in the sky, but the low overcast above the treetops was beginning to lighten at their backs.

The first twelve hundred meters through the woods, though they covered it cautiously enough, turned out to be just what Lee had called it—a Sunday walk. It was when Donal, in the lead with the first half-Group, came out on the edge of the river that things began to tighten up.

"Scouts out!" he said. Two of the men from the Group sloshed into the smoothly flowing water, and, rifles held high, waded across its gray expanse to the far side. The glint of their rifles, waved in a circle, signaled the all clear and Donal led the rest of the men into the water and across.

Arrived on the far side, he threw out scouts in three directions—ahead, and along the bank each way—and waited until Suki and his men appeared on the far side of the river. Then, his scouts having returned with no sight of the enemy, Donal spread his men out in light skirmish order and went forward.

The day was growing rapidly. They proceeded by

fifty meter jumps, sending the scouts out ahead, then moving the rest of the men up when the signal came back that the ground was clear ahead. Jump succeeded jump and there was no contact with the enemy. A little over an hour later, with the large orange disk of E. Eridani standing clear of the horizon, Donal looked out through a screen of bushes at a small, battle-torn village that was silent as the grave.

Forty minutes later, the three Forces of the Third Command, Battle Unit 176 were united and dug in about the small town of Faith Will Succour. They had uncovered no local inhabitants.

They had had no encounter with the enemy.

FORCE-LEADER II

The name of Force-Leader Graeme was mud.

The Third Command, or at least that portion of it that was dug in around the village, made no great attempt to hide the fact from him. If he had shown at all that he was sensitive to their opinion of him, they would have made even less. But there was something about his complete indifference to their attitude that put a check to their obvious contempt. Nevertheless, the hundred and fifty men that had been forced by him to make their approach on the village under full equipment and maximum security effort, and the three hundred other men who had made a much more casual and easy approach, and were congratulating themselves on being out from under such an officer, agreed in an opinion of Donal that had reached its nadir! There is only one thing that veterans hate worse than being made to sweat unnecessarily in garrison; and that is being made to sweat unnecessarily in the field. The word had gone out that the day's work was to be a Sunday walk. And it *had* been a Sunday walk, except for those serving under a green young Dorsai officer, name of Graeme. The men were not happy.

Along about twilight, as the sunset was fading through the bushy-limbed trees that were the local mutant variform of the Earthly conifer that had been imported when this planet was terraformed, a runner came from Hugh at Command HQ, just outside the enemy end of the village. He found Donal seated astride a fallen log, studying a map of the local area.

"Signal from Battles," said the runner, squatting beside the log.

"Stand up," said Donal, quietly. The runner stood. "Now, what's the signal?"

"Second and Third Commands won't be moving up until tomorrow morning," said the runner, sulkily.

"Signal acknowledged," said Donal, waving him off. The runner turned and hurried away with another instance of the new officer's wax-and-braid to relate to the other enlisted men back at HQ.

Left to himself, Donal continued to study the map as long as the light lasted. When it was completely gone, he put the map away, produced a small black whistle from his pocket and peeped for his ranking Senior Groupman.

A moment later a thin body loomed up against the faintly discernible sky beyond the treetops.

"Morphy, sir. Reporting," came the voice of the Senior Groupman.

"Yes—" said Donal. "Sentries all posted, Groupman?"

"Yes, sir." The quality of Morphy's tone was completely without inflection.

"Good. I want them alert at all times. Now, Morphy—"

"Yes, sir?"

"Who do we have in the Force that has a good sense of smell?"

"Smell, sir?"

Donal merely waited.

"Well, sir," said Morphy, finally and slowly. "There's Lee, he practically grew up in the mines, where you have to have a good sense of smell. That's the mines on Coby, Force-Leader."

"I assumed those were the mines you meant," said Donal, dryly. "Get Lee over here, will you?"

Morphy took out his own whistle and blew for the Senior Groupman, Third Group. They waited.

"He's about the camp isn't he?" said Donal, after a moment. "I want all the men within whistle sound that aren't on sentry duty."

"Yes, sir," said Morphy. "He'll be here in a moment. He knows it's me. Everybody sounds a little different on these whistles and you get to know them like voices after a while, sir."

"Groupman," said Donal. "I'd be obliged if you didn't feel the need to keep telling me things I already know."

"Yes, sir," said Morphy, subsiding.

Another shadow loomed up out of the darkness.

"What is it, Morphy?" said the voice of Lee.

"I wanted to see you," spoke up Donal, before the Senior Groupman had a chance to answer. "Morphy tells me you have a good sense of smell."

"I do pretty well," said Lee.

"Sir!"

"I do pretty well, sir."

"All right," said Donal. "Both of you take a look at

the map here. Look sharp. I'm going to make a light."
He flicked on a little flash, shielded by his hand. The
map was revealed, spread out on the log before them.
"Look here," said Donal, pointing. "Three kilometers
off this way. Do you know what that is?"

"Small valley," said Morphy. "It's way outside our
sentry posts."

"We're going there," Donal said. The light went
out and he got up from the log.

"Us? Us, sir?" the voice of Lee came at him.

"The three of us," said Donal. "Come along." And
he led the way surefootedly out into the darkness.

Going through the woods, he was pleased to discover the two Groupmen were almost as sure-footed
in the blackness as himself. They went slowly but
carefully for something over a mile; and then they felt
the ground beginning to slope upward under their
feet.

"All right. Down and easy," said Donal quietly. The
three men dropped to their bellies and began in
skilled silence to work their way up to the crest of
the slope. It took them a good half-hour; but at the
end of that time they lay side by side just under the
skyline of a ridge, looking over into a well of blackness that was a small, hidden valley below. Donal
tapped Lee on the shoulder and when the other
turned his face toward him in the gloom, Donal
touched his own nose, pointed down into the valley
and made sniffing motions. Lee turned his face back
to the valley and lay in that position for several minutes, apparently doing nothing at all. However, at the
end of that time, he turned toward Donal again, and
nodded. Donal motioned them all back down the
slope.

Donal asked no questions and the two Groupmen
volunteered nothing until they were once more back

safely within the lines of their own sentry posts. Then Donal turned toward Lee.

"Well, Groupman," he said. "What did you smell?"

Lee hesitated. His voice, when he answered, had a note of puzzlement in it.

"I don't know, sir," he answered. "Something—sour, sort of. I could just barely smell it."

"That's the best you can do?" inquired Donal. "Something sour?"

"I don't know, sir," said Lee. "I've got a pretty good nose, Force—in fact," a note of belligerence crept into his voice. "I've got a damned good nose. I never smelled anything like this before. I'd remember."

"Have either of you men ever contracted on this planet before?"

"No," said Lee.

"No, sir," answered Morphy.

"I see," said Donal. They had reached the same log from which they had started a little less than three hours before. "Well, that'll be all. Thank you, Groupmen."

He sat down on the log again. The other two hesitated a moment; and then went off together.

Left alone, Donal consulted the map again; and sat thinking for a while. Then he rose, and hunting up Morphy, told him to take over the Force, and stay awake. Donal himself was going to Command HQ. Then he took off.

Command HQ was a blackout shell containing a sleepy orderly, a map viewer and Skuak.

"The commandant around?" asked Donal, as he came in.

"Been asleep three hours," said Skuak. "What're you doing up? I wouldn't be if I didn't have the duty."

"Where's he sleeping?"

"About ten meters off in the bush, at eleven o'clock,"

said Skuak. "What's it all about? You aren't going to wake him, are you?"

"Maybe he'll still be awake," said Donal; and went out.

Outside the shell, and the little cleared space of the HQ area, he cat-footed around to the location Skuak had mentioned. A battle hammock was there, slung between two trees, with a form mounding its climate cover. But when Donal reached in to put his hand on the form's shoulder, it closed only on the soft material of a rolled-up battle jacket.

Donal breathed out and turned about. He went back the way he had come, past the Command HQ area, and was stopped by a sentry as he approached the village.

"Sorry, Force," said the sentry. "Commandant's order. No one to go into the village area. Not even himself, he says. Booby traps."

"Oh, yes—thank you, sentry," said Donal; and, turning about, went off into the darkness.

As soon as he was safely out of sight, however, he turned again, and worked his way back past the sentry lines and in among the houses of the village. The small but very bright moon which the Harmonites called The Eye of the Lord, was just rising, and throwing, through the ruined walls, alternate patches of tricky silver and black. Slipping in and out of the black places, he began patiently to search the place, house by house, and building by building.

It was a slow and arduous process, carried out the way he was doing it, in complete silence. And the moon mounted in the sky. It was nearly four hours later that he came upon what he was searching for.

In the moonlit center of a small building's roofless shell, stood Hugh Killien, looking very tall and efficient in his chameleon battle-dress. And close to him—almost close enough to be in his arms—was Anea, the Select of Kultis. Beyond them both, blurred by action of the polarizer that had undoubtedly been the means of allowing it to carry her invisibly to this spot, was a small flying platform.

". . . Sweet," Hugh was saying, his resonant voice pitched so low it barely carried to the ears of Donal, shrouded in shadow outside the broken wall, "Sweet, you must trust me. Together we can stop him; but you must let me handle it. His power is tremendous—"

"I know, I know!" she interrupted, fiercely, all but wringing her hands. "But every day we wait makes it more dangerous for you, Hugh. Poor Hugh—" gently she raised her hand to touch his cheek, "what I've dragged you into."

"Dragged? Me?" Hugh laughed, low and confidently. "I went into this with my eyes open." He reached out for her. "For you—"

But she slipped away from him.

"Now's not the time for that," she said. "Anyway, it's not me you're doing this for. It's Kultis. He's not going to use me," she said fiercely, "to get *my* world under his thumb!"

"Of course, it's for Kultis," said Hugh. "But you *are* Kultis, Anea. You're everything I love about the Exotics. But don't you see; all we have to work on are your suspicions. You *think* he's planning against the Bond, against Sayona, himself. But thats' not enough for us to go to Kultis with."

"But what can I do?" she cried. "I can't use his own methods against him. I can't lie, or cheat, or set agents on him while he still holds my contract. I . . . I just *can't*. That's what being Select means!" She clenched her fists. "I'm trapped by my own mind, my own body." She turned on him suddenly. "You said when

I first spoke to you, two months ago you said you had evidence!"

"I was mistaken," Hugh's tone was soothing. "Something came to my attention—at any rate I was wrong. I have my own built-in moral system, too, Anea. It may not reach the level of psychological blockage like yours," he drew himself up, looking very martial in the moonlight. "But I know what's honorable and right."

"Oh, I know. I know, Hugh—" she was all contrition. "But I get so desperate. You don't know—"

"If he had only made some move against you personally—"

"Me?" She stiffened. "He wouldn't dare! A Select of Kultis—and besides," she added with more of a touch of common sense than Donal had heretofore given her credit for possessing, "that'd be foolish. He'd have nothing to gain; and Kultis would be alerted against him."

"I don't know," Hugh scowled in the moonlight. "He's a man like anyone else. If I thought—"

"Oh, Hugh!" she giggled suddenly, like any schoolgirl. "Don't be absolutely ridiculous!"

"Ridiculous!" His tone rang with wounded feelings.

"Oh, now—I didn't mean that. Hugh, now stop looking like an elephant that just had his trunk stung by a bee. There's no point in making things up. He's far too intelligent to—" she giggled again, then sobered. "No, it's his head we have to worry about; not his heart."

"Do you worry about my heart?" he asked in a low voice.

She looked down at the ground.

"Hugh—I do like you," she said. "But you don't understand. A Select is a . . . a symbol."

"If you mean you can't—"

"No, no, not that—" she looked up quickly. "I've no block against love, Hugh. But if I was involved in something . . . something small, and mean, it's what it would do to those back on Kultis to whom a Select means something—You *do* understand?"

"I understand that I'm a soldier," he said. "And that I never know whether I'll have a tomorrow or not."

"I know," she said. "And they send you out on things like this, dangerous things."

"My dear little Anea," he said, tenderly. "How little you understand what it is to be a soldier. I volunteered for this job."

"Volunteered?" She stared at him.

"To go look for danger—to go look for opportunities to prove myself!" he said, fiercely. "To make myself a name, so that the stars will believe I'm the kind of man a Select of Kultis could want and belong with!"

"Oh, Hugh!" she cried on a note of enthusiasm. "If you only could! If only something would make you famous. Then we could really fight him!"

He checked, staring at her in the moonlight with such a sandbagged expression that Donal, in the shadows, nearly chuckled.

"Must you always be talking about politics?" he cried.

But Donal had already turned away from the two of them. There was no point in listening further. He moved silently out of earshot; but after that he went quickly, not caring about noise. His search for Hugh had taken him clear across the village, so that what was closest to him now was his own Force area. The short night of Harmony's northern continent was already beginning to gray toward dawn. He headed toward his own men, one of his odd certainties chilling him.

"Halt!" cried one of his own sentries, as Donal broke clear of the houses. "Halt and give—sir!"

"Come with me!" snapped Donal. "Where's the Third Group Area from here?"

"This way, sir," said the man; and led the way, trotting to keep up with Donal's long strides.

They burst into the Third Group area. Donal put his whistle to his lips and blew for Lee.

"What—?" mumbled a sleepy voice from half a dozen meters' distance. A hammock heaved and disgorged the bony figure of the ex-miner. "What the hell ... sir?"

Donal strode up to him and with both hands swung him about so that he faced toward the enemy territory from which the dawn breeze was coming. "Smell!" he ordered.

Lee blinked, scrubbed his nose with one knotty fist, and stifled a yawn. He took a couple of deep breaths, filling his lungs, his nostrils spread—and suddenly he snapped into complete awakedness.

"Same thing, sir," he said, turning to Donal. "Stronger."

"All right!" Donal wheeled about on the sentry. "Take a signal to Senior Groupmen, First and Second Groups. Get their men into trees, high up in trees, and get themselves up, too."

"Trees, sir?"

"Get going! I want every man in this Force a dozen meters off the ground in ten minutes—*with* their weapons!" The sentry turned to make off. "If you've got time after making that signal, try to get through to Command HQ with it. If you see you can't, climb a tree yourself. Got that?"

"Yes, sir."

"Then get going!"

Donal wheeled about and started himself on the business of getting the sleeping Third Group soldiers

out of their hammocks and up the trunks of tall trees.
It was not done in ten minutes. It was closer to twenty by the time they were all off the ground. A group
of Dorsai schoolboys would have made it in a quarter
of the time, from the sounder sleep of youth. But
on the whole, thought Donal, pulling himself at last
up into a tree, they had been in time; and that was
what counted.

He did not stop as the others had, at a height of a
dozen meters. Automatically, as he hurried the others
out of their hammocks, he had marked the tallest tree
in the area; and this he continued to climb until he
had a view out over the tops of the lesser vegetation
of the area. He shaded his eyes against the new-ris-
ing sun, peering off toward enemy territory, and between the trees.

"Now, what d'we do?" floated up an aggrieved
voice from below and off to one side of his own lofty
perch. Donal took his palm from his eyes and tilted
his head downward.

"Senior Groupman Lee," he said in a low, but carrying voice. "You will shoot the next man who opens
his mouth without being spoken to first by either you,
or myself. That is a direct order."

He raised his head again, amid a new silence, and
again peered off under his palm through the trees.

The secret of observation is patience. He saw nothing, but he continued to sit, looking at nothing in particular, and everything in general; and after four slow
minutes he was rewarded by a slight flicker of movement that registered on his gaze. He made no effort to
search it out again, but continued to observe in the
same general area; and gradually, as if they were
figures developing on a film out of some tangled
background, he became aware of men slipping from
cover to cover, a host of men, approaching the camp.

He leaned down again through the branches.

"No firing until I blow my whistle," he said, in an even lower voice than before. "Pass the word—quietly."

He heard, like the murmur of wind in those same branches, the order being relayed on to the last man in the Third Group and—he hoped—to the Second and First Groups as well.

The small, chameleon-clad figures continued to advance. Squinting at them through the occulting leaves and limbs, he made out a small black cross sewn to the right shoulder of each battle-dress. These were no mercenaries. These were native elite troops of the United Orthodox Church itself, superb soldiers and wild fanatics both. And even as the recognition confirmed itself in his mind, the advancing men broke into a charge upon the camp, bursting forth all at once in the red-gray dawnlight into full-throated yips and howls, underlaid a second later by the high-pitched singing of their spring-gun slivers as they ripped air and wood and flesh.

They were not yet among the trees where Donal's force was hiding. But his men were mercenaries, and had friends in the camp the Orthodox elite were attacking. He held them as long as he could, and a couple of seconds longer; and then, putting his whistle to lips, he blew with the damper completely off —a blast that echoed from one end of the camp to the other.

Savagely, his own men opened up from the trees. And for several moments wild confusion reigned on the ground. It is not easy to tell all at once from which direction a sliver gun is being fired at you. For perhaps five minutes, the attacking Orthodox soldiers labored under the delusion that the guns cutting them down were concealed in some ground-level ambush. They killed ruthlessly, everything they could see on their own eye-level; and, by the time they had discovered their mistake, it was too late. On their dwindled numbers was concentrated the fire of a hundred and fifty-one rifles; and if the marksmanship of only one of these was up to Dorsai standards, that of the rest was adequate to the task. In less than forty minutes from the moment in which Donal had begun to harry his sleep-drugged men up into the trees, the combat was over.

The Third Group slid down out of their trees and one of the first down—a soldier named Kennebuc—calmly lifted his rifle to his shoulder and sent a sliver through the throat of an Orthodox that was writhing on the ground, nearby.

"None of that!" cried Donal, sharply and clearly; and his voice carried out over the area. A mercenary hates wanton killing, it not being his business to slaughter men, but to win battles. But not another shot was fired. The fact said something about a significant change in the attitude of the men of the Third Command toward a certain new officer by the name of Graeme.

Under Donal's orders, the wounded on both sides were collected and those with serious wounds medicated. The attacking soldiery had been wiped out almost to a man. But it had not been completely one-sided. Of the three hundred-odd men who had been on the ground at the time of the attack, all but forty-three—and that included Force-Leader Skuak—were casualties.

"Prepare to retreat," ordered Donal—and, at that moment, the man facing him turned his head to look past at something behind Donal. Donal turned about. Pounding out of the ruined village, hand gun in his fist, was Commandant Killienn.

In silence, not moving, the surviving soldiers of the Command watched him race up to them. He checked at their stare; and his eyes swung about to focus on Donal. He dropped to a walk and strode up to within a few meters of the younger officer.

"Well, Force-Leader!" he snapped. "What happened? Report?"

Donal did not answer him directly. He raised his hand and pointed to Hugh; and spoke to two of the enlisted men standing by.

"Soldiers," he said. "Arrest that man. And hold him for immediate trial under Article Four of the Mercenaries Code."

VETERAN

Directly after getting into the city, with his canceled contract stiff in his pocket, and cleaning up in his hotel room, Donal went down two flights to pay his visit to Marshal Hendrik Galt. He found him in, and concluded certain business with him before leaving to pay his second call at a different hotel across the city.

In spite of himself, he felt a certain weakness in the knees as he announced his presence to the doorbot. It was a weakness most men would have excused him. William, Prince of Ceta, was someone few persons would have cared to beard in his own den; and Donal, in spite of what he had just experienced, was still a young—a very young—man. However, the doorbot invited him in, and summoning up his calmest expression, Donal strode into the suite.

William was, as the last time Donal had seen him, busy at his desk. This was no affectation on William's part, as a good many people between the stars could testify. Seldom has one individual accomplished in a single day what William accomplished in the way of business, daily, as a matter of routine. Donal walked up to the desk and nodded his greeting. William looked up at him.

"I'm amazed to see you," he said.

"Are you, sir?" said Donal.

William considered him in silence for perhaps half a minute.

"It's not often I make mistakes," he said. "Perhaps I can console myself with the thought that when I do they turn out to be on the same order of magnitude as my successes. What inhuman kind of armor are you wearing, young man, that leads you to trust yourself in my presence, again?"

"Possibly the armor of public opinion," replied Donal. "I've been in the public eye, recently. I have something of a name, nowadays."

"Yes," said William. "I know that type of armor from personal experience, myself."

"And then," said Donal, "you did send for me."

"Yes." And then, without warning, William's face underwent a change to an expression of such savagery as Donal had never seen before. "How dare you!" snarled the older man, viciously. "How dare you!"

"Sir," said Donal, wooden-faced, "I had no alternative."

"No alternative! You come to me and have the effrontery to say—no alternative?"

"Yes, sir," said Donal.

William rose in swift and lithe motion. He stalked around the desk to stand face to face, his eyes uptilted a little to bore into the eyes of this tall young Dorsai.

"I took you on to follow my orders, nothing else!" he said icily. "And you—grandstand hero that you are —wreck everything."

"Sir?"

"Yes—'*sir*'. You backwoods moron! You imbecile! Who told you to interfere with Hugh Killien? Who told you to take any action about him?"

"Sir," said Donal. "I had no choice."

"No choice? How—no choice?"

"My command was a command of mercenaries," answered Donal, without moving a muscle. "Commandant Killien had given his assurance in accordance with the Mercenaries Code. Not only had his assurance proved false, he himself had neglected his command while in the field and in enemy territory. Indirectly, he had been responsible for the death of over half his men. As ranking field officer present, I had no choice but to arrest him and hold him for trial."

"A trial held on the spot?"

"It is the code, sir," said Donal. He paused. "I regret it was necessary to shoot him. The court-martial left me no alternative."

"Again!" said William. "No alternative! Graeme, the space between the stars does not go to men who can find *no alternatives!*" He turned about abruptly, walked back around his desk and sat down.

"All right," he said, coldly but with all the passion gone, "get out of here." Donal turned and walked toward the door as William picked up a paper from before him. "Leave your address with my doorbot," said William. "I'll find some kind of a post for you on some other world."

"I regret, sir—" said Donal.

William looked up.

"It didn't occur to me that you would have any

further need of me. Marshal Galt has already found me another post."

William continued to look at him for a long moment. His eyes were as cold as the eyes of a basilisk.

"I see," he said at last, slowly. "Well, Graeme, perhaps we shall have something to do with each other in the future."

"I'll hope we will," said Donal. He went out. But, even after he had closed the door behind him, he thought he could feel William's eyes still coming at him through all the thickness of its panel.

He had yet one more call to make, before his duty on this world was done. He checked the directory out in the corridor and went down a flight.

The doorbot invited him in; and ArDell Montor, as large and untidy as ever, with his eyes only slightly blurred from drink, met him halfway to the entrance.

"You!" said ArDell, when Donal explained what it was he wanted. "She won't see *you*." He hunched his heavy shoulders, looking at Donal; and for a second his eyes cleared. Something sad and kind looked out of them, to be replaced with bitter humor. "But the old fox won't like it. I'll ask her."

"Tell her it's about something she needs to know," said Donal.

"I'll do that. Wait here," ArDell went out the door. He returned in some fifteen minutes.

"You're to go up," he said. "Suite 1890." Donal turned toward the door. "I don't suppose," said the Newtonian, almost wistfully, "I'll be seeing you again."

"Why, we may meet," answered Donal.

"Yes," said ArDell. He stared at Donal penetratingly. "We may at that. We may at that."

Donal went out and up to Suite 1890. The doorbot let him in. Anea was waiting for him, slim and rigid in one of her high-collared, long dresses of blue.

"Well?" she said. Donal considered her almost sorrowfully.

"You really hate me, don't you?" he said.

"You killed him!" she blazed.

"Oh, of course." In spite of himself, the exasperation she was always so capable of tapping in him, rose to the surface. "I had to—for your own good."

"For my good!"

He reached into his tunic pocket and withdrew a small telltale. But it was unlighted. For a wonder this apartment was unbugged. And then he thought—*of course, I keep forgetting who she is.*

"Listen to me," he said. "You've been beautifully equipped by gene selection and training to be a Select—but not to be anything else. Why can't you understand that interstellar intrigue isn't your dish?"

"Interstellar . . . what're you talking about?" she demanded.

"Oh, climb down for a moment," he said wearily—and more youngly than he had said anything since leaving home. "William is your enemy. You understand that much; but you don't understand why or how, although you think you do. And neither do I," he confessed, "although I've got a notion. But the way for you to confound William isn't by playing his game. Play your own. Be the Select of Kultis. As the Select, you're untouchable."

"If," she said, "you've nothing more to say than that—"

"All right," he took a step toward her. "Listen, then. William was making an attempt to compromise you. Killien was his tool—"

"How dare you?" she erupted.

"How dare I?" he echoed wearily. "Is there anyone in this interstellar community of madmen and madwomen who doesn't know that phrase and use it to me on sight? I dare because it's the truth."

"Hugh," she stormed at him, "was a fine, honest man. A soldier and a gentleman! Not a . . . a—"

"Mercenary?" he inquired. "But he was."

"He was a career officer," she replied haughtily. "There's a difference."

"No difference." He shook his head. "But you wouldn't understand that. Mercenary isn't necessarily the dirty word somebody taught you it is. Never mind. Hugh Killien was worse than any name you might be mistaken enough to call me. He was a fool."

"Oh!" she whirled about.

He took her by one elbow and turned her around. She came about in shocked surprise. Somehow, it had never occurred to her to imagine how strong he was. Now, the sudden realization of her physical helplessness in his hands shocker her into abrupt and unusual silence.

"Listen to the truth, then," he said. "William dangled you like an expensive prize before Killien's eyes. He fed him full of the foolish hope that he could have *you*— the Select of Kultis. He made it possible for you to visit Hugh that night at Faith Will Succour— yes," he said, at her gasp, "I know about that. I saw you there with him. He also made sure Hugh would meet you, just as he made sure that the Orthodox soldiers would attack."

"I don't believe it—" she managed.

"Don't you be a fool, too," Donal said, roughly. "How else do you think an overwhelming force of Orthodox elite troops happened to move in on the encampment at just the proper time? What other men than fanatic Orthodox soldiery could be counted on to make sure none of the men in our unit escaped alive? There was supposed to be only one man to escape from that affair—Hugh Killien, who would be in a position then to make a hero's claim on you. You see how much your good opinion is worth?"

"Hugh wouldn't—"

"Hugh didn't," interrupted Donal. "As I said, he was a fool. A fool but a good soldier. Nothing more was needed for William. He knew Hugh would be fool enough to go and meet you, and good soldier enough not to throw his life away when he saw his command was destroyed. As I say, he would have come back alone—and a hero."

"But you saw through this!" she snapped. "What's your secret? A pipeline to the Orthodox camp?"

"Surely it was obvious from the situation; a command exposed, a commandant foolishly making a love-tryst in a battleground, that something like the attack was inevitable. I simply asked myself what kind of troops would be used and how they might be detected. Orthodox troops eat nothing but native herbs, cooked in the native fashion. The odor of their cooking permeates their clothing. Any veteran of a Harmony campaign would be able to recognize their presence the same way."

"If his nose was sensitive enough. If he knew where to look for them—"

"There was only one logical spot—"

"Anyway," she said coldly. "This is beside the point. The point is"—suddenly she fired up before him—"Hugh wasn't guilty. You said it yourself. He was, even according to you, only a fool! And you had him murdered!"

He sighed in weariness.

"The crime," he said, "for which Commandant Killien was executed was that of misleading his men and abandoning them in enemy territory. It was *that* he paid with his life for."

"Murderer!" she said. "Get out!"

"But," he said, staring baffledly at her, "I've just explained."

"You've explained nothing," she said, coldly, and from a distance. "I've heard nothing but a mountain of lies, lies, lies, about a man whose boots you aren't fit to clean. Now, will you get out, or do I have to call the hotel guard?"

"You don't believe—?" He stared at her, wide-eyed.

"Get out." She turned her back on him. Like a man in a daze, he turned himself and walked blindly to door and numbly out into the corridor. Still walking, he shook his head, like a person who finds himself in a bad dream and unable to wake up.

What was this curse upon him? She had not been lying—she was not capable of doing so successfully. She had really heard his explanation and—it had meant nothing to her. It was all so obvious, so plain —the machinations of William, the stupidity of Killien. And she had not seen it when Donal pointed it out to her. *She*, of all people, a Select of Kultis!

Why? Why? Why?

Scourged by the devils of self-doubt and loneliness, Donal moved off down the corridor, back in the direction of Galt's hotel.

AIDE-DE-CAMP

They met in the office of Marshal Galt, in his Freiland home; and the enormous expanse of floor and the high vaulted ceiling dwarfed them as they stood three men around a bare desk.

"Captain Lludrow, this is my Aide, Commandant Donal Graeme," said Galt, brusquely. "Donal, this is Russ Lludrow, Patrol Chief of my Blue Patrol."

"Honored, sir," said Donal, inclining his head.

"Pleased to meet you, Graeme," answered Lludrow. He was a fairly short, compact man in his early forties, very dark of skin and eye.

"You'll trust Donal with all staff information," said Galt. "Now, what's your reconnaissance and intelligence picture?"

"There's no doubt about it, they're planning an expeditionary landing on Oriente." Lludrow turned toward the desk and pressed buttons on the map keyboard. The top of the desk cleared to transparency and they looked through at a non-scale map of the Sirian system. "Here we are," he said, stabbing his finger at the world of Freiland, "Here's New Earth" —his finger moved to Freiland's sister planet—"and here's Oriente"—his finger skipped to a smaller world inward toward the sun—"in the positions they'll be in, relative to one another twelve days from now. You see, we'll have the sun between the two of us and also almost between each of our worlds and Oriente. They couldn't have picked a more favorable tactical position."

Galt grunted, examining the map. Donal was watching Lludrow with quiet curiosity. The man's accent betrayed him for a New Earthman, but here he was high up on the Staff of Freiland's fighting forces. Of course, the two Sirian worlds were natural allies, being on the same side as Old Earth against the Mars-Venus-Newton-Cassida group; but simply because they were so close, there was a natural rivalry in some things, and a career officer from one of them usually did best on his home world.

"Don't like it," said Galt, finally. "It's a fool stunt from what I can see. The men they land will have to wear respirators; and what the devil do they expect to do with their beachhead when they establish it? Oriente's too close to the sun for terraforming, or we would have done it from here long ago."

"It's possible," said Lludrow, calmly, "they could intend to mount an offensive from there against our two planets here."

"No, no," Galt's voice was harsh and almost irritable. His heavy face loomed above the map. "That's as wild a notion as terraforming Oriente. They couldn't keep a base there supplied, let along using it to attack two large planets with fully established population and industry. Besides, you don't conquer civilized worlds. That's a maxim."

"Maxims can become worn out, though," put in Donal.

"What?" demanded Galt, looking up. "Oh—Donal. Don't interrupt us now. From the looks of it," he went on to Lludrow, "it strikes me as nothing so much as a live exercise—you know what I mean."

Lludrow nodded—as did Donal unconsciously. Live exercises were something that no planetary Chief of Staff admitted to, but every military man recognized. They were actual small battles provoked with a handy enemy either for the purpose of putting a final edge on troops in training, or to keep that edge on troops that had been too long on a standby basis. Galt, almost alone among the Planetary Commanders of his time, was firmly set against this action, not only in theory, but in practice. He believed it more honest to hire his troops out, as in the recent situation on Harmony, when they showed signs of going stale. Donal privately agreed with him; although there was always the danger that when you hired troops out, they lost the sense of belonging to you, in particular, and were sometimes spoiled through mismanagement.

"What do you think?" Galt was asking his Patrol chief.

"I don't know, sir," Lludrow answered. "It seems the only sensible interpretation."

"The thing," interrupted Donal, again, "would be to go over some of the nonsensible interpretations as well, to see if one of them doesn't constitute a possible danger. And from that—"

"Donal," broke in Galt, dryly, "you are my aide, not my Battle Op."

"Still—" Donal was persisting, when the marshal cut him off in a tone of definite command.

"That will be all!"

"Yes, sir," said Donal, subsiding.

"Then," said Galt, turning back to Lludrow, "we'll regard this as a heaven-sent opportunity to cut an arm or two off the fighting strength of the Newton-Cassidan fleet and field force. Go back to your Patrol. I'll send orders."

Lludrow inclined his head and was just about to turn and go when there was an interruption—the faint swish of air from one of the big office doors sliding back, and the tap of feminine heels approaching over the polished floor. They turned to see a tall, dazzlingly beautiful woman with red hair coming at them across the office.

"Elvine!" said Galt.

"Not interrupting anything, am I?" she called, even before she came up to them. "Didn't know you had a visitor."

"Russ," said Galt. "You know my sister-in-law's daughter, The Elvine Rhy? Elvine, this is my Blue Patrol Chief, Russ Lludrow."

"Very deeply honored," said Lludrow, bowing.

"Oh, we've met—or at least I've seen you before."

She gave him her hand briefly, then turned to Donal. "Donal, come fishing with me."

"I'm sorry," said Donal. "I'm on duty."

"No, no," Galt waved him off with a large hand. "There's nothing more at the moment. Run along, if you want."

"At your service, then," said Donal.

"But what a cold acceptance!" she turned on Lludrow. "I'm sure the Patrol chief wouldn't have hesitated like that."

Lludrow bowed again.

"I'd never hesitate where the Rhy was concerned."

"There!" she said. "There's your model, Donal. You should practice manners—and speeches like that."

"If you suggest it," said Donal.

"Oh, Donal." She tossed her head. "You're hopeless. But come along, anyway." She turned and left; and he followed her.

They crossed the great central hall and emerged into the garden terrace above the blue-green bay of the shallow, inland sea that touched the edges of Galt's home. He expected her to continue down to the docks, but instead she whirled about in a small arbor, and stood facing him.

"Why do you treat me like this?" she threw at him. "Why?"

"Treat you?" He looked down at her.

"Oh, you wooden man!" Her lips skinned back over her perfect teeth. "What're you afraid of—that I'll eat you up?"

"Wouldn't you?" he asked her quite seriously—and she checked at his answer.

"Come on. Let's go fishing!" she cried, and whirled about and ran down toward the dock.

So, they went fishing. But even slicing through the water in pursuit of a twisting fish at sixty fathoms depth, Donal's mind was not on the sport. He let the small jet unit on his shoulders push him whither the chase led him; and, in the privacy of his helmet, condemned himself darkly for his own ignorance. For it was this crime of ignorance which he abhorred above all else—in this case his ignorance of the ways of women—that had led him to believe he could allow himself the luxury of a casual and friendly acquaintanceship with a woman who wanted him badly, but whom he, himself, did not want at all.

She had been living here, in this household, when Galt had brought him here as a personal aide. She was, by some intricate convolution of Freiland inheritance laws, the marshal's responsibility; in spite of the distance of their relationships and the fact that her own mother and some other relatives were still living. She was some five years older than Donal, although in her wild energy and violence of emotion, this difference was lost. He had found her excitements interesting, at first; and her company a balm to what —though he would not admit it to himself in so many words—was a recently bruised and very tender portion of his ego. That had been at first.

"You know," she had said to him in one of her peculiar flashes of directness. "Anybody would want me."

"Anybody would," he admitted, considering her beauty. It was not until later that he discovered, to his dismay, that he had accepted an invitation he had not even suspected was there.

For four months now, he had been established at the marshal's estate, learning some of the elements of Freilander Staff Control; and learning also, to his increasing dismay, some of the intricacies of a woman's mind. And, in addition to it all, he found himself puzzled as to why he did not want her. Certainly he liked Elvine Rhy. Her company was enjoyable, her

attractiveness was undeniable, and a certain brightness and hunger in her personality matched similar
traits in his own. Yet, he did not want her. No, not the
least bit, not at all.

They gave up their fishing after several hours. Elvine had caught four, averaging a good seven or eight
kilograms. He had caught none.

"Elvine—" he began, as he went up the steps of
the terrace with her. But, before he could finish his
carefully thought out speech, an annunciator hidden
in a rosebush chimed softly.

"Commandant," said the rosebush, gently, "the
doorbot announces a Senior Groupman Tage Lee to
see you. Do you wish to see him?"

"Lee—" murmured Donal. He raised his voice.
"From Harmony?"

"He says he is from Harmony," answered the rosebush.

"I'll see him," said Donal, striding quickly toward
the house. He heard the sound of running feet behind
him and Elvine caught at his arm.

"Donal—" she said.

"This'll just take a minute," he answered. "I'll see
you in the library in a few minutes."

"All right—" She let go and fell behind him. He
went in and to the entrance hall.

Lee, the same Lee who had commanded his Third
Group, was waiting for him.

"Well, Groupman," said Donal, shaking hands.
"What brings you here?"

"You do, sir," said Lee. He looked Donal in the eye
with something of the challenge Donal had marked
the first time Donal had seen him. "Could you use a
personal orderly?"

Donal considered him.

"Why?"

"I've been carrying my contract around since they let us all go after that business with Killien," said Lee. "If you want to know, I've been on a bat. That's my cross. Out of uniform I'm an alcoholic. In uniform, it's better, but sooner or later I get into a hassle with somebody. I've been putting off signing up again because I couldn't make up my mind what I wanted. Finally, it came to me. I wanted to work for you."

"You look sober enough now," said Donal.

"I can do anything for a few days—even stop drinking. If I'd come up here with the shakes, you'd never have taken me."

Donal nodded.

"I'm not expensive," said Lee. "Take a look at my contract. If you can't afford me yourself, I'll sign up as a line soldier and you pull strings to get me assigned to you. I don't drink if I've got something to do; and I can make myself useful. Look here—"

He extended his hand in a friendly manner, as if to shake hands again, and suddenly there was a knife in it.

"That's a back-alley, hired killer trick," said Donal. "Do you think it'd work with me?"

"With you—no." Lee made the knife vanish again. "That's why I want to work for you. I'm a funny character, commandant. I need something to hang to. I need it the way ordinary people need food and drink and home and friends. It's all there in the psychological index number on my contract, if you want to copy it down and check on me."

"I'll take your word for it, for now," said Donal. "What *is* wrong with you?"

"I'm borderline psycho," Lee answered, his lean face expressionless. "Not correctable. I was born with a deficiency. What they tell me is, I've got no sense of right or wrong; and I can't manage just by abstract rules. The way the doctors put it when I first got my contract, I need my own, personal, living god in front of me all the time. You take me on and tell me to cut the throat of all the kids under five I meet, and that's fine. Tell me to cut my own throat—the same thing. Everything's all right, then."

"You don't make yourself sound very attractive."

"I'm telling you the truth. I can't tell *you* anything else. I'm like a bayonet that's been going around all my life looking for a rifle to fit on to; and now I've found it. So, don't trust me. Take me on probation for five years, ten years—the rest of my life. But don't shut me out." Lee half-turned and pointed one bony finger at the door behind him. "Out there is hell for me, commandant. Anything inside here is heaven."

"I don't know," said Donal, slowly. "I don't know that I'd want the responsibility."

"No responsibility." Lee's eyes were shining; and it struck home to Donal suddenly that the man was terrified: terrified of being refused. "Just tell me. Try me, now. Tell me to get down and bark like a dog. Tell me to cut my left hand off at the wrist. As soon as they've grown me a new one I'll be back to do whatever you want me to do." The knife was suddenly back in his hand. "Want to see?"

"Put that away!" snapped Donal. The knife disappeared. "All right, I'll buy your contract personally. My suite of rooms are third door to the right, the head of the stairs. Go up there and wait for me."

Lee nodded. He offered no word of thanks. He only turned and went.

Donal shook himself mentally as if the emotional charge that had crackled in the air about him the last few seconds was a thing of physical mass draped heavily upon his shoulders. He turned and went to the library.

Elvine was standing looking out the great expanse of open wall at the ocean, as he came in. She turned quickly, at the sound of his steps and came to meet him.

"What was it?" she asked.

"One of my soldiers from the Harmony business," he said. "I've taken him on as my personal orderly." He looked down at her. "Ev—"

Instantly, she drew a little away from him. She looked out the wall, one hand falling down to play with a silver half-statuette that sat on a low table beside her.

"Yes?" she said.

He found it very hard to get the words out.

"Ev, you know I've been around here a long time," he said.

"A long time?" At that, she turned to face him with a slight look of startlement. "Four months? It seems like hours, only."

"Perhaps," he said, doggedly. "But it *has* been a long time. So perhaps it's just as well I'm leaving."

"Leaving?" Her eyes shot wide; hazel eyes, staring at him. "Who said you were leaving?"

"I have to, of course," he said, "But I thought I ought to clear something up before I go. I've liked you a great deal, Ev—"

But she was too quick for him.

"Liked me?" she cried. "I should think you should! Why, I haven't hardly had a minute to myself for entertaining you. I swear I hardly know what it looks like any more outside of this place! Liked me! You certainly ought to like me after the way I've put myself out for you!"

He gazed at her furious features for a long moment and then he smiled ruefully.

"You're quite right," he said. "I've put you to a great deal of trouble. Pardon me for being so dense as not to notice it." He bent his head to her. "I'll be going now."

He turned and walked away. But he had hardly taken a dozen steps across the sunlit library before she called his name.

"Donal!"

He turned and saw her staring after him, her face stiff, her fists clenched at her side.

"Donal, you . . . you can't go," she said, tightly.

"I beg your pardon?" He stared at her.

"You can't go," she repeated. "Your duty is here. You're assigned here."

"No." He shook his head. "You don't understand, Ev. This business of Oriente's come up. I'm going to ask the marshal to assign me to one of the ships."

"You can't." Her voice was brittle. "He isn't here. He's gone down to the Spaceyard."

"Well, then, I'll go there and ask him."

"You can't. I've already asked him to leave you here. He promised."

"You *what?*" The words exploded from his lips in a tone more suited to the field than to this quiet mansion.

"I asked him to leave you here."

He turned and stalked away from her.

"Donal!" He heard her voice crying despairingly after him, but there was nothing she, or anyone in that house could have done, to stop him then.

He found Galt examining the new experimental model of a two-man anti-personnel craft. The older man looked up in surprise as Donal came up.

"What is it?" he asked.

"Could I see you alone for a minute, sir?" said Donal. "A private and urgent matter."

Galt shot him a keen glance, but motioned aside with his head and they stepped over into the privacy of a tool control booth.

"What is it?" asked Galt.

"Sir," said Donal. "I understand Elvine asked you if I couldn't continue to be assigned to your household during the upcoming business we talked about with Patrol Chief Lludrow earlier today."

"That's right. She did."

"I did not know of it," said Donal, meeting the older man's eyes. "It was not my wish."

"Not your wish?"

"No, sir."

"Oh," said Galt. He drew a long breath and rubbed his chin with one thick hand. Turning his head aside, he gazed out through the screen of the control booth at the experimental ship. "I see," he said. "I didn't realize."

"No reason why you should." Donal felt a sudden twist of emotion inside him at the expression on the older man's face. "I should have spoken to you before, sir."

"No, no," Galt brushed the matter aside with a wave of his hand. "The responsibility's mine. I've never had children. No experience. She has to get herself settled in life one of these days; and . . . well, I have a high opinion of you, Donal."

"You've been too kind to me already, sir," Donal said miserably.

"No, no . . . well, mistakes will happen. I'll see you have a place with the combat forces right away, of course."

"Thank you," said Donal.

"Don't thank me, boy." Abruptly, Galt looked old. "I should have remembered. You're a Dorsai."

STAFF LIAISON

"Welcome aboard," said a pleasant-faced Junior Captain, as Donal strode through the gas barrier of the inner lock. The Junior Captain was in his early twenties, a black-haired, square-faced young man who looked as if he had gone in much for athletics. "I'm J. C. Allmin Clay Andresen."

"Donal Graeme." They saluted each other. Then they shook hands.

"Had any ship experience?" asked Andresen.

"Eighteen months of summer training cruises in the Dorsai," answered Donal. "Command and armament —no technical posts."

"Command and armament," said Andresen, "are plenty good enough on a Class 4J ship. Particularly Command. You'll be senior officer after me—if anything happens." He made the little ritual gesture, reaching out to touch a close, white, carbon-plastic wall beside him. "Not that I'm suggesting you take over in such a case. My First can handle things all right. But you may be able to give him a hand, if it should happen."

"Be honored," said Donal.

"Care to look over the ship?"

"I'm looking forward to it."

"Right. Step into the lounge, then." Andersen led the way across the small reception room, and through a sliding bulkhead to a corridor that curved off ahead of them to right and left. They went through another door in the wall of the corridor directly in front of them, down a small passage, and emerged through a final door into a large, pleasantly decorated, circular room.

"Lounge," said Andresen. "Control center's right under our feet; reverse gravity." He pressed a stud on the wall and a section of the floor slid back. "You'll have to flip," he warned, and did a head-first dive into the hole.

Donal, who knew what to expect, followed the J. C.'s example. The momentum of his dive shot him through and into another circular chamber of the same size as the lounge, in which everything would have been upside down and nailed to the ceiling, except for the small fact that here the gravity was reversed; and what had been down, was up, and up was down instead.

"Here," said Andresen, as Donal landed lightly on the floor at one side of the opening, "is our Control Eye. As you probably saw when you were moving in to come aboard, the Class 4J is a ball-and-hammer ship." He pressed several studs and in the large globe floating in the center of the floor, that which he had referred to as the Control Eye, a view formed of their craft, as seen from some little distance outside the ship. Half-framed against the star-pricked backdrop of space, and with just a sliver of the curved edge of Freiland showing at the edge of the scene, she floated. A sphere thirty meters in diameter, connected by two slim shafts a hundred meters each in length to a rhomboid-shape that was the ship's thrust unit, some five meters in diameter at its thickest and looking like a large child's spinning top, pivoted on two wires that clamped it at the middle. This was the "hammer." The ship, proper, was the "ball."

"No phase-shift equipment?" asked Donal. He was

thinking of the traditional cylinder shape of the big
ships that moved between the stars.

"Don't fool yourself," answered Andresen. "The
grid's there. We just hope the enemy doesn't see it,
or doesn't hit it. We can't protect it, so we try to make
it invisible." His finger stabbed out to indicate the
apparently bare shafts. "There's a covering grid running the full length of the ship, from thrust to nose.
Painted black."

Donal nodded thoughtfully.

"Too bad a polarizer won't work in the absence of
atmosphere," he said.

"You can say that," agreed Andresen. He flicked off
the Eye. "Let's look around the rest of the ship by
hand."

He led out a door and down a passage similar to
the one by which they had entered the lounge. They
came out into a corridor that was the duplicate of the
curving one they had passed in the other half of the
ship.

"Crew's quarters, mess hall, on the other one," explained Andresen. "Officer's quarters, storage and sup-
pliers, repair section, on this one." He pushed open a
door in the corridor wall opposite them and they
stepped into a section roughly the size of a small hotel
room, bounded on its farther side by the curving outer
shell of the ship, proper. The shell in this secion was,
at the moment, on transparent; and the complicated
"dentist's chair" facing the bank of controls at the foot
of the transparency was occupied; although the figure in it was dressed in coveralls only.

"My First," said Andresen. The figure looked up
over the headrest of the chair. It was a woman in her
early forties.

"Hi, All," she said. "Just checking the override."
Andresen made a wry grimace at Donal.

"Antipersonnel weapons," he explained. "Nobody likes to shoot the poor helpless characters out of the sky as they fall in for an assault—so it's an officer's job. I usually take it over myself if I'm not tied up with something else at the moment. Staff Liaison Donal Graeme—First Officer Coa Benn."

Donal and she shook hands.

"Well, shall we get on?" asked Andresen. They toured the rest of the ship and ended up before the door of Donal's stateroom in Officer's Country.

"Sorry," said Andresen. "But we're short of bunk space. Full complement under battle conditions. So we had to put your orderly in with you. If you've no objection—"

"Not at all," said Donal.

"Good," Andresen looked relieved. "That's why I like the Dorsai. They're so sensible." He clapped Donal on the shoulder, and went hurriedly off back to his duties of getting his ship and crew ready for action.

Entering his stateroom, Donal found Lee had already set up both their gear, including a harness hammock for himself to supplement the single bunk that would be Donal's.

"All set?" asked Donal.

"All set," answered Lee. He still chronically forgot the "sir"; but Donal, having already had some experience with the fanatic literal-mindedness with which the man carried out any command given him, had refrained from making an issue of it. "You settle my contract, yet?"

"I haven't had time," said Donal. "It can't be done in a day. You knew that, didn't you?"

"No," said Lee. "All I ever did was hand it over. And then, later on when I was through my term of service they gave it back to me; and the money I had coming."

"Well, it usually takes a number of weeks or months," Donal said. He explained what it had never occurred to him that anyone should fail to know, that the contracts are owned entirely by the individual's home community or world, and that a contract agreement was a matter for settlement between the employer and the employee's home government. The object was not to provide the individual so much with a job and a living wage, as to provide the home government with favorable monetary and "contractual" balances which would enable them to hire, in their turn, the trained specialists *they* needed. In the case of Lee's contract, since Donal was a private employer and had money to offer, but no contractual credits, the matter of Lee's employment had to be cleared with the Dorsai authorities, as well as the authorities on Coby, where Lee came from.

"That's more of a formality than anything else, though," Donal assured him. "I'm allowed an orderly, since I've been commandant rank. And the intent to hire's been registered. That means your home government won't draft you for any special service some place else."

Lee nodded, which was almost his utmost expression of relief.

". . . Signall" chimed the annunciator in the state-room wall by the door, suddenly. "Signal for Staff Liaison Graeme. Report to Flagship, immediately. Staff Liaison Graeme report to Flagshlip immediately."

Donal cautioned Lee to keep from under the feet of the ship's regular crew; and left.

The Flagship of the Battle made up by the Red and Green Patrols of the Freilander Space Force was, like the Class 4J Donal had just left, already in temporary loose orbit around Oriente. It took him some forty minutes to reach here; and when he entered her lock reception room and gave his name and rank, he was assigned a guide who took him to a briefing room in the ship's interior.

The room was filled by some twenty-odd other Staff Liaisons.

They ranged in rank from Warrant Couriers to a Sub-Patrol Chief in his fifties. They were already seated facing a platform; and, as Donal entered—he was, apparently, the last to arrive—a Senior Captain of flag rank entered, followed closely by Blue Patrol Chief Lludrow.

"All right, gentlemen," said the Senior Captain; and the room came to order. "Here's the situation." He waved a hand and the wall behind him dissolved to reveal an artist's extrapolation of the coming battle. Oriente floated in black space, surrounded by a number of ships in various patterns. The size of the ships had been grossly exaggerated in order to make them visible in comparison with the planet which was roughly two-thirds the diameter of Mars. The largest of these, the Patrol Class—long cylindrical interstellar warships—were in varying orbit eighty to five hundred kilometers above the planet's surface, so that the integration of their pattern enclosed Oriente in web of shifting movement. A cloud of smaller craft, C4Js, A(subclass)9s, courier ships, firing platforms, and individual and two-man gnat class boats, held position out beyond and planetward of them, right down into the atmosphere.

"We think," said the Senior Captain, "that the enemy, at effective speed and already braking, will come into phase about here—" a cloud of assault ships winked into existence abruptly, a half million kilometers sunward of Oriente, and in the sun's eye. They fell rapidly toward the planet, swelling visibly in size. As they approached, they swung into a circular landing orbit about the planet. The smaller craft closed in, and the two fleets came together in a myriad of patterns whose individual motions the eye could not follow all at once. Then the attacking fleet emerged below the mass of the defenders, spewing a sudden cloud of tiny objects that were the assault troops. These drifted down, attacked by the smaller craft, while the majority of the assault ships from Newton and Cassida began to disappear like blown-out candles as they sought safety in a phase shift that would place them light-years from the scene of battle.

To Donal's fine-trained professional mind it was both beautifully thrilling—and completely false. No battle since time began had ever gone off with such ballet grace and balance and none ever would. This was only an imaginative guess at how the battle would take place, and it had no place in it for the inevitable issuance of wrong orders, the individual hesitations, the underestimation of an opponent, the navigational errors that resulted in collisions, or firing upon a brother ship. These all remained for the actual event, like harpies roosting upon the yet-unblasted limbs of a tree, as dawn steals like some gray thief onto the field where men are going to fight. In the coming action off Oriente there would be good actions and bad, wise decisions, and stupid ones—and none of them would matter. Only their total at the end of the day.

". . . Well, gentlemen," the Senior Captain was saying, "there you have it as Staff sees it. Your job—yours personally, as Staff Liaisons—is to observe. We want to know anything you can see, anything you can discover, anything you can, or think you can, deduce. And of course"—he hesitated, with a wry smile

—"there's nothing we'd appreciate quite so much as a prisoner."

There was a ripple of general laughter at this, as all men there knew the fantastic odds against being able to scoop up a man from an already broken-open enemy ship under the velocities and other conditions of a space battle—and find him still alive, even if you succeeded.

"That's all," said the Senior Captain. The Staff Liaisons rose and began to crowd out the door.

"Just a minute, Graeme!"

Donal turned. The voice was the voice of Lludrow. The Patrol Chief had come down from the platform and was approaching him. Donal turned back to meet him.

"I'd like to speak to you for a moment," said Lludrow. "Wait until the others are out of the room." They stood together in silence until the last of the Staff Liaisons had left, and the Senior Captain had disappeared.

"Yes, sir?" said Donal.

"I'm interested in something you said—or maybe were about to say the other day—when I met you at Marshal Galt's in the process of assessing this Oriente business. You said something that seemed to imply doubt about the conclusions we came to. But I never did hear what it was you had in mind. Care to tell me now?"

"Why, nothing, sir," said Donal. "Staff and the marshal undoubtedly know what they're doing."

"It isn't possible, then, you saw something in the situation that we didn't?" Donal hesitated.

"No, sir. I don't know any more about enemy intensions and plans than the rest of you. Only—" Donal looked down into the dark face below his, wavering on the verge of speaking his mind. Since the affair

with Anea he had been careful to keep his flights of
mental perception to himself. "Possibly I'm just sus-
picious, sir."

"So are all of us, man!" said Lludrow, with a hint of
impatience. "What about it? In our shoes what would
you be doing?"

"In your shoes," said Donal, throwing discretion to
the winds, "I'd attack Newton."

Lludrow's jaw fell. He stared at Donal.

"By heaven," he said, after a moment. "You're not
shy about expedients, are you? Don't you know a
civilized world can't be conquered?"

Donal allowed himself the luxury of a small sigh.
He made an effort to explain himself, once again, in
terms others could understand.

"I remember the marshal saying that," he said "I'm
not so sanguine, myself. In fact, that's a particular
maxim I'd like to try to disprove some day. However
—that's not what I meant. I didn't mean to suggest
we attempt to *take* Newton; but that we *attack* it. I
suspect the Newtonians are as maxim-ridden as ourselves. Seeing us try the impossible, they're very like
to conclude we've suddenly discovered some way to
make it possible. From their reactions to such a conclusion we might learn a lot—including about the
Oriente affair."

Lludrow's look of amazement was tightening into a
frown.

"Any force attacking Newton would suffer fantastic
losses," he began.

"Only if they intended to carry the attack through,"
interrupted Donal, eagerly. "It could be a feint—
nothing more than that. The point wouldn't be to do
real damage, but to upset the thinking of the enemy
strategy by introducing an unexpected factor."

"Still," said Lludrow, "to make their feint effective,

the attacking force would have to run the risk of being wiped out."

"Give me a dozen ships—" Donal was beginning; when Lludrow started and blinked like a man waking up from a dream.

"Give you—" he said; and smiled. "No, no, commandant, we were speaking theoretically. Staff would never agree to such a wild, unplanned gamble; and I've no authority to order it on my own. And if I did —how could I justify giving command of such a force to a young man with only field experience, who's never held command in a ship in his life?" He shook his head. "No, Graeme—but I will admit your idea's interesting. And I wish one of us at least had thought of it."

"Would it hurt to mention it—"

"It wouldn't do any good—to argue with a plan Staff has already had in operation for over a week, now." He was smiling broadly. "In fact, my reputation would find itself cut rather severely. But it was a good idea, Graeme. You've got the makings of a strategist. I'll mention the fact in my report to the marshal."

"Thank you, sir," said Donal.

"Back to your ship, then," said Lludrow.

"Good-by, sir."

Donal saluted and left. Behind him, Lludrow frowned for just a moment more over what had just been said—before he turned his mind to other things.

ACTING CAPTAIN

Space battles, mused Donal, are said to be held only by mutual consent. It was one of those maxims he distrusted; and which he had privately determined to disprove whenever he should get the chance. However—as he stood now by the screen of the Control Eye in the main control room of the C4J, watching the enemy ships appearing to swell with the speed of their approach—he was forced to admit that in this instance, it was true. Or true at least to the extent that mutual consent is involved when you attack an enemy point that you know that enemy will defend.

But what if he should not defend it after all? What if he should do the entirely unexpected—

"Contact in sixty seconds. Contact in sixty seconds!" announced the speaker over his head.

"Fasten all," said Andresen, calmly into the talker before him. He sat, with his First and Second Officers duplicating him on either side, in a "dentist's chair" across the room—"seeing" the situation not in actual images as Donal was doing, but from the readings of his instruments. And his knowledge was therefore the more complete one. Cumbersome in his survival battle suit, Donal climbed slowly into the similar chair that had been rigged for him before the Eye, and connected himself to the chair. In case the ship should be broken apart, he and it would remain together as long as possible. With luck, the two of them would be able to make it to a survival ship in orbit around Oriente in a forty or fifty hours—if none of some dozens of factors intervened.

He had time to settle himself before the Eye before contact was made. In those last few seconds, he glanced around him; finding it a little wonderful in spite of all he knew, that this white and quiet room, undisturbed by the slightest tremor, should be perched on the brink of savage combat and its own quite possible destruction. Then there was no more time for thinking. Contact with the enemy had been made and he had to keep his eyes on the scene.

Orders had been to harry the enemy, rather than close with him. Estimates had been twenty per cent casualties for the enemy, five per cent for the defending forces. But such figures, without meaning to be, are misleading. To the man in the battle, twenty per cent, or even five per cent casualties do not mean that he will be twenty per cent or five per cent wounded. Nor, in a space battle, does it mean that one man out of five, or one man out of twenty will be a casualty. It means one *ship* out of five, or one *ship* out of twenty—and every living soul aboard her; for, in space, one hundred per cent casualties mean ninety-eight per cent dead.

There were three lines of defense. The first were the light craft that were meant to slow down the on-coming ships so that the larger, more ponderous craft, could try to match velocities well enough to get to work with heavy weapons. Then there were the large craft themselves in their present orbits. Lastly, there were the second line of smaller craft that were essentially antipersonnel, as the attackers dropped their space-suited assault troops. Donal in a C4J was in the first line.

There was no warning. There was no full moment

of battle. At the last second before contact, the gun crews of the C4J had opened fire. Then—

It was all over.

Donal blinked and opened his eyes, trying to remember what had happened. He was never to remember. The room in which he lay, fastened to his chair, had been split as if by a giant hatchet. Through the badly-lit gap, he could see a portion of an officer's stateroom. A red, self-contained flare was burning somewhere luridly overhead, a signal that the control room was without air. The Control Eye was slightly askew, but still operating. Through the transparency of his helmet, Donal could see the dwindling lights that marked the enemy's departure on toward Oriente. He struggled upright in his chair and turned his head toward the Control panel.

Two were quite dead. Whatever had split the room open had touched them, too. The Third officer was dead, Andresen was undeniably dead. Coa Benn still lived, but from the feeble movements she was making in the chair, she was badly hurt. And there was nothing anyone could do for her now that they were without air and all prisoners in their suits.

Donal's soldier-trained body began to react before his mind had quite caught up to it. He found himself breaking loose the fastenings that connected him to his chair. Unsteadily, he staggered across the room, pushed the lolling head of Andresen out of the way, and thumbed the intership button.

"C4J One-twenty-nine," he said. "C4J One-twenty-nine—" he continued to repeat the calabalistic numbers until the screen before him lit up with a helmeted face as bloodless as that of the dead man in the chair underneath him.

"KL," said the face. "A-twenty-three?" Which was code for: *"Can you still navigate?"*

Donal looked over the panel. For a wonder, it had

been touched by what had split the room—but barely.
Its instruments were all reading.

"A-twenty-nine," he replied affirmatively.

"M-Forty," said the other, and signed off. Donal let
the intership button slip from beneath his finger. M-
Forty was—*Proceed as ordered.*

Proceed as ordered, for the C4J One-twenty-nine,
the ship Donal was in, meant—get in close to Oriente
and pick off as many assault troops as you can. Donal
set about the unhappy business of removing his dead
and dying from their control chairs.

Coa, he noted, as he removed her, more gently than
the others, seemed dazed and unknowing. There
were no broken bones about her, but she appeared to
have been pinched, or crushed on one side by just a
touch of what had killed the others. Her suit was tight
and intact. He thought she might make it, after all.

Seating himself in the captain's chair, he called the
gun stations and other crew posts.

"Report," he ordered.

Gun stations One and Five through Eight answered.

"We're going in planetward," he said. "All able
men abandon the weapon stations for now and form
a working crew to seal ship and pump some air back
in here. Those not sealed off, assemble in lounge.
Senior surviving crewman to take charge."

There was a slight pause. Then a voice spoke back
to him.

"Gun Maintenanceman Ordovya," it said. "I seem to
be surviving Senior, sir. Is this the captain?"

"Staff Liaison Graeme, Acting Captain. Your officers
are dead. As ranking man here, I've taken command.
You have your orders, Maintenanceman."

"Yes, sir." The voice signed off.

Donal set himself about the task of remembering

his ship training. He got the C4J underway toward Oriente and checked all instruments. After a while, the flare went out abruptly overhead and a slow, hissing noise registered on his eardrums—at first faintly, then scaling rapidly up in volume and tone to a shriek. His suit lost some of its drum-tightness.

A few moments later, a hand tapped him on his shoulder. He turned around to look at a blond-headed crewman with his helmet tilted back.

"Ship tight, sir," said the crewman. "I'm Ordovya."

Donal loosened his own helmet and flipped it back, inhaling the room air gratefully.

"See to the First Officer," he ordered. "Do we have anything in the way of a medic aboard?"

"No live medic, sir. We're too small to rate one. Freeze unit, though."

"Freeze her, then. And get the men back to their posts. We'll be on top of the action again in another twenty minutes."

Ordovya went off. Donal sat at his controls, taking the C4J in cautiously and with the greatest possible margins of safety. In principle, he knew how to operate the craft he was seated in; but no one knew better than he what a far cry he was from being an experienced pilot and captain. He could handle this craft the way someone who has taken half a dozen riding lessons can handle a horse—that is, he knew what to do, but he did none of it instinctively. Where Andresen had taken in the readings of all his instruments at a glance and reacted immediately, Donal concentrated on the half dozen main telltales and debated with himself before acting.

So it was, that they came late to the action on the edges of Oriente's atmosphere; but not so late that the assault troops were already safely down out of range. Donal searched the panel for the override button on the antipersonnel guns and found it.

"Override on the spray guns," he announced into the mike before him. He looked at the instruments, but he saw in his imagination the dark and tumbling, spacesuited bodies of the assault troops, and he thought of the several million, tiny slivers of carbon steel that would go sleeting among them at the touch of his finger. There was a slight pause before answering; and then the voice of Ordovya came back.

"Sir . . . if you like, the gunmen say they're used to handling the weapons—"

"Maintenanceman!" snapped Donal. "You heard the order. Override!"

"Override, sir."

Donal looked at his scope. The computer had his targets in the gunsights. He pressed the button, and held it down.

Two hours later, the C4J, then in standby orbit, was ordered to return to rendezvous and its captain to report to his Sub-Patrol chief. At the same time came a signal for all Staff Liaisons to report to the flagship; and one for Staff Liaison Donal Graeme to report personally to Blue Patrol Chief Lludrow. Considering the three commands, Donal called Ordovya on the ship's phone and directed him to take care of the first errand. He himself, he decided, could take care of the other two, which might—or might not—be connected.

Arriving at the flagship, he explained his situation to the Reception Officer, who made a signal both to the Staff Liaison people and to the Blue Patrol chief.

"You're to go directly to Lludrow," he informed Donal; and assigned him a guide.

Donal found Lludrow in a private office on the flagship that was not much bigger than Donal's stateroom in the C4J.

"Good!" said Lludrow, getting up from behind a desk as Donal came in and coming briskly around it.

He waited until the guide had left, and then he put a dark hand on Donal's arm.

"How'd your ship come through?" he asked.

"Navigating," said Donal. "There was a direct hit on the control room though. All officers casualties."

"All officers?" Lludrow peered sharply at him. "And you?"

"I took command, of course. There was nothing left, though, but antipersonnel mop-up."

"Doesn't matter," said Lludrow. "You were Acting Captain for part of the action?"

"Yes."

"Fine. That's better than I hoped for. Now," said Lludrow, "tell me something. Do you feel like sticking your neck out?"

"For any cause I can approve of, certainly," answered Donal. He considered the smaller, rather ugly man; and found himself suddenly liking the Blue Patrol chief. Directness like this had been a rare experience for him, since he had left the Dorsai.

"All right. If you agree, we'll both stick our necks out." Lludrow looked at the door of the office, but it was firmly closed. "I'm going to violate top security and enlist you in an action contrary to Staff orders, if you don't mind."

"Top security?" echoed Donal, feeling a sudden coolness at the back of his neck.

"Yes. We've discovered what was behind this Newton-Cassida landing on Oriente . . . you know Oriente?"

"I've studied it, of course," said Donal. "At school—and recently when I signed with Freiland. Temperatures up to seventy-eight degrees centigrade, rock, desert, and a sort of native vine and cactus jungle. No large bodies of water worth mentioning and too much carbon dioxide in the atmosphere."

"Right. Well," said Lludrow, "the important point is, it's big enough to hide in. They're down there now and we can't root them out in a hurry—and not at all unless we go down there after them. We thought they were making the landing as a live exercise and we could expect them to run the gauntlet back out in a few days or weeks. We were wrong."

"Wrong?"

"We've discovered their reason for making the landing on Oriente. It wasn't what we thought at all."

"That's fast work," said Donal. "What's it been . . . four hours since the landing?"

"*They* made fast work of it," said Lludrow. "The news is being sat on; but they are firing bursts of a new kind of radiation from projectors that fire once, move, and fire again from some new hiding place—a large number of projectors. And the bursts they fire hit old Sirius himself. We're getting increased sunspot activity." He paused and looked keenly at Donal, as if waiting for comment. Donal took his time, considering the situation.

"Weather difficulties?" he said at last.

"That's it!" said Lludrow, energetically, as though Donal had been a star pupil who had just shone again. "Meteorological opinion says it can be serious, the way they're going about it. And we've already heard their price for calling it off. It seems there's a trade commission of theirs on New Earth right now. No official connection—but the Commission's got the word across."

Donal nodded. He was not at all surprised to hear that trade negotiations were going on in normal fashion between worlds who were at the same time actively fighting each other. That was the normal course of existence between the stars. The ebb and flow of trained personnel on a contractual basis was the lifeblood of civilization. A world who tried to go it on its own would be left behind within a matter of years, to wither on the vine—or at last buy the mere necessities of existence at ruinous cost to itself. Competition meant the trading of skilled minds, and that meant contracts, and contracts meant continuing negotiations.

"They want a reciprocal brokerage agreement," Lludrow said.

Donal looked at him sharply. The open market trading of contracts had been abandoned between the worlds for nearly fifty years. It amounted to speculating in human lives. It removed the last shreds of dignity and security from the individual and treated him as so much livestock or hardware to be traded for no other reason than the greatest possible gain. The Dorsai, along with the Exotics, Mara and Kultis, had led the fight against it. There was another angle as well. On "tight" worlds such as those of the Venus Group—which included Newton and Cassida—the Friendlies, and Coby, the open market became one more tool of the ruling group; while on "loose" worlds like Freiland, it became a spot of vulnerability where foreign credits could take advantage of local situations.

"I see," said Donal.

"We've got three choices," Lludrow said. "Give in—accept the agreement. Suffer the weather effects over a period of months while we clean out Oriente by orthodox military means. Or pay a prohibitive price in casualties by a crash campaign to clean up Oriente in a hurry. We'd lose as many lives to the conditions down there as we would to the enemy in a crash campaign. So, it's my notion that it's a time to gamble—my notion, by the way, not Staff's. They don't know anything about this; and wouldn't stand for it if they did. Care to try your idea of throwing a scare into Newton, after all?"

"With pleasure!" said Donal, quickly, his eyes glowing.

"Save your enthusiasm until you hear what you're going to have to do it with," replied Lludrow, dryly. "Newton maintains a steady screen of ninety ships of the first class, in defensive orbit around it. I can give you five."

SUB-PATROL CHIEF

"Five!" said Donal. He felt a small crawling sensation down his spine. He had, before Lludrow turned him down the first time, worked out rather carefully what could be done with Newton and how a man might go about it. His plan had called for a lean and compact little fighting force of thirty first-class ships in a triangular organization of three sub-patrols, ten ships to each.

"You see," Lludrow was explaining, "it's not what craft I have available—even with what losses we've just suffered, my Blue Patrol counts over seventy ships of the first class, alone. It's what ships I can trust to you on a job where at least the officers and probably the men as well will realize that it's a mission that should be completely volunteer and that's being sneaked off when Staff's back is turned. The captains of these ships are all strongly loyal to me, personally, or I couldn't have picked them." He looked at Donal. "All right," he said. "I know it's impossible. Just agree with me and we can forget the matter."

"Can I count on obedience?" asked Donal.

"That," said Lludrow, "is the one thing I can guarantee you."

"I'll have to improvise," said Donal. "I'll go in with them, look at the situation, and see what can be done."

"Fair enough. It's decided then."

"It's decided," said Donal.

"Then come along." Lludrow turned and led him out of the office and through corridors to a lock. They passed through the lock to a small courier ship, empty and waiting for them there; and took it to a ship of the first class, some fifteen minutes off.

Ushered into this ship's large and complex main control room, Donal found five senior captains waiting for him. Lludrow accepted a salute from a gray-haired powerful-looking man, who by saluting revealed himself as captain of this particular ship.

"Captain Bannerman," said Lludrow, introducing him to Donal, "Captain Graeme." Donal concealed a start well. In the general process of his thinking, he had forgotten that a promotion for himself would be necessary. You could hardly put a Staff Liaison with a field rank of commandant over men captaining ships of the first class.

"Gentlemen," said Lludrow, turning to the other executive officers. "I've been forced to form your five ships rather hastily into a new Sub-Patrol unit. Captain Graeme will be your new chief. You'll form a reconnaissance outfit to do certain work near the very center of the enemy space area; and I want to emphasize the point that Captain Graeme's command is absolute. You will obey any and all of his orders without question. Now, are there any questions any of you would like to ask before he assumes command?"

The five captains were silent.

"Fine, then." Lludrow led Donal down the line. "Captain Graeme, this is Captain Aseini."

"Honored," said Donal, shaking hands.

"Captain Cole."

"Honored."

"Captain Sukaya-Mendez."

"At your service, captain."

"Captain el Man."

"Honored," said Donal. A scarred Dorsai face in it's mid-thirties looked at him. "I believe I know your family name, captain. South Continent near Tamlin, isn't it?"

"Sir, near Bridgevort," answered el Man. "I've heard of the Graemes." Donal moved on.

"And Captain Ruoul."

"Honored."

"Well, then," said Lludrow, stepping back briskly. "I'll leave the command in your hands, Captain Graeme. Anything in the way of special supplies?"

"Torpedoes, sir," answered Donal.

"I'll have Armaments Supply contact you," said Lludrow. And left.

Five hours later, with several hundred extra torpedoes loaded, the five-ship Sub-Patrol moved out for deep space. It was Donal's wish that they get clear of the home base as soon as possible and off where the nature of their expedition could not be discovered and countermanded. With the torpedoes, Lee had come aboard; Donal having remembered that his orderly had been left aboard the C4J. Lee had come through the battle very well, being strapped in his hammock harness throughout in a section of the ship that was undamaged by the hit that had pierced to the control room. Now, Donal had definite instructions for him.

"I want you with me, this time," he said. "You'll stay by me. I doubt very much I might need you; but if I do, I want you in sight."

"I'll be there," said Lee, unemotionally.

They had been talking in the Patrol chief's state-room, which had been opened to Donal. Now, Donal headed for the main control room, Lee following be-hind. When Donal reached that nerve center of the ship, he found all three of the ship's officers engaged in calculating the phase shift, with Bannerman over-seeing.

"Sir!" said Bannerman as Donal came up. Looking at him, Donal was reminded of his mathematics in-structor at school; and he was suddenly and painfully reminded of his own youth.

"About ready to shift?" asked Donal.

"In about two minutes. Since you specified no par-ticular conclusion point, the computer run was a short one. We've merely been making the usual checks to make sure there's no danger of collision with any object. A four light-year jump, sir."

"Good," said Donal. "Come here with me, Banner-man.

He led the way over to the larger and rather more elaborate Control Eye that occupied the center of this control room; and pressed keys. A scene from the library file of the ship filled the globe. It showed a green-white planet with two moons floating in space and lit by the illumination from a GO type sun.

"The orange and the two pips," said Bannerman, revealing a moonless Freilander's dislike for natural planetary satellites.

"Yes," said Donal. "Newton." He looked at Banner-man. "How close can we hit it?"

"Sir?" said Bannerman, looking around at him. Donal waited, holding his eyes steady on the older man. Bannerman's gaze shifted and dropped back to the scene in the Eye.

"We can come out as close as you want, sir," he answered. "See, in deep space jumps, we have to stop to make observations and establish our location precisely. But the precise location of any civilized planet's already established. To come out at a safe distance from their defenses, I'd say, sir—"

"I didn't ask you for a safe distance from their defenses," said Donal, quietly. "I said—how close?"

Bannerman looked up again. His face had not paled; but there was now a set quality about it. He looked at Donal for several seconds.

"How close?" he echoed. "Two planetary diameters."

"Thank you, captain," said Donal.

"Shift in ten seconds," announced the First Officer's voice; and began to count down. "Nine seconds— eight—seven—six—five—four—three—two—*shift!*"

They shifted.

"Yes," said Donal, as if the shift itself had never interrupted what he was about to say, "out here where it's nice and empty, we're going to set up a maneuver, and I want all the ship's to practice it. If you'll call a captain's conference, captain."

Bannerman walked over to the control board and put in the call. Fifteen minutes later, with all junior officers dismissed, they gathered in the privacy of the control room of Bannerman's ship and Donal explained what he had in mind.

"In theory," he said, "our Patrol is just engaged in reconnaissance. In actuality, we're going to try to simulate an attacking force making an assault on the planet Newton."

He waited a minute to allow the weight of his words to register on their minds; and then went on to explain his intentions.

They were to set up a simulated planet on their ship's instruments. They would approach this planet, which was to represent Newton, according to a random pattern and from different directions, first a single ship, then two together, then a series of single ships—and so on. They would, theoretically, appear into phase just before the planet, fire one or more torpedoes, complete their run past the planet and immediately go out of phase again. The intention would be to simulate the laying of a pattern of explosions covering the general surface of the planet.

There was, however to be one main difference. Their torpedoes were to be exploded well without the outer ring of Newton's orbits of defense, as if the torpedoes were merely intended as a means to release some radiation or material which was planned to fall in toward the planet, spreading as it went.

And, one other thing, the runs were to be so timed that the five-ship force, by rotation, could appear to be a large fleet engaged in continuous bombardment.

". . . Any suggestions or comments?" asked Donal, winding it up. Beyond the group facing him, he could see Lee, lounging against the control room wall and watching the captains with a colorless gaze.

There was no immediate response; and then Bannerman spoke up slowly, as if he felt it had devolved upon him, the unwelcome duty of being spokesman for the group.

"Sir," he said, "what about the chances of collision?"

"They'll be high, I know," said Donal. "Especially with the defending ships. But we'll just have to take our chances."

"May I ask how many runs we'll be making?"

"As many," said Donal, "as we can." He looked deliberately around the group. "I want you gentlemen to understand. We're going to make every possible attempt to avoid open battle or accidental casualties. But these things may not be avoidable considering the necessarily high number or runs."

"How many runs did you have in mind, captain?" asked Sukaya-Mendez.

"I don't see," replied Donal, "how we can effectively present the illusion of a large fleet engaged in saturation bombardment of a world in under a full two hours of continuous runs."

"Two hours!" said Bannerman. There was an instinctive murmur from the group. "Sir," continued Bannerman. "Even at five minutes a run, that amounts with five ships to better than two runs an hour. If we double up, or if there's casualties it could run as high as four. That's eight phase shifts to an hour—sixteen in a two-hour period. Sir, even doped to the ears, the men on our ships can't take that."

"Do you know of anyone who ever tried, captain?" inquired Donal.

"No, sir—" began Bannerman.

"Then how do we know it can't be done?" Donal did not wait for an answer. "The point is, it must be done. You're being required only to navigate your ships and fire possibly two torpedoes. That doesn't require the manpower it would to fight your ships under ordinary conditions. If some of your men become unfit for duty, make shift with the ones you have left."

"*Shai Dorsai!*" murmured the scarred el Man; and Donal glanced toward him, as grateful for the support as for the compliment.

"Anyone want out?" Donal asked cirsply.

There was a slow, but emphatic, mutter of negation from all of them.

"Right," Donal took a step back from them. "Then let's get about our practice runs. Dismissed, gentlemen."

He watched the four from other ships leave the control room.

"Better feed and rest the crews," Donal said, turning to Bannerman. "And get some rest yourself. I intend to. Have a couple of meals sent to my quarters."

"Sir," acknowledged Bannerman. Donal turned and left the control room, followed by Lee as by a shadow.

The Cobyman was silent until they were in the state-room; then he growled: "What did that scarface mean by calling you shy?"

"Shy?" Donal turned about in surprise.

"Shaey, shy—something like that."

"Oh," Donal smiled at the expression on the other's face. "That wasn't an insult, Lee. It was a pat on the back. *Shai* was what he said. It means something like —true, pure, the actual."

Lee grunted. Then he nodded.

"I guess you can figure on him," he said.

The food came, a tray for each of them. Donal ate lightly and stretched himself out on the couch. It seemed he dropped instantly into sleep; and when he awoke at the touch of Lee's hand on his shoulder he knew he had been dreaming—but of what, he could not remember. He remembered only a movement of shapes in obscurity, as of some complex physics problem resolving itself in terms of direction and mass, somehow given substance.

"Practice about to start," said Lee.

"Thank you, orderly," he said automatically. He got to his feet and headed toward the control room, shedding the druggedness of his sleep as he went. Lee had followed him, but he was not aware of this until the Cobyman pushed a couple of small white tablets into his hand.

"Medication," said Lee. Donal swallowed them automatically. Bannerman, over by the control board, had seen him come in, and now turned and came across the floor.

"Ready for the first practice run, sir," he said. "Where would you like to observe—controls, or Eye?"

Donal looked and saw they had a chair set up for him in both locations.

"Eye," he said. "Lee, you can take the other chair, as long as there does not seem to be one for you."

"Captain, you—"

"I know, Bannerman," said Donal, "I should have mentioned the fact I meant to have my orderly up here. I'm sorry."

"Not at all, sir." Bannerman went over and fitted himself into his own chair, followed by Lee. Donal turned his attention to the Eye.

The five ships were in line, in deep space, at thousand-kilometer intervals. He looked at their neat Indian file and stepped up the magnification slightly so that in spite of the distance that should have made even the nearest invisible, they appeared in detail, in-lighted by the Eye.

"Sir," said Bannerman; and his quiet voice carried easily across the room. "I've arranged a key-in. When we make our phase shift, that library tape will replace the image in the Eye, so you can see what our approach will actually look like."

"Thank you, captain."

"Phase shift in ten seconds—"

The count-down ticked off like the voice of a clock. Then, there was the sensation of a phase shift; and abruptly Donal was sweeping closely over a planet, barely fifty thousand kilometers distance from its surface. "Fire—" and "Fire—" spoke the speaker in the control room ceiling. Again, the indescribable destruction and rebuilding of the body. The world was gone and they were again in deep space.

Donal looked at the four other ships in line. Abruptly the leading one disappeared. The rest continued, seemingly, to hang there, without motion. There was no sound in the control room about him. The seconds crept by, became minutes. The minutes crawled. Suddenly—a ship appeared in front of Bannerman's craft.

Donal looked back at the three behind. Now, there were only two.

The run continued until all the ships had made their pass.

"Again," ordered Donal.

They did it again; and it went off without a hitch.

"Rest," said Donal, getting out of the chair. "Captain, pass the word for all ships to give their personnel a break of half an hour. Make sure everyone is fed, rested, and supplied with medication. Also supply every person with extra medication to be taken as needed. Then, I'd like to talk to you, personally."

When Bannerman had accomplished these orders and approached Donal, Donal took him aside.

"How about the reactions of the men?" he asked.

"Fine, captain," Bannerman said; and Donal was surprised to read a true enthusiasm in his voice. "We've got good crews, here. High level-ratings, and experience."

"I'm glad to hear it," said Donal, thankfully. "Now ... about the time interval—"

"Five minutes exactly, sir," Bannerman looked at him inquiringly. "We can shorten slightly, or lengthen as much as you want."

"No," said Donal. "I just wanted to know. Do you have battle dress for me and my orderly?"

"It's coming up from stores."

The half hour slid by quickly. As it approached its end and they prepared to tie into their chairs, Donal noticed the chronometer on the control room wall. It stood at 23:10 and the half hour would be up at 23:12.

"Make that start at 23:15," he directed Bannerman. The word was passed to the other ships. Everyone was in battle dress in their chairs and at their posts, waiting. Donal felt a strange metallic taste in his mouth and the slow sweat began to work out on the surface of his skin.

"Give me an all-ship hookup," he said. There was a few seconds pause, and then a Third Officer spoke from the control panel.

"You're hooked in, sir."

"Men," said Donal. "This is Captain Graeme." He paused. He had no idea what he had intended to say. He had asked for the hookup on impulse, and to break the strain of the last few moments which must be weighing on all the rest as much as him. "I'll tell you one thing. This is something Newton's never going to forget. Good luck to all of you. That's all."

He wigwagged to the Third Officer to cut him off; and looked up at the clock. A chime sounded softly through the ship.

It was 23:15.

SUB-PATROL CHIEF II

Newton was not to forget.

To a world second only to Venus in its technical accomplishments—and some said not even second— to a world rich in material wealth, haughty with its knowledge, and complacent in the contemplation of its lavish fighting forces, came the shadow of the invader. One moment its natives were secure as they had always been behind the ringing strength of their ninety ships in orbit—and then enemy craft were upon them, making runs across the skies of their planet, bombing them with—*what?*

No, Newton was never to forget. But that came afterward.

To the men in the five ships, it was the here and now that counted. Their first run across the rich world below them seemed hardly more than another exercise. The ninety ships were there—as well as a host of other spacecraft. They—or as many of them as were not occluded by the body of the planet—registered on the instruments of the Freilander ships. But that was all. Even the second run was almost without incident. But by the time Donal's leading ship came through for the start of the third run, Newton was beginning to buzz like a nest of hornets, aroused.

The sweat was running freely down Donal's face as they broke into the space surrounding the planet; and it was not tension alone that was causing it. The psychic shocks of five phase shifts were taking their toll. Halfway in their run there was a sudden sharp tremor that shook their small white-walled world that was the control room, but the ship continued as if unhurt, released its second torpedo and plunged into the safety of its sixth phase shift.

"Damage?" called Donal—and was surprised to hear his voice issue on an odd croaking note. He swallowed and asked again, in a more normal, conrolled tone. "Damage?"

"No damage—" called an officer sharply, from the control panel. "Close burst."

Donal turned his eyes almost fiercely back onto the scene in the Eye. The second ship appeared. Then the third. The fourth. The fifth.

"Double up this time!" ordered Donal harshly. There was a short minute or two of rest and then the sickening wrench of the phase shift again.

In the Eye, it's magnification jumping suddenly,

Donal caught sight of two Newtonian ships, one planetward, the other in a plane and at approximately two o'clock to the line of the bombing run they had begun.

"Defensive—" began Donal; but the gun crews had waited for no order. Their tracking has been laid and the computers were warm. As he watched, the Newtonian ship which was ahead and in their plane opened out like a burst balloon in slow motion and seemed to fall away from them.

—Another phase shift.

The room swam for a second in Donal's blurred eyes. He felt a momentary surge of nausea; and, on the heels of it, heard someone over at the panel, retching. He blazed up inside, forcing an anger to fight the threatening sickness.

It's in your mind—it's all in your mind—he slapped the thought at himself like a curse. The room steadied; the sickness retreated a little way.

"Time—" It was Bannerman, calling in a half-gasping voice from the panel. Donal blinked and tried to focus on the scene in the Eye. The rank odor of his own sweat was harsh in his nostrils—or was it simply that the room was permeated with the stink of all their sweating?

In the Eye he could make out that four ships had come through on this last run. As he watched, the fifth winked into existence.

"Once more!" he called, hoarsely. "In at a lower level, this time." There was a choked, sobbing-like sound from the direction of the panel; but he deliberately did not turn his head to see who it was.

Again the phase shift.

Blur of planet below. A sharp shock. Another.

Again the phase shift.

The control room—full of mist? No—his own eyes. Blink them. Don't be sick.

"Damage?"

No answer.

"Damage!"

"—Light hit. Aft. Sealed—"

"Once more."

"Captain—" Bannerman's voice, "we can't make it again. One of our ships—"

Check in the Eye. Images dancing and wavering —yes, only four ships.

"Which one?"

"I think—" Bannerman, gasping, "Mendez."

"Once more."

"Captain, you can't ask—"

"Give me a hookup then." Pause. "You hear me? Give me a hookup."

"Hookup—" some officer's voice. "You're hooked up, captain."

"All right, this is Captain Graeme." Croak and squeak. Was that *his* voice speaking. "I'm calling for volunteers—one more run. Volunteers only. Speak up, anyone who'll go."

Long pause.

"Shai Dorsai!"

"Shai el Man!—any others?"

"Sir—" Bannerman—"The other two ships aren't receiving."

Blink at Eye. Focus. True. Two of three ships there yawing out of line.

"Just the two of us then. Bannerman?"

"At"—croaking—"your orders, sir."

"Make the run."

Pause . . .

Phase shift!

Planet, whirling—shock—dark space. Can't black out now—

"Pull her out of it!" Pause. "*Bannerman!*"
Weakly responding: "Yes sir—"
PHASE SHIFT
—Darkness . . .

"—Up!"

It was a snarling, harsh, bitter whisper in Donal's ear. He wondered, eyes-closed, where it was coming from. He heard it again, and once again. Slowly it dawned on him that he was saying it to himself.

He fought his eyes open.

The control room was still as death. In the depths of the eye before him three small tiny shapes of ships could be seen, at full magnification, far-flung from each other. He fumbled with dead fingers at the ties on his suit, that bound them to his chair. One by one they came free. He pushed himself out of the chair and fell to his knees on the floor.

Swaying, staggering, he got to his feet. He turned himself toward the five chairs at the control panel, and staggered to them.

In four of the chairs, Bannerman and his three officers sagged unconscious. The Third officer seemed more than unconscious. His face was milkish white and he did not seem to be breathing. All four men had been sick.

In the fifth chair, Lee hung twisted in his ties. He was not unconscious. His eyes were wide on Donal as he approached, and a streak of blood had run down from one corner of the orderly's mouth. He had apparently tried to break his ties by main strength, like a mindless animal, and go directly to Donal. And yet his eyes were not insane, merely steady with an unnatural fixity of purpose. As Donal reached him Lee tried to speak; but all he was able to manage for a second was a throttled sound, and a little more blood came out of the corner of his mouth.

"Y'arright?" he mumbled, finally.

"Yes," husked Donal. "Get you loose in a minute. What happened to your mouth?"

"Bit tongue—" mumbled Lee thickly. "M'arright."

Donal unfastened the last of the ties and, reaching up, opened Lee's mouth with his hands. He had to use real strength to do so. A little more blood came out, but he was able to see in. One edge of Lee's tongue, halfway back from the tip, had been bitten entirely through.

"Don't talk," directed Donal. "Don't use that tongue at all until you can get it fixed."

Lee nodded, with no mark of emotion, and began painfully to work out of the chair.

By the time he was out, Donal had managed to get the ties loose on the still form of the Third Officer. He pulled the man out of the chair and laid him on the floor. There was no perceptible heartbeat. Donal stretched him out and attempted to begin artificial respiration; but at the first effort his head swam dizzily and he was forced to stop. Slowly he pulled himself erect and began to break loose the ties on Bannerman.

"Get the Second, if you feel up to it," he told Lee. The Cobyman staggered stiffly around to the Second Officer and began work on his ties.

Between the two of them, they got the three Freilanders stretched out on the floor and their helmets off. Bannerman and the Second Officer began to show signs of regaining consciousness and Donal left them to make another attempt at respiration with the Third Officer. But he found the body, when he touched it, was already beginning to cool.

He turned back and began work on the First Officer, who was still laxly unconscious. After a while the First Officer began to breathe deeply and more steadily; and his eyes opened. But it was apparent from his gaze that he did not see the rest of them, or know where he was. He stared at the control panel with blank eyes like a man in a heavily drugged condition.

"How're you feeling?" Donal asked Bannerman. The Freiland captain grunted, and made an effort to raise himself up on one elbow. Donal helped, and between the two of them they got him, first sitting up, then to his knees, and finally—with the help of the back of a chair to pull him up—to his feet.

Bannerman's eyes had gone directly to the control panel, from the first moment they had opened. Now, without a word, he pulled himself painfully back into his chair and began clumsily to finger studs.

"All ship sections," he croaked into the grille before him. "Report."

There was no answer.

"Report!" he said. His forefinger came down on a button and an alarm bell rang metallically loud through the ship. It ceased and a faint voice came from the speaker overhead.

"Fourth Gun Section reporting as ordered, sir—"

The battle of Newton was over.

HERO

Sirius himself had just set; and the small bright disk of that white dwarf companion that the Freilanders and the New Earthmen had a number of uncomplimentary names for, was just beginning to show strongly through the wall of Donal's bedroom. Donal sat, bathed in the in-between light, dressed in only a pair of sport trunks, sorting through some of the interesting messages that had come his way, recently— since the matter of the raid on Newton.

So engrossed was he that he paid no attention until Lee tapped him on one brown-tanned shoulder.

"Time to dress for the party," said the Cobyman. He had a gray dress uniform of jacket and trousers, cut in the long-line Freiland style, over one arm. It was fashionably free of any insignia of rank. "I've got a couple of pieces of news for you. First, *she* was here again."

Donal frowned, getting into the uniform. Elvine had conceived the idea of nursing him after his return from the short hospital stay that had followed the Newton affair. It was her convenient conclusion that he was still suffering from the psychological damage of the overdose of phase-shifting they had all gone through. Medical opinion and Donal's to the contrary, she had insisted on attaching herself to him with a constancy which lately had led him to wonder if perhaps he would not have preferred the phase shifting itself. The frown now vanished, however.

"I think I see an end to that," he said. "What else?"

"This William of Ceta you're so interested in," answered Lee. "He's here for the party."

Donal turned his head to look sharply at the man. But Lee was merely delivering a report. The bony face was empty of even those small signs of expression which Donal had come to be able to read, in these past weeks of association.

"Who told you I was interested in William?" he demanded.

"You listen when people talk about him," said Lee. "Shouldn't I mention him?"

"No, that's all right," Donal said. "I want you to tell

me whenever you find out anything about him you think I might not know. I just didn't know you observed that closely."

Lee shrugged. He held the jacket for Donal to slide his arms into.

"Where'd he come from?" asked Donal.

"Venus," said Lee. "He's got a Newton man with him—big young drunk named Montor. And a girl—one of those special people from the Exotics."

"The Select of Kultis?"

"That's right."

"What're they doing here?"

"He's top-level," said Lee. "Who is on Freiland and not here for your party?"

Donal frowned again. He had almost managed to forget that it was in his honor these several hundred well-known people would be gathered here tonight. Oh—not that he would be expected to place himself on show. The social rules of the day and this particular world made lionizing impolite. Direct lionizing, that is. You honored a man by accepting his hospitality, that was the theory. And since Donal had little in the way of means to provide hospitality for the offering, the marshal had stepped into the breach. Nevertheless, this was the sort of occasion that went against Donal's instinctive grain.

He put that matter aside and returned to that of William. If the man happened to be visiting Freiland it would be unthinkable that he should not be invited, and hardly thinkable that he should decline to come. It could be just that. Perhaps, thought Donal with a weariness beyond his years, I'm starting at shadows. But even as his mind framed the thought, he knew it was not true. It was that oddness in him, now more pronounced than ever since the psychic shaking-up of the Newtonian battle, with its multiple phase shifts. Things seen only dimly before were now beginning to take on shape and substance for him. A pattern was beginning to form, with William as its center, and Donal did not like what he saw of the pattern.

"Let me know what you can find out about William," he said.

"Right," replied Lee. "And the Newton man?"

"And the girl from the Exotics." Donal finished dressing and took a back slipway down to the marshal's office. Elvine was there, and with her and the marshal, as guests, were William and Anea.

"Come in, Donal!" called Galt, as Donal hesitated in the entrance. "You remember William and Anea, here!"

"I'd be unlikely to forget." Donal came in and shook hands. William's smile was warm, his handclasp firm; but the hand of Anea was cool and quickly withdrawn from Donal's grasp, and her smile perfunctory. Donal caught Elvine watching them closely; and a faint finger of warning stirred the surface of Donal's mind.

"I've looked forward to seeing you again," said William. "I owe you an apology, Donal. Indeed I do. I've underestimated your genius considerably."

"Not genius," said Donal.

"Genius," insisted William. "Modesty's for little men." He smiled frankly. "Surely you realize this affair with Newton's made you the newest nova on our military horizon?"

"I'll have to watch out your flattery doesn't go to my head, Prince." Donal could deal in double meaning, too. William's first remark had put him almost at his ease. It was not the wolves among people who embarrassed and confused him; but the sheep dogs gone wrong. Those, in fact, who were equipped by nature and instinct to be one thing and through chance and wrongheadedness found themselves acting contrary to their own natures. Possibly, he had thought, that was the reason he found men so much easier to deal with than women—they were less prone to self-deception. Now, however, a small intake of breath drew his attention to Anea.

"You're modest," she said; but two touches of color high on the cheek-bones of her otherwise slightly pale face, and her unfriendly eyes, did not agree with her.

"Maybe," he said, as lightly as he could, "that's because I don't really believe I've got anything to be modest about. Anyone could have done what I did above Newton—and, in fact, several hundred other men did. Those that were there with me."

"Oh, but it was your idea," put in Elvine.

Donal laughed.

"All right," he said. "For the idea, I'll take credit."

"Please do," said Anea.

"Well," put in Galt, seeing that things were getting out of hand. "We were just about to go in and join the party, Donal. Will you come along?"

"I'm looking forward to it," answered Donal, smoothly.

They proceeded, a small knot of people, out through the big doors of the office and into the main hall of the mansion. It was already full of guests interspersed with drifting floats laden with food and drinks. Into this larger body of people, their small group melted like one drop of coloring matter into a glass of water. Their individual members were recognized, captured and dispersed by other guests; and in a few seconds they were all separated—all but Donal and Elvine, who had taken his arm possessively, as they had come out of the office.

She pulled him into the privacy of a small alcove.

"So that's what you've been mooning over!" she said, fiercely. "It's her!"

"Her?" he pulled his arm loose. "What's wrong with you, Ev?"

"You know who I mean!" she snapped. "That Select girl. It's her you're after—though why, I don't know. She's certainly nothing special to look at. And she's hardly even grown up yet."

He chilled suddenly. And she—abruptly realizing that this time she had gone too far, took a sudden, frightened step back from him. He fought to control himself; but this was the authentic article, one of the real Dorsai rages that was his by inheritance. His limbs were cold, he saw everything with an unnatural clarity, and his mind ticked away like some detached machine in the far depths of his being. There was murder in him at the moment. He hung balanced on the knife edge of it.

"Good-by, Ev," he said. She took another, stiff-legged step back from him, then another, and then she turned and fled. He turned about to see the shocked faces of those nearby upon him.

His glance went among them like a scythe, and they fell away before it. He walked forward through them and out of the hall as if he had been alone in the room.

He was pacing back and forth in the bare isolation of the marshal's office, walking off the charge of adrenalin that had surged through him on the heels of his emotion, when the door opened. He turned like a wolf; but it was only Lee.

"You need me?" asked Lee.

The three words broke the spell. The tension in him snapped suddenly; and he burst out laughing. He laughed so long and loud that the Cobyman's eyes became shadowed first with puzzlement, and then with a sort of fear.

"No . . . no . . . it's all right," he gasped at last. He

had a fastidiousness about casually touching people; but now he clapped Lee on the shoulder to reassure him, so unhappy did the lean man look. "See if you can find me a drink—some Dorsai whisky."

Lee turned and left the room. He was back in seconds with a tulip-shaped glass holding perhaps a deciliter of the bronze whisky. Donal drank it down, grateful for the burn in his throat.

"Learn anything about William?" He handed the glass back to Lee.

Lee shook his head.

"Not surprised," murmured Donal. He frowned. "Have you seen ArDell Montor around—that Newtonian that came with William?"

Lee nodded.

"Can you show me where I can find him?"

Lee nodded again. He led Donal out onto the terrace, down a short distance, and in through an open wall to the library. There, in one of the little separate reading cubicles, he found ArDell alone with a bottle and some books.

"Thanks, Lee," said Donal. Lee vanished. Donal came forward and sat down at the small table in the cubicle opposite ArDell and his bottle.

"Greetings," said ArDell, looking up. He was not more than slightly drunk by his own standards. "Hoping to talk to you."

"Why didn't you come up to my room?" asked Donal.

"Not done," ArDell refilled his glass, glanced about the table for another and saw only a vase with some small native variform lilies in it. He dumped these on the floor, filled the vase and passed it politely to Donal.

"No thanks," said Donal.

"Hold it anyway," ArDell said. "Makes me uncomfortable, drinking with a man who won't drink. No, besides, better to just bump into each other." He looked at Donal suddenly with one of his unexpected flashes of soberness and shrewdness. "He's at it again."

"William?"

"Who else?" ArDeall drank. "But what would he be doing with Project Blaine?" ArDell shook his head. "*There's* a man. And a scientist. Make two of any of the rest of us. Can't see *him* leading Blaine around by the nose—but still . . ."

"Unfortunately," said Donal, "we are all tied to the business end of our existence by the red tape in our contracts. And it's in business William shines."

"But he doesn't make sense!" ArDell twisted the glass in his hands. "Take me. Why would he want to ruin me? But he does." He chuckled suddenly. "I've got him scared now."

"You have?" asked Donal. "How?"

ArDell tapped the bottle with one forefinger.

"This. He's afraid I may kill myself. Evidently he doesn't want that."

"Will you?" asked Donal, bluntly.

ArDell shook his head.

"I don't know. Could I come out of it, now? It's been five years. I started it deliberately to spite him —didn't even like the stuff, like you. Now, I wonder. I'll tell you"—he leaned forward over the table—"they can cure me, of course. But would I be any good now, if they did? Math—it's a beautiful thing. Beautiful like art. That's the way I remember it; but I'm not sure. Not sure at all any more." He shook his head again. "When the time comes to dump this," he ·pointed again at the bottle, "you need something that means more to you. I don't know if work does, any more."

"How about William?" asked Donal.

"Yes," said ArDell, slowly, "there is him. That

would do it. One of these days I'm going to find out why he did this to me. Then—"

"What does he seem to be after?" asked Donal. "I mean, in general?"

"Who knows?" ArDell threw up his hands. "Business. More business. Contracts—more contracts. Agreements with every government, a finger in every honeypot. That's our William."

"Yes," said Donal. He pushed back his float and stood up.

"Sit down," said ArDell. "Stop and talk. You never sit still for more than a second or two. For the love of peace, you're the only man between the stars I can talk to, and you won't sit still."

"I'm sorry," Donal said. "But there're things I have to do. A day'll come, maybe, when we can sit down and talk."

"I doubt it," muttered ArDell. "I doubt it very much."

Donal left him there, staring at his bottle.

He went in search of the marshal; but it was Anea he encountered first, standing upon a small balcony, deserted except for herself; and gazing out over the hall, directly below, with an expression at the same time so tired and so longing that he was suddenly and deeply moved by the sight of it.

He approached her, and she turned at the sound of his footsteps. At the sight of him, her expression changed.

"You again," she said, in no particularly welcome tone.

"Yes," said Donal, brusquely. "I meant to search you out later, but this is too good a chance to pass up."

"Too good."

"I mean you're alone . . . I mean I can talk to you privately," said Donal, impatiently.

She shook her head.

"We've got nothing to talk about," she said.

"Don't talk nonsense," said Donal. "Of course we have—unless you've given over your campaign against William."

"Well!" The word leaped from her lips and her eyes flashed their green fire at him. "Who do you think you are!" she cried furiously. "Who ever gave you the right to have any say about what I do?"

"I'm part Maran through both my grandmothers," he said. "Maybe that's why I feel a sense of responsibility to you."

"I don't believe it!" she snapped. "About you being part Maran, that is. You couldn't be part Maran, someone like you, a—" she checked, fumbling for words.

"Well?" He smiled a little grimly at her. "A what?"

"A . . . *mercenary!*" she cried triumphantly, finding at last the word that would hurt him the most, in her misinterpretation of it.

He *was* hurt, and angered; but he managed to conceal it. This girl had the ability to get through his defenses on the most childish level, where a man like William could not.

"Never mind that," he said. "My question was about you and William. I told you not to try intriguing against him the last time I saw you. Have you followed that advice?"

"Well, I certainly don't have to answer that question," she blazed directly at him. "And I won't."

"Then," he said, finding suddenly an insight into her that was possibly a natural compensation for her unusual perceptiveness where he was concerned. "You have. I'm glad to know that." He turned to go. "I'll leave you now."

"Wait a minute," she cried. He turned back to her. I didn't do it because of you!"

"Didn't you?"

Surprisingly, her eyes wavered and fell.

"All right!" she said. "It just happened your ideas coincided with mine."

"Or, that what I said was common sense," he retorted, "and being the person you are, you couldn't help seeing it."

She looked fiercely up at him again.

"So he just goes on . . . and I'm chained to him for another ten years with options—"

"Leave that part to me," said Donal.

Her mouth opened.

"You!" she said; and her astonishment was so great that the word came out in a tone of honest weakness.

"I'll take care of it."

"*You!*" she cried. And the word was entirely different this time. "*You* put yourself in opposition to a man like William—" she broke off suddenly, turning away. "Oh!" she said, angrily, "I don't know why I keep listening to you as if you were actually telling the truth—when I know what kind of person you are."

"You don't know anything at all about what kind of person I am!" he snapped, nettled again. "I've done a few things since you first saw me."

"Oh, yes," she said, "you've had a man shot, and pretended to bomb a planet."

"Good-by," he said, wearily, turning away. He went out through the little balcony entrance, abruptly leaving her standing there; and unaware that he had left her, not filled with the glow of righteous indignation and triumph she had expected, but oddly disconcerted and dismayed.

He searched throughout the rest of the mansion

and finally located the marshal back in his office, and alone.

"May I come in, sir?" he said from the doorway.

"Of course, of course—" Galt looked up from his desk. "Lock the door behind you. I've had nothing but people drifting in, thinking this was an extra lounge. Why'd they think I had it set up without any comfortable floats or cushions in the first place?"

Donal locked the door behind him and came across the wide floor to the desk.

"What is it, boy?" asked the marshal. He raised his heavy head and regarded Donal intently. "Something up?"

"A number of things," agreed Donal. He took the bare float beside the desk that Galt motioned him into. "May I ask if William came here tonight with the intention of transacting any business with you?"

"You may ask," answered Galt, putting both his massive forearms on the desk, "but I don't know why I should answer you."

"Of course you needn't," said Donal. "Assuming he did, however, I'd like to say that in my opinion it would be exceedingly unwise to do any business with Ceta at this time—and particularly William of Ceta."

"And what causes this to be your opinion?" asked Galt, with a noticeable trace of irony. Donal hesitated.

"Sir," he said, after a second. "I'd like to remind you that I was right on Harmony, and right about Newton; and that I may be right here, as well."

It was a large pill of impertinence for the marshal to swallow; since, in effect, it pointed out that if Donal had twice been right, Galt had been twice wrong—first about his assessment of Hugh Killien as a responsible officer, and second about his assessment of the reasons behind the Newtonian move on Oriente. But if he was Dorsai enough to be touchy about his pride, he was also Dorsai enough to be honest when he had to.

"All right," he said. "William did come around with a proposition. He wants to take over a large number of our excess land forces, not for any specific campaign, but for re-leasing to other employers. They'd remain our troops. I was against it, on the grounds that we'd be competing against ourselves when it came to offering troops to outside markets, but he proved to me the guarantee he's willing to pay would more than make up for any losses we might have. I also didn't see how he intended to make his own profit out of it, but evidently he intends training the men to finer specializations than a single planet can afford to do, and maintain a balanced force. And God knows Ceta's big enough to train all he wants, and that its slightly lower gravity doesn't hurt either —for our troops, that is."

He got his pipe out of a compartment in the desk and began to fill it.

"What's your objection?" he asked.

"Can you be sure the troops won't be leased to someone who might use them against you?" Donal asked.

Galt's thick fingers ceased suddenly to fill his pipe. "We can insist on guarantees."

"But how much good are guarantees in a case like that?" asked Donal. "The man who gives you the guarantee—William—isn't the man who might move the troops against you. If Freilander leased troops were suddenly found attacking Freilander soil, you might gain the guarantee, but lose the soil."

Galt frowned.

"I still don't see," he said, "how that could work out to William's advantage."

"It might," said Donal, "in a situation where what

he stood to gain by Freilander fighting Freilander was worth more than the guarantee."

"How could that be?"

Donal hesitated on the verge of those private suspicions of his own. Then he decided that they were not yet solid enough to voice to the marshal; and might, indeed, even weaken his argument.

"I don't know," he replied. "However, I think it'd be wise not to take the chance."

"Hah!" Galt snorted and his fingers went back to work, filling the pipe. "*You* don't have to turn the man down—and justify your refusal to Staff and Government."

"I don't propose that you turn him down outright," said Donal. "I suggest you only hesitate. Say that in your considered opinion the interstellar situation right now doesn't justify your leaving Freiland short-handed of combat troops. Your military reputation is good enough to establish such an answer beyond question."

"Yes"—Galt put the pipe in his mouth and lit it thoughtfully—"I think I may just act on that recommendation of yours. You know, Donal, I think from now on you better remain as my aide, where I can have the benefit of your opinions handy when I need them."

Donal winced.

"I'm sorry, sir," he said. "But I was thinking of moving on—if you'll release me."

Galt's eyebrows abruptly drew together in a thicket of dense hair. He took the pipe from his mouth.

"Oh," he said, somewhat flatly. "Ambitious, eh?"

"Partly," said Donal. "But partly—I'll find it easier to oppose William as a free agent." Galt bent a long, steady look upon him.

"By heaven," he said, "what is this personal vendetta of yours against William?"

"I'm afraid of him," answered Donal.

"Leave him alone and he'll certainly leave you alone. He's got bigger fish to fry—" Galt broke off, jammed his pipe into his mouth and bit hard on the stem.

"I'm afraid," said Donal, sadly, "there are some men between the stars that are just not meant to leave each other alone." He straightened in his chair. "You'll release my contract, then?"

"I won't hold any man against his will," growled the marshal. "Except in an emergency. Where were you thinking of going?"

"I've had a number of offers," said Donal. "But I was thinking of accepting one from the Joint Church Council of Harmony and Association. Their Chief Elder's offered me the position of War Chief for both the Friendlies."

"Eldest Bright? He's driven every commander with a spark of independence away from him."

"I know," said Donal. "And just for that reason I expect to shine the more brightly. It should help build my reputation."

"By—" Galt swore softly. "Always thinking, aren't you?"

"I suppose you're right," said Donal, a trifle unhappily. "It comes of being born with a certain type of mind."

WAR CHIEF

The heels of his black boots clicking against the gray floor of the wide office of the Defense Headquarters on Harmony, the aide approached Donal's desk.

"Special, urgent and private, sir." He placed a signal tape in the blue shell of ordinary communications on the desk pad.

"Thank you," said Donal, and waved him off. He broke the seal on the tape, placed it in his desk unit, and—waiting until the aide had left the room—pressed the button that would start it.

His father's voice came from the speaker, deep-toned.

"Donal, my son—

"We were glad to get your last tape; and to hear of your successes. No one in this family has done so well in such a short time, in the last five generations. We are all happy for you here, and pray for you and wait to hear from you again.

"But I am speaking to you now on an unhappy occasion. Your uncle, Kensie, was assassinated one night shortly over a month ago in the back streets of the city of Blauvain, on St. Marie, by a local terrorist group in opposition to the government there. Ian, who was, of course, an officer in the same unit, later somehow managed to discover the headquarters of the group in some alley or other and killed the three men he found there with his hands. However, this does not bring Kensie back. He was a favorite of us all; and we are all hard hit, here at home, by his death.

"It is Ian, however, who is presently the cause of our chief concern. He brought Kensie's body home, refusing burial on St. Marie, and has been here now several weeks. You know he was always the dark-natured of the twins, just as it seemed that Kensie had twice the brightness and joy in life that is the usual portion of the normal man. Your mother says it is now as if Ian had lost his good angel, and is abandoned to the forces of darkness which have always had such a grip on him.

"She does not say it in just that way, of course. It is the woman and the Maran in her, speaking—but I have not lived with her thirty-two years without realizing that she can see further into the soul of a man or woman than I can. You have in some measure inherited this same gift, Donal; so maybe you will understand better what she means. At any rate, it is at her urging that I am sending you this signal; although I would have been speaking to you about Kensie's death, in any case.

"As you know, it has always been my belief that members of the same immediate family should not serve too closely together in field or garrison—in order that family feelings should not be tempted to influence military responsibilities. But it is your mother's belief that Ian should not now be allowed to sit in his dark silence about the place, as he has been doing; but that he should be once more in action. And she asks me to ask you if you could find a place for him on your staff, where you can keep your eye on him. I know it will be difficult for both of you to have him filling a duty post in a position subordinate to you; but your mother feels it would be preferable to the present situation.

"Ian has expressed no wish to return to an active

life; but if I speak to him as head of the family, he will go. Your brother Mor is doing well on Venus and has recently been promoted to commandant. Your mother urges you to write him, whether he has written you or not, since he may be hesitant to write you without reason, you having done so well in so short a time, although he is the older.

"All our love. Eachan."

The spool, seen through the little transparent cover, stopped turning. The echoes of Eachan Khan Graeme's voice died against the gray walls of the office. Donal sat still at his desk, his eyes fixed on nothing, remembering Kensie.

It seemed odd to him, as he sat there, to discover that he could remember so few specific incidents. Thinking back, his early life seemed to be filled with his smiling uncle—and yet Kensie had not been home much. He would have thought that it would be the separate occasions of Kensie's going and coming that would be remembered—but instead it was more as if some general presence, some light about the house, had been extinguished.

Donal sighed. It seemed he was accumulating people at a steady rate. First Lee. Then the scarfaced el Man had asked to accompany him, when he left Freiland. And now Ian. Well, Ian was a good officer, aside from whatever crippling the death of his twin brother had caused him now. It would be more than easy for Donal to find a place for him. In fact, Donal could use him handily.

Donal punched a stud and turned his mouth to the little grille of the desk's signal unit.

"Eachan Khan Graeme, Graeme-house, South District, Foralie Canton, the Dorsai," he said. "Very glad to hear from you, although I imagine you know how I feel about Kensie. Please ask Ian to come right along. I will be honored to have him on my staff; and, to tell the truth, I have a real need for someone like him here. Most of the ranking officers I inherited as War Chief have been browbeaten by these Elders into a state of poor usefulness. I know I won't have to worry about Ian on that score. If he would take over supervision of my training program, he would be worth his weight in diamonds—natural ones. And I could give him an action post either on my personal staff, or as Patrol Chief. Tell Mother I'll write Mor but that the letter may, be a bit sketchy right at present. I am up to my ears in work at the moment. These are good officers and men; but they have been so beaten about the ears at every wrong move that they will not blow their nose without a direct order. My love to all at home. Donal."

He pressed the button again, ending the recording and sealing it ready for delivery with the rest of the outgoing signals his office sent daily on their way. A soft chime from his desk reminded him that it was time for him to speak once more with Eldest Bright. He got up and went out.

The ranking elder of the joint government of the Friendly Worlds of Harmony and Association maintained his own suite of offices in Government Center, not more than half a hundred meters from the military nerve center. This was not fortuitous. Eldest Bright was a Militant, and liked to keep his eye on the fighting arm of God's True Churches. He was at work at his desk, but rose as Donal came in.

He advanced to meet Donal, a tall, lean man, dressed entirely in black, with the shoulders of a back-alley scrapper and the eyes of a Torquemada, that light of the Inquisition in ancient Spain.

"God be with you," he said. "Who authorized this requisition order for sheathing for the phase shift grids on the sub-class ships?"

"I did," said Donal.

"You spend credit like water." Bright's hard, middle-aged face leaned toward Donal. "A tithe on the churches, a tithe of a tithe on the church members of our two poor planets is all we have to support the business of government. How much of this do you think we can afford to spend on whims and fancies?"

"War, sir," said Donal, "is hardly a matter of whims and fancies."

"Then why shield the grids?" snapped Bright. "Are they liable to rust in the dampness of space? Will a wind come along between the stars and blow them apart?"

"Sheathe, not shield," replied Donal. "The point is to change their appearance; from the ball-and-hammer to the cylindrical. I'm taking all ships of the first three classes through with me. When they come out before the Exotics, I want them all looking like ships of the first class."

"For what reason?"

"Our attack on Zombri cannot be a complete surprise," explained Donal, patiently. "Mara and Kultis are as aware as anyone else that from a military standpoint it is vulnerable to such action. If you'll permit me—" He walked past Bright to the latter's desk and pressed certain keys there. A schematic of the Procyon system sprang into existence on one of the large gray walls of the office, the star itself in outline to the left. Pointing, Donal read off the planets in their order, moving off to the right. "Coby—Kultis —Mara—St. Marie. As close a group of habitable planets as we're likely to discover in the next ten generations. And simply because they are habitable —and close, therefore—we have this escaped moon, Zombri, in its own eccentric orbit lying largely between Mara and St. Marie—"

"Are you lecturing me?" interrupted Bright's harsh voice.

"I am," said Donal. "It's been my experience that the things people tend to overlook are those they learned earliest and believe they know best. Zombri is not habitable and too small for terraforming. Yet it exists like the Trojan horse, lacking only its complement of latter-day Acheans to threaten the Procyon peace—"

"We've discussed this before," broke in Bright.

"And we'll continue to discuss it," continued Donal, pleasantly, "whenever you wish to ask for the reason behind any individual order of mine. As I was saying —Zombri is the Trojan horse of the Procyon city. Unfortunately, in this day and age, we can hardly smuggle men onto it. We can, however, make a sudden landing in force and attempt to set up defenses before the Exotics are alerted. Our effort, then, must be to make our landing as quickly and effectively as possible. To do that best, is to land virtually unopposed in spite of the fact that the Exotics will undoubtedly have a regular force keeping its eye on Zombri. The best way to achieve that, is to appear in overwhelming strength, so that the local commanders will realize it is foolish to attempt to interfere with our landing. And the best way to put on a show of strength is to appear to have three times the ships of the first class that we do have. Therefore the sheathing."

Donal stopped talking, walked back across to the desk, and pressed the keys. The schematic disappeared.

"Very well," said Bright. The tone of his voice showed no trace of defeat or loss of arrogance. "I will authorize the order."

"Perhaps," said Donal, "you'll also authorize another

order to remove the Conscience Guardians from my ships and units."

"Heretics—" began Bright.

"Are no concern of mine," said Donal. "My job is to get these people ready to mount an assault. But I've got over sixty per cent native troops of yours under me; and their morale is hardly being improved, on an average of three trials for heresy a week."

"This is a church matter," said Bright. "Is there anything else you wished to ask me, War Chief?"

"Yes," said Donal. "I ordered mining equipment. It hasn't arrived."

"The order was excessive," said Bright. "There should be no need to dig in anything but the command posts, on Zombri."

Donal looked at the black-clad man for a long moment. His white face and white hands—the only uncovered part of him, seemed rather the false part than the real, as if they were mask and gloves attached to some black and alien creature.

"Let's understand each other," said Donal. "Aside from the fact that I don't order men into exposed positions where they'll be killed—whether they're mercenaries or your own suicide-happy troops, just what do you want to accomplish by this move against the Exotics?"

"They threaten us," answered Bright. "They are worse than the heretics. They are Satan's own legion —the deniers of God." The man's eyes glittered like ice in the sunlight. "We must establish a watchtower over them that they may not threaten us without warning; and we may live in safety."

"All right," said Donal. "That's settled then. I'll get you your watchtower. And you get me the men and equipment I order without question and without delay. Already, these hesitations of your government mean I'll be going into Zombri ten to fifteen per cent understrength."

"What?" Bright's dark brows drew together. "You've got two months yet until Target Date."

"Target Dates," said Donal, "are for the benefit of enemy intelligence. We'll be jumping off in two weeks."

"Two weeks!" Bright stared at him. "You can't be ready in two weeks."

"I earnestly hope Colmain and his General Staff for Mara and Kultis agrees with you," replied Donal. "They've the best land and space forces between the stars."

"How?" Bright's face paled with anger. "You dare to say that our own organization's inferior?"

"Facing facts is definitely preferable to facing defeat," said Donal, a little tiredly. "Yes, Eldest, our forces are definitely inferior. Which is why I'm depending on surprise rather than preparation."

"The Soldiers of the Church are the bravest in the universe!" cried Bright. "They wear the armor of righteousness and never retreat."

"Which explains their high casualty rate, regular necessity for green replacements, and general lower level of training," Donal reminded him. "A willingness to die in battle is not necessarily the best trait in a soldier. Your mercenary units, where you've kept them free of native replacements, are decidedly more combat-ready at the moment. Do I have your backing from now on, for anything I feel I need?"

Bright hesitated. The tension of fanaticism relaxed out of his face, to be replaced by one of thoughtfulness. When he spoke again his voice was cold and businesslike.

"On everything but the Conscience Guardians," he answered. "They have authority, after all, only over our own Members of the Churches." He turned and walked around once more behind his desk. "Also," he said, a trifle grimly, "you may have noticed that there are sometimes small differences of opinion concerning dogma between members of differing Churches. The presence of the Conscience Guardians among them makes them less prone to dispute, one with the other —and this you'll grant, I'm sure, is an aid to military discipline."

"It's effective," said Donal, shortly. He turned himself to go. "Oh, by the way, Eldest," he said. "That true Target Date of two weeks from today. It's essential it remain secret; so I've made sure it's known only to two men and will remain their knowledge exclusively until an hour or so before jump-off."

Bright's head came up.

"Who's the other?" he demanded sharply.

"You, sir," said Donal. "I just made my decision about the true date a minute ago."

They locked eyes for a long minute.

"May God be with you," said Bright, in cold, even tones.

Donal went out.

WAR CHIEF II

Genéve bar-Colmain was, as Donal had said, commander of the best land-and-space forces between the stars. This because the Exotics of Mara and Kultis, though they would do no violence in their own proper persons, were wise enough to hire the best available in the way of military strength. Colmain, himself, was one of the top military minds of his time, along with Galt on Freiland, Kamal on the Dorsai, Issac on Venus, and that occasional worker of military miracles—Dom Yen, Supreme Commander on the single world of Ceta where William had his home office. Colmain had his troubles (including a young wife who no longer cared for him) and his faults (he was a gambler—in a military as well as a monetary sense) but there was nothing wrong with either the intelligence that had its home in his skull, or the Intelligence that made its headquarters in his Command Base, on Mara.

Consequently, he was aware that the Friendly Worlds were preparing for a landing on Zombri within three weeks of the time when the decision to do so had become an accomplished fact. His spies adequately informed him of the Target Date that had been established for that landing; and he himself set about certain plans of his own for welcoming the invaders when they came.

The primary of these was the excavation of strong points on Zombri, itself. The assault troops would find they had jumped into a hornet's nest. The ships of the Exotic fleet would meanwhile be on alert not too far off. As soon as action had joined on the surface of Zombri, they would move in and drive the space forces of the invasion inward. The attackers would be caught between two fires; their assault troops lacking the chance to dig in and their ships lacking the support from below that intrenched ground forces could supply with moon-based heavy weapons.

The work on the strong points was well under way one day as, at the Command Base, back on Mara, Colmain was laying out a final development of strategy with his General Staff. An interruption occurred in the shape of an aide who came hurrying into the conference room without even the formality of asking permission first.

"What's this?" growled Colmain, looking up from the submitted plans before him with a scowl on his swarthy face, which at sixty was still handsome enough to provide him compensation in the way of other female companionship for his wife's lack of interest.

"Sir," said the aide, "Zombri's attacked—"

"*What?*" Colmain was suddenly on his feet; and the rest of the heads of the General Staff with him.

"Over two hundred ships, sir. We just got the signal." The aide's voice cracked a little—he was still in his early twenties. "Our men on Zombri are fighting with what they have—"

"Fighting?" Colmain took a sudden step toward the aide almost as if he would hold the man personally responsible. "They've started to land assault troops?"

"They've landed, sir—"

"How many?"

"We don't know sir—"

"Knucklehead! How many ships went in to drop men?"

"None, sir," gasped the aide. "They didn't drop any men. They all landed."

"Landed?"

For the fraction of a second, there was no sound at all in the long conference room.

"Do you mean to tell me—" shouted Colmain. "They landed two hundred ships of the first class on Zombri?"

"Yes, sir," the aide's voice had thinned almost to a squeak. "They're cleaning out our forces there and digging in—"

He had no chance to finish. Colmain swung about on his Battle Ops and Patrol Chiefs.

"Hell and damnation!" he roared. "Intelligence!"

"Sir?" answered a Freilander officer halfway down the length of the table.

"What's the meaning of this?"

"Sir—" stammered the officer. "I don't know how it happened. The latest reports I had from Harmony, three days ago—"

"Damn the latest reports. I want every ship and every man we can get into space in five hours! I want every patrol ship of any class to rendezvous with everything we can muster here, off Zombri in ten hours. Move!"

The General Staff of the Exotics moved.

It was a tribute to the kind of fighting force that Colmain commanded that they were able to respond at all in so short a time as ten hours to such orders. The fact that they accomplished the rendezvous with nearly four hundred craft of all classes, all carrying near their full complement of crews and assault troops, was on the order of a minor miracle.

Colmain and his chief officers, aboard the flagship, regarded the moon, swimming below them in the Control Eye of the ship. There had been reports of fighting down there up until three hours ago. Now there was a silence that spoke eloquently of captured troops. In addition, Observation reported—in addition to the works instigated by the Exotic forces—another hundred and fifty newly mined entrances in the crust of the moon.

"They're in there," said Colmain, "ships and all." Now that the first shock of discovery had passed, he was once more a cool and capable commander of forces. He had even found time to make a mental note to get together with this Dorsai, Graeme. Supreme command was always sweet bait to a brilliant youngster; but he would find the Council of United Churches a difficult employer in time—and the drawback of a subordinate position under Colmain himself could be compensated for by the kind of salary the Exotics were always willing to pay. Concerning the outcome of the actual situation before him, Colmain saw no real need for fear, only for haste. It was fairly obvious now that Graeme had risked everything on one bold swoop. He had counted on surprise to get him onto the moon and so firmly intrenched there that the cost of rooting him out would be prohibitive —before reinforcements could arrive.

He had erred only—and Colmain gave him full credit for all but that single error—in underestimating the time it would take for Colmain to gather his strength to retaliate. And even that error was forgiveable. There was no other force on the known worlds that could have been gotten battle-ready in under three times the time.

"We'll go in," said Colmain. "All of us—and fight it out on the moon." He looked around his officers. "Any comment?"

"Sir," said his Blue Patrol chief, "maybe we could wait them out up here?"

"Don't you think it," said Colmain, good-humoredly. "They would not come and dig in, in our own system, without being fully supplied for long enough to establish an outpost we can't take back." He shook his head. "The time to operate is now, gentlemen, before the infection has a chance to get its hold. All ships down—even the ones without assault troops. We'll fight them as if they were ground emplacements."

His staff saluted and went off to execute his orders.

The Exotic fleet descended on the moon of Zombri like locusts upon an orchard. Colmain, pacing the floor of the control room in the flagship—which had gone in with the rest—grinned as the reports began to flood in of strong points quickly cleaned of the

Friendly troops that had occupied them—or dug in ships quickly surrendering and beginning to dig themselves out of the deep shafts their mining equipment had provided for them. The invading troops were collapsing like cardboard soldiers; and Colmain's opinion of their commander—which had risen sharply with the first news of the attack—began to slip decidedly. It was one thing to gamble boldly; it was quite another to gamble foolishly. It appeared from the morale and quality of the Friendly troops that there had, after all, been little chance of the surprise attack succeeding. This Graeme should have devoted a little more time to training his men and less to dreaming up dramatic actions. It was, Colmain thought, very much what you might expect of a young commander in supreme authority for the first time in his life.

He was enjoying the roseate glow of anticipated victory when it was suddenly all rudely shattered. There was a sudden ping from the deep-space communicator and suddenly two officers at the board spoke at once.

"Sir, unidentified call from—"

"Sir, ships above us—"

Colmain, who had been watching the Zombri surface through his Control Eye, jabbed suddenly at his buttons and the seeker circuit on it swung him dizzily upward and toward the stars, coming to rest abruptly, on full magnification, on a ship of the first class which unmistakably bore the mark of Friendly design and manufacture. Incredulously, he widened his scope, and in one swift survey, picked out more than twenty such ships in orbit around Zombri, within the limited range of his ground-restricted Eye, alone.

"Who is it?" he shouted, turning on the officer who had reported a call.

"Sir—" the officer's voice was hesitantly incredulous, "he says he's the Commander of the Friendlies."

"What?" Colmain's fist came down on a stud beside the controls of the Eye. A wall screen lit up and a lean young Dorsai with odd, indefinite-colored eyes looked out at him.

"Graeme!" roared Colmain. "What kind of an imitation fleet are you trying to bluff me with?"

"Look again, commander," answered the young man. "The imitations are digging their way out down there on the surface by you. They're my sub-class ships. Why'd you think they would be taken so easily? These are my ships of the first class—one hundred and eighty-three of them."

Colmain jammed down the button and blanked the screen. He turned on his officers at the control panel.

"Report!"

But the officers had already been busy. Confirmations were flooding in. The first of the attacking ships had been dug out and proved to be sub-class ships with sheathing around their phase-shift grids, little weapons, and less armor. Colmain swung back to the screen again, activated it, and found Donal in the same position, waiting for him.

"We'll be up to see you in ten minutes," he promised, between his teeth.

"You've got more sense than that, commander," replied Donal, from the screen. "Your ships aren't even dug in. They're sitting ducks as they are; and in no kind of formation to cover each other as they try to jump off. We can annihilate you if you try to climb up here, and lying as you are we can pound you to pieces on the ground. You're not equipped from the standpoint of supplies to dig in there; and I'm well enough informed about your total strength to know you've got no force left at large that's strong enough to do us any damage." He paused. "I suggest you come up here yourself in a single ship and discuss terms of surrender."

Colmain stood, glaring at the screen. But there was, in fact, no alternative to surrender. He would not have been a commander of the caliber he was, if he had not recognized the fact. He nodded, finally, grudgingly.

"Coming up," he said; and blanked the screen. Shoulders a little humped, he went off to take the little courier boat that was attached to the flagship for his own personal use.

"By heaven," were the words with which he greeted Donal, when he at last came face to face with him aboard the Friendly flagship, "you've ruined me. I'll be lucky to get the command of five C-class and a tender, on Dunnin's World, after this."

It was not far from the truth.

Donal returned to Harmony two days later, and was cheered in triumph even by the sourest of that world's fanatics, as he rode through the streets to Government Center. A different sort of reception awaited him there, however, when he arrived and went alone to report to Eldest Bright.

The head of United Council of Churches for the worlds of Harmony and Association looked up grimly as Donal came in, still wearing the coverall of his battle dress under a barrel-cut jacket he had thrown on hastily for the ride from the spaceport. The platform on which he had ridden had been open for the admiration of the crowds along the way; and Harmony was in the chill fall of its short year.

"Evening, gentlemen," said Donal, taking in not only Bright in the greeting, but two other members of the Council who sat alongside him at his desk. These two did not answer. Donal had hardly expected them to. Bright was in charge here. Bright nodded at three armed soldiers of the native elite guard that had been holding post by the door and they went out, closing the door behind them.

"So you've come back," said Bright.

Donal smiled.

"Did you expect me to go some place else?" he asked.

"This is no time for humor!" Bright's large hand came down with a crack on the top of the desk. "What kind of an explanation have you got for us, for this outrageous conduct of yours?"

"If you don't mind, Eldest!" Donal's voice rang against the gray walls of the room, with a slight cutting edge the three had never heard before and hardly expected on this occasion. "I believe in politeness and good manners for myself; and see no reason why others shouldn't reciprocate in kind. What're you talking about?"

Bright rose. Standing wide-legged and shoulder-bent above the smooth, almost reflective surface of the gray desk, the resemblance to the back-alley scrapper for the moment outweighed the Torquemada in his appearance.

"You come back to us," he said, slowly and harshly, "and pretend not to know how you betrayed us?"

"Betrayed you?" Donal considered him with a quietness that was almost ominous. "How—betrayed you?"

"We sent you out to do a job."

"I believe I did it," said Donal dryly. "You wanted a watchtower over the Godless. You wanted a permanent installation on Zombri to spot any buildup on the part of the Exotics to attack you. You remember I asked you to set out in plain terms what you were after, a few days back. You were quite explicit about that being just what you wanted. Well—you've got it."

"You limb of Satan!" blared Bright, suddenly losing

control. "Do you pretend to believe that you thought that was all we wanted? Did you think the anointed of the Lord would hesitate on the threshold of the Godless?" He turned and stalked suddenly around the desk to stand face to face with Donal. "You had them in your power and you asked them only for an unarmed observation station on a barren moon. You had them by the throat and you slew none of them, when you should have wiped them from the face of the stars, to the last ship—to the last man!"

He paused and Donal could hear his teeth gritting in the sudden silence.

"How much did they pay you?" Bright snarled.

Donal stood in an unnatural stillness.

"I will pretend," he said, after a moment, "that I didn't hear that last remark. As for your questions as to why I asked only for the observation station, that was all you had said you wanted. As to why I did not wipe them out—wanton killing is not my trade. Nor the needless expenditure of my own men in the pursuit of wanton killing." He looked coldly into Bright's eyes. "I suggest you could have been a little more honest with me, Eldest, about what you wanted. It was the destruction of the Exotic power, wasn't it?"

"It was," gritted Bright.

"I thought as much," said Donal. "But it never occurred to you that I would be a good enough commander to find myself in the position to accomplish that. I think," said Donal, letting his eyes stray to the other two black-clad elders as well, "you are hoist by your own petard, gentlemen." He relaxed; and smiling slightly, turned back to Bright. "There are reasons," he said, "why it would be very unwise tactically for the Friendly Worlds to break the back of Mara and Kultis. If you'll allow me to give you a small lesson in power dis—"

"You'll come up with better answers than you

have!" burst out Bright. "Unless you want to be tried for betrayal of your employer!"

"Oh, come now!" Donal laughed out loud.

Bright whirled away from him and strode across the gray room. Flinging wide the door by which Donal had entered, and they had exited, he revealed the three elite guard soldiers. He whirled about, arm outstretched to its full length, finger quivering.

"Arrest that traitor!" he cried.

The guards took a step toward Donal—and in that same moment, before they had any of them moved their own length's-worth of distance toward him— three faint blue beams traced their way through the intervening space past Bright, leaving a sharp scent of ionized air behind them. And the three dropped.

Like a man stunned by a blow from behind, Bright stared down at the bodies of his three guards. He swayed about to see Donal reholstering his handgun.

"Did you think I was fool enough to come here unarmed?" asked Donal, a little sadly. "And did you think I'd submit to arrest?" He shook his head. "You should have wit enough to see now I've just saved you from yourselves."

He looked at their disbelieving faces.

"Oh, yes," he said. He gestured to the open wall at the far end of the office. Sounds of celebration from the city outside drifted lightly in on the evening breeze. "The better forty per cent of your fighting forces are out there. Mercenaries. Mercenaries who appreciate a commander who can give them a victory at the cost of next to no casualties at all. What do you suppose their reaction would be if you tried me for betrayal, and found me guilty, and had me executed?" He paused to let the thought sink in. "Consider it, gentlemen."

He pinched his jacket shut and looked grimly at

the three dead elite guards; and then turned back to the elders, again.

"I consider this sufficient grounds for breach of contract," he said. "You can find yourself another War Chief."

He turned and walked toward the door. As he passed through it, Bright shouted after him.

"Go to them, then! Go to the Godless on Mara and Kultis!"

Donal paused and turned. He inclined his head gravely.

"Thank you, gentlemen," he said. "Remember—the suggestion was yours."

PART-MORON

There remained the interview with Sayona the Bond. Going up some wide and shallow steps into the establishment—it could not be called merely a building, or group of buildings—that housed the most important individual of the two Exotic planets, Donal found cause for amusement in the manner of his approach.

Farther out, among some shrubbery at the entrance to the—estate?—he had encountered a tall, gray-eyed woman; and explained his presence.

"Go right ahead," the woman had said, waving him onward. "You'll find him." The odd part of it was, Donal had no doubt that he would. And the unreasonable certainty of it tickled his own strange sense of humor.

He wandered on by a sunlit corridor that broadened imperceptibly into a roofless garden, past paintings, and pools of water with colorful fish in them —through a house that was not a house, in rooms and out until he came to a small sunken patio, half-roofed over; and at the far end of it, under the shade of the half-roof was a tall bald man of indeterminate age, wrapped in a blue robe and seated on a little patch of captive turf, surrounded by a low, stone wall.

Donal went down three stone steps, across the patio, and up the three stone steps at the far side until he stood over the tall, seated man.

"Sir," said Donal. "I'm Donal Graeme."

The tall man waved him down on the turf.

"Unless you'd rather sit on the wall, of course," he smiled. "Sitting cross-legged doesn't agree with everyone."

"Not at all, sir," answered Donal, and sat down cross-legged himself.

"Good," said the tall man; and apparently lost himself in thought, gazing out over the patio.

Donal also relaxed, waiting. A certain peace had crept into him in the way through this place. It seemed to beckon to meditation; and—Donal had no doubt—was probably cleverly constructed and designed for just that purpose. He sat, comfortably now, and let his mind wander where it chose; and it happened—not so oddly at all—to choose to wander in the direction of the man beside him.

Sayona the Bond, Donal had learned as a boy in school, was one of the human institutions peculiar to the Exotics. The Exotics were two planetsful of strange people, judged by the standards of the rest of the human race—some of whom went so far as to wonder if the inhabitants of Mara and Kultis had developed wholly and uniquely out of the human race, after all. This, however, was speculation half in humor and half in superstition. In truth, they were human enough.

They had, however, developed their own forms of wizardry. Particularly in the fields of psychology and its related branches, and in that other field which you could call gene selection or planned breeding depending on whether you approved or disapproved of it. Along with this went a certain sort of general mysticism. The Exotics worshiped no god, overtly, and laid claim to no religion. On the other hand they were nearly all—they claimed, by individual choice—vegetarians and adherents of nonviolence on the ancient Hindu order. In addition, however, they held to another cardinal nonprinciple; and this one was the principle of noninterference. The ultimate violence, they believed, was for one person to urge a point of view on another—in any fashion of urging. Yet, all these traits had not destroyed their ability to take care of themselves. If it was their creed to do violence to no man, it was another readily admitted part of their same creed that no one should therefore be wantonly permitted to do violence to them. In war and business, through mercenaries and middlemen, they more than held their own.

But, thought Donal—to get back to Sayona the Bond, and his place in Exotic culture. He was one of the compensations peculiar to the Exotic peoples, for their different way of life. He was—in some way that only an Exotic fully understood—a certain part of their emotional life made manifest in the person of a living human being. Like Anea, who—devastatingly normal and female as she was—was, to an Exotic, *literally* one of the select of Kultis. She was their best selected qualities made actual—like a living work of art that they worshiped. It did not matter that she was not always joyful, that indeed, her life must bear as much or more of the normal human sorrow of situation and existence. That was where most people's appreciation of the matter went astray. No, what was important was the capabilities they had bred and trained into her. It was the capacity in her for living, not the life she actually led, that pleasured them. The actual achievement was up to her, and was her own personal reward. They appreciated the fact that —if she chose, and was lucky—she could appreciate life.

Similarly, Sayona the Bond. Again, only in a sense that an Exotic would understand, Sayona was the actual bond between their two worlds made manifest in flesh and blood. In him was the capability for common understanding, for reconciliation, for an expression of the community of feeling between people . . .

Donal awoke suddenly to the fact that Sayona was speaking to him. The older man had been speaking some time, in a calm, even voice, and Donal had been letting the words run through his mind like water of a stream through his fingers. Now, something that had been said had jogged him to a full awareness.

". . . Why, no," answered Donal, "I thought this was standard procedure for any commander before you hired him."

Sayona chuckled.

"Put every new commander through all that testing and trouble?" he said. "No, no. The word would get around and we'd never be able to hire the men we wanted."

"I rather enjoy taking tests," said Donal, idly.

"I know you do," Sayona nodded. "A test is a form of competition, after all; and you're a competitor by nature. No, normally when we want a military man we look for military proofs like everyone else—and that's as far as we go."

"Why the difference with me, then?" asked Donal, turning to look at him. Sayona returned his gaze with pale brown eyes holding just a hint of humor in the wrinkles at their corners.

"Well, we weren't just interested in you as a commander," answered Sayona. "There's the matter of your ancestors, you know. You're actually part-Maran; and those genes, even when outmatched, are of interest to us. Then there's the matter of you, yourself. You have astonishing potentials."

"Potentials for what?"

"A number of rather large things," said Sayona soberly. "We only glimpse them, of course, in the results of our tests."

"Can I ask what those large things are?" asked Donal, curiously.

"I'm sorry, no. I can't answer that for you," said Sayona. "The answers would be meaningless to you, personally, anyway—for the reason you can't explain anything in terms of itself. That's why I thought I'd have this talk with you. I'm interested in your philosophy."

"Philosophy!" Donal laughed. "I'm a Dorsai."

"Everyone, even Dorsai, every living thing has its own philosophy—a blade of grass, a bird, a baby. An individual philosophy is a necessary thing, the touchstone by which we judge our own existence. Also—you're only part Dorsai. What does the other part say?"

Donal frowned.

"I'm not sure the other part says anything," he said. "I'm a soldier. A mercenary. I have a job to do; and I intend to do it—always—in the best way I know how."

"But beyond this—" urged Sayona.

"Why, beyond this—" Donal fell silent, still frowning. "I suppose I would want to see things go well."

"You said *want* to see things go well—rather than *like* to see things go well." Sayona was watching him. "Don't you see any significance in that?"

"Want? Oh—" Donal laughed. "I suppose that's an unconscious slip on my part. I suppose I was thinking of *making* them go well."

"Yes," said Sayona, but in a tone that Donal could not be sure was meant as agreement or not. "You're a doer, aren't you?"

"Someone has to be," said Donal. "Take the civilized worlds now—" he broke off suddenly.

"Go on," said Sayona.

"I meant to say—take civilization. Think how short a time it's been since the first balloon went up back on Earth. Four hundred years? Five hundred years? Something like that. And look how we've spread out and split up since then."

"What about it?"

"I don't like it," said Donal. "Aside from the inefficiency, it strikes me as unhealthy. What's the point of technological development if we just split in that many more factions—everyone hunting up his own type of aberrant mind and hiving with it? That's no progress."

"You subscribe to progress?"

Donal looked at him.

"Don't you?"

"I suppose," said Sayona. "A certain type of progress. *My* kind of progress. What's yours?"

Donal smiled.

"You want to hear that, do you? You're right. I guess I do have a philosophy after all. You want to hear it?"

"Please," said Sayona.

"All right," said Donal. He looked out over the little sunken garden. "It goes like this—each man is a tool in his own hands. Mankind is a tool in *its* own hands. Our greatest satisfaction doesn't come from the rewards of our work, but from the working itself; and our greatest responsibility is to sharpen, and improve the tool that is ourselves so as to make it capable of tackling bigger jobs." He looked at Sayona. "What do you think of it?"

"I'd have to think about it," answered Sayona. "My own point of view is somewhat different, of course. I see Man not so much as an achieving mechanism, but as a perceptive link in the order of things. I would say the individual's role isn't so much to *do* as it is to *be*. To realize to the fullest extent the truth already and inherently in him—if I make myself clear."

"Nirvana as opposed to Valhalla, eh?" said Donal, smiling a little grimly. "Thanks, I prefer Valhalla."

"Are you sure?" asked Sayona. "Are you quite sure you've no use for Nirvana?"

"Quite sure," said Donal.

"You make me sad," said Sayona, somberly. "We had had hopes."

"Hopes?"

"There is," said Sayona, lifting one finger, "this possibility in you—this great possibility. It may be exercised in only one direction—that direction you choose. But you have freedom of choice. There's room for you here."

"With you?"

"The other worlds don't know," said Sayona, "what we've begun to open up here in the last hundred years. We are just beginning to work with the butterfly implicit in the matter-bound worm that is the present human species. There are great opportunities for anyone with the potentialities for this work."

"And I," said Donal, "have these potentialities?"

"Yes," answered Sayona. "Partly as a result of your Maran genes, partly as a result of a lucky genetic accident that is beyond our knowledge to understand, now. Of course—you would have to be retrained. That other part of your character that rules you now would have to be readjusted to a harmonious integration with the other part *we* consider more valuable."

Donal shook his head.

"There would be compensations," said Sayona, in a sad, almost whimsical tone, "things would become possible to you—do you know that you, personally, are the sort of man who, for example, could walk on air if only you believed you could?"

Donal laughed.

"I am quite serious," said Sayona. "Try believing it some time."

"I can hardly try believing what I instinctively disbelieve," said Donal. "Beside, that's beside the point. I am a soldier."

"But what a strange soldier," murmured Sayona. "A soldier full of compassion, of whimsical fancies and wild daydreams. A man of loneliness who wants to be like everyone else; but who finds the human race a conglomeration of strange alien creatures whose twisted ways he cannot understand—while still he understands them too well for their own comfort."

He turned his eyes calmly onto Donal's face, which had gone set and hard.

"Your tests *are* quite effective, aren't they?" Donal said.

"They are," said Sayona. "But there's no need to look at me like that. We can't use them as a weapon, to make you do what we would like to have you do. That would be an action so self-crippling as to destroy all its benefits. We can only make the offer to you."

He paused. "I can tell you that on the basis of our knowledge we can assure you with better than fair certainty that you'll be happy if you take our path."

"And if not?" Donal had not relaxed.

Sayona sighed.

"You are a strong man," he said. "Strength leads to responsibility, and responsibility pays little heed to happiness."

"I can't say I like the picture of myself going through life grubbing after happiness." Donal stood up. "Thanks for the offer, anyway. I appreciate the compliment it implies."

"There is no compliment in telling a butterfly he is a butterfly and need not crawl along the ground," said Sayona.

Donal inclined his head politely.

"Good-by," he said. He turned about and walked the few steps to the head of the shallow steps leading down into the sunken garden and across it to the way he had come in.

"Donal—" The voice of Sayona stopped him. He turned back and saw the Bond regarding him with an expression almost impish. "*I* believe you can walk on air," said Sayona.

Donal stared; but the expression of the other did not alter. Swinging about, Donal stepped out as if onto level ground—and to his unutterable astonishment his foot met solidity on a level, unsupported, eight inches above the next step down. Hardly thinking why he did it, Donal brought his other foot forward into nothingness. He took another step—and another. Unsupported on the thin air, he walked across above the sunken garden to the top of the steps on the far side.

Striding once more onto solidity, he turned about and looked across the short distance. Sayona still regarded him; but his expression now was unreadable. Donal swung about and left the garden.

Very thoughtful, he returned to his own quarters in the city of Portsmouth, which was the Maran city holding the Command Base of the Exotics. The tropical Maran night had swiftly enfolded the city by the time he reached his room, yet the soft illumination that had come on automatically about and inside all the buildings by some clever trick of design failed to white-out the overhead view of the stars. These shone down through the open wall of Donal's bedroom.

Standing in the center of the bedroom, about to change for the meal which would be his first of the day—he had again forgotten to eat during the earlier hours—Donal paused and frowned. He gazed up at the gently domed roof of the room, which reached its highest point some twelve feet above his head. He frowned again and searched about through his writing desk until he found a self-sealing signal-tape capsule. Then, with this in one hand, he turned toward the ceiling and took one rather awkward step off the ground.

His foot caught and held in air. He lifted himself off the floor. Slowly, step by step he walked up through nothingness to the high point of the ceiling. Opening the capsule, he pressed its self-sealing edges against the ceiling, where they clung. He hung there a second in air, staring at them.

"Ridiculous!" he said suddenly— and, just as suddenly, he was falling. He gathered himself with the instinct of long training in the second of drop and, landing on hands and feet, rolled over and came to his feet like a gymnast against a far wall. He got up, brushing himself off, unhurt—and turned to look up at the ceiling. The capsule still clung there.

He lifted the little appliance that was strapped to his wrist and keyed its phone circuit in.

"Lee," he said.

He dropped his wrist and waited. Less than a minute later, Lee came into the room. Donal pointed toward the capsule on the ceiling. "What's that?" he asked.

Lee looked.

"Tape capsule," he said. "Want me to get it down?"

"Never mind," answered Donal. "How do you suppose it got up there?"

"Some joker with a float," answered Lee. "Want me to find out who?"

"No—never mind," said Donal. "That'll be all."

Bending his head at the dismissal, Lee went out of the room. Donal took one more look at the capsule, then turned and wandered over to the open wall of his room, and looked out. Below him lay the bright carpet of the city. Overhead hung the stars. For longer than a minute he considered them.

Suddenly he laughed, cheerfully and out loud.

"No, no," he said to the empty room. "I'm a Dorsai!"

He turned his back on the view and went swiftly to work at dressing for dinner. He was surprised to discover how hungry he actually was.

PROTECTOR

Battle Commander of Field Forces Ian Ten Graeme, that cold, dark man, strode through the outer offices of the Protector of Procyon with a *private-and-secret* signal in his large fist. In the three outer offices, no one got in his way. But at the entrance to the Protector's private office, a private secretary in the green-and-gold of a staff uniform ventured to murmur that the Protector had left orders to be undisturbed. Ian merely looked at her, placed one palm flat against the lock of the inner office door—and strode through.

Within, he discovered Donal standing by an open wall, caught by a full shaft of Procyon's rich-yellow sunlight, gazing out over Portsmouth and apparently deep in thought. It was a position in which he was to be discovered often, these later days. He looked up now at the sound of Ian's measured tread approaching.

Six years of military and political successes had laid their inescapable marks upon Donal's face, marks plain to be seen in the sunlight. At a casual glance he appeared hardly older than the young man who had left the Dorsai half a dozen years before. But a closer inspection showed him to be slightly heavier of build now—even a little taller. Only this extra weight, slight increase as it was, had not served to soften the clear lines of his features. Rather these same features had grown more pronounced, more hard of line. His eyes seemed a little deeper set now; and the habit of command—command extended to the point where it became unconscious—had cast an invisible shadow upon his brows, so that it had become a face men obeyed without thinking, as if it was the natural thing to do.

"Well?" he said, as Ian came up.

"They've got New Earth," his uncle answered; and handed over the signal tape. "Private-and-secret to you from Galt."

Donal took the tape automatically, that deeper, more hidden part of him immediately taking over his mind. If the six years had wrought changes upon his person and manner, they had worked to even greater ends below the surface of his being. Six years of command, six years of estimate and decision had beaten broad the path between his upper mind and that dark, oceanic part of him, the depthless waters of which lapped on all known shores and many yet unknown. He had come—you could not say to terms —but to truce with the source of his oddness; hiding it well from others, but accepting it to himself for the sake of the tool it placed in his hands. Now, this information Ian had just brought him was like one more stirring of the shadowy depths, a rippled vibration spreading out to affect all, integrate with all— and make even more clear the vast and shadowy ballet of purpose and counter-purpose that was behind all living action; and—for himself—a call to action.

As Protector of Procyon, now responsible not only for the defense of the Exotics, but of the two smaller inhabited planets in that system—St. Marie, and Coby—that action was required of him. But even more; as himself, it was required of him. So that what it now implied was not something he was eager to avoid. Rather, it was due, and welcome. Indeed, it was almost too welcome—fortuitous, even.

"I see—" he murmured. Then, lifting his face to his uncle, "Galt'll need help. Get me some figures on available strength, will you Ian?"

Ian nodded and went out, as coldly and martially as he had entered.

Left alone, Donal did not break open the signal tape immediately. He could not now remember what he had been musing about when Ian entered, but the sight of his uncle had initiated a new train of thought. Ian seemed well, these days—or at least as well as could be expected. It did not matter that he lived a solitary life, and little to do with the other commanders of his own rank, and refused to go home to the Dorsai, even for a trip to see his family. He devoted himself to his duties of training field troops—and did it well. Aside from that, he went his own way.

The Maran psychiatrists had explained to Donal that no more than this could be expected of Ian. Gently, they had explained it. A normal mind, gone sick, they could cure. The unfortunate thing was that—at least in so far as his attachment to his twin had been —Ian was not normal. Nothing in this universe could replace the part of him that had died with Kensie— had, indeed, *been* Kensie—for the peculiar psychological make-up of the twins had made them two halves of a whole.

"Your uncle continued to live," the psychiatrists had explained to Donal, "because of an unconscious desire to punish himself for letting his brother die. He is, in fact, seeking death—but it must be a peculiar sort of death which will include the destruction of all that matters to him. 'If they right hand offend thee, cut it off.' To his unconscious, the Ian-Kensie gestalt holds the Ian part of it to blame for what happened and is hunting a punishment to fit the crime. That is why he continues to practice the—for him—morbid abnormality of staying alive. The normal thing for such a personality would be to die, or get himself killed.

"And that is why," they had concluded, "he refuses to see or have anything to do with his wife or children. His unconscious recognizes the danger of pulling them down to destruction with him. We would advise against his being urged to visit them against his will."

Donal sighed. Thinking about it now, it seemed to him strange that the people who had come to group around him had none of them come—really—because of the fame he had won or the positions he could offer them. There was Ian, who had come because the family had sent him. Lee, who had found the supply of that which his own faulty personality lacked—and would have followed if Donal had been Protector of nothing, instead of being Protector of Procyon. There was Lludrow, Donal's now assistant Chief of Staff, who had come to him not under his own free will, but under the prodding of his wife. For Lludrow had ended up marrying Elvine Rhy, Galt's niece, who had not let even marriage impose a barrier to her interest in Donal. There was Genéve bar-Colmain, who was on Donal's staff because Donal had been kind; and because he had no place else to go that was worthy of his abilities. And, lastly, there was Galt, himself, whose friendship was not a military matter, but the rather wistful affection of a man who had never had a son, and saw its image in Donal—though it was not really fair to count Galt, who was apart, as still Marshal of Freiland.

And—in contradistinction to all the rest—there was Mor, the one Donal would have most liked to have at his side; but whose pride had driven him to place himself as far from his successful younger brother as possible. Mor had finally taken service with Venus, where in the open market that flourished on that technological planet, he had had his contract sold to Ceta; and now found himself in the pay of Donal's enemy, which would put them on opposite sides if conflict finally came.

Donal shook himself abruptly. These fits of depression that took him lately were becoming more frequent—possibly as a result of the long hours of work he found himself putting in. Brusquely, he broke open the signal from Galt.

Donal:

The news about New Earth will have reached you by this time. The *coup d'état* that put the Kyerly government in control of the planet was engineered with troops furnished by Ceta. I have never ceased to be grateful to you for your advice against leasing out units to William. But the pattern here is a bad one. We will be facing the same sort of internal attack here through the local proponents of an open exchange for the buying and selling of contracts. One by one, the worlds are falling into the hands of manipulators, not the least of which is William himself. Please furnish us with as many field units as you can conveniently spare.

There is to be a General Planetary Discussion, meeting on Venus to discuss recognition of the new government on New Earth. They would be wise not to invite you; so come anyway. I, myself, must be there; and I need you, even if no other reason impels you to come.

Hendrik Galt
Marshal, Freiland.

Donal nodded to himself. But he did not spring immediately into action. Where Galt was reacting against the shock of a sudden discovery, Donal, in the situation on New Earth, recognized only the revelation of something he had been expecting for a long time.

The sixteen inhabited worlds of the eight stellar systems from Sol to Altair survived within a complex of traded skills. The truth of the matter was that present day civilization had progressed too far for each planet to maintain its own training systems and keep up with progress in the many necessary fields. Why support a thousand mediocre school systems when it was possible to have fifty superb ones and trade the graduates for the skilled people you needed in other areas of learning? The overhead of such systems was tremendous, the number of top men in each field necessarily limited; moreover, progress was more effective if all the workers in one area of knowledge were kept closely in touch with each other.

The system seemed highly practical. Donal was one of the few men of his time to see the trouble inherent in it.

The joker to such an arrangement comes built in to the question—how much is a skilled worker an individual in his own right, and how much is he a piece of property belonging to whoever at the moment owns his contract? If he is too much an individual, barter between worlds breaks down to a series of individual negotiations; and society nowadays could not exist except on the basis of community needs. If he is too much a piece of property, then the field is opened for the manipulators—the buyers and sellers of flesh, those who would corner the manpower market and treat humanity like cattle for their own gain.

Among the worlds between the stars, this question

still hung in argument. "Tight" societies, like the technological worlds of the so-called Venus group— Venus herself, Newton and Cassia—and the fanatic worlds of Harmony and Association, and Coby, which was ruled by what amounted to a criminal secret society—had always favored the piece of property view more strongly than the individual one. "Loose" societies, like the republican worlds of Old Earth, and Mars, the Exotics—Mara and Kultis—and the violently individualistic society of the Dorsai, held to the individual side of the question. In between were the middling worlds—the ones with strong central governments like Freiland and New Earth, the merchandising world of Ceta, the democratic theocracy of St. Marie, and the pioneer, underpopulated fisher-planet of Dunnin's World, ruled by the co-operative society known as the Corbel.

Among the "tight" societies, the contract exchange mart had been in existence for many years. On these worlds, unless your contract was written with a specific forbidding clause, you might find yourself sold on no notice at all to a very different employer—possibly on a completely different world. The advantages of such a mart were obvious to an autocratic government, since the government itself was in a position to control the market through its own vast needs and resources, which no individual could hope to match. On a "loose" world, where the government was hampered by its own built in system of checks from taking advantage of opposing individual employers, the field was open for the sharp practices not only of individuals, but of other governments.

Thus, an agreement between two worlds for the establishment of a reciprocal open market worked all to the advantage of the "tighter" of the two governments—and must inevitably end in the tighter government gaining the lion's share of the talent available on the two worlds.

This, then, was the background for the inevitable conflict that had been shaping up now for fifty years between two essentially different systems of controlling what was essentially the lifeblood of the human race—it's skilled minds. In fact, thought Donal, standing by the open wall—the conflict was here, and now. It had already been under way that day he had stepped aboard the ship on which he was to meet Galt, and William, and Anea, the Select of Kultis. Behind the scenes, the build-up for a final battle had been already begun, and his own role in that battle, ready and waiting for him.

He went over to his desk and pressed a stud, speaking into a grille.

"I want all Chiefs of Staff here immediately," he said. "For a top-level conference."

He took his finger from the stud and sat down at the desk. There was a great deal to be done.

PROTECTOR II

Arriving at Holmstead the capital city of Venus five days later, Donal went immediately to a conference with Galt in the latter's suite of rooms at Government Hotel.

"There were things to take care of," he said, shaking hands with the older man and sitting down, "or

I'd have been here sooner." He examined Galt. "You're looking tired."

The marshal of Freiland had indeed lost weight. The skin of his face sagged a little on the massive bones, and his eyes were darkened with fatigue.

"Politics—politics—" answered Galt. "Not my line at all. It wears a man down. Drink?"

"No thanks," said Donal.

"Don't care for one myself," Galt said. "I'll just light my pipe . . . you don't mind?"

"I never did before. And," said Donal, "you never asked me before."

"Heh . . . no," Galt gave vent to something halfway between a cough an a chuckle; and, getting out his pipe, began to fill it with fingers that trembled a little. "Damned tired, that's all. In fact I'm ready to retire —but how can a man quit just when all hell's popping? You got my message—how many field units can you let me have?"

"A couple and some odds and ends. Say twenty thousand of first-line troops—" Galt's head came up. "Don't worry," Donal smiled. They will be moved in by small, clumsy stages to give the impression I'm letting you have five times that number, but the procedure's a little fouled up in getting them actually transferred."

Galt grunted.

"I might've known you'd think of something," he said. "We can use that mind of yours here, at the main Conference. Officially, we're gathered here just to agree on a common attitude to the new government on New Earth—but you know what's really on the fire, don't you?"

"I can guess," said Donal. "The open market."

"Right." Galt got his pipe alight; and puffed on it gratefully. "The split's right down the middle, now that New Earth's in the Venus Group's camp and we

—Freiland, that is—are clear over on the nonmarket side by way of reaction. We're in fair enough strength counting heads as we sit around the table; but that's not the problem. They've got William—and that white-haired devil Blaine." He looked sharply over at Donal. "You know Project Blaine, don't you?"

"I've never met him. This is my first trip to Venus," said Donal.

"There's a shark," said Galt with feeling. "I'd like to see him and William lock horns on something. Maybe they'd chew each other up and improve the universe. Well . . . about your status here—"

"Officially I'm sent by Sayona the Bond as an absorver."

"Well, that's no problem then. We can easily get you invited to step from observer to delegate status. In fact, I've already passed the word. We were just waiting for you to arrive." Galt blew a large cloud of smoke and squinted at Donal through it. "But how about it, Donal? I trust that insight of yours. What's really in the wind here at the Conference?"

"I'm not sure," answered Donal. "It's my belief somebody made a mistake."

"A mistake?"

"New Earth," explained Donal. "It was a fool's trick to overthrow the government there right now—and by force, at that. Which is why I believe we'll be getting it back."

Galt sat up sharply, taking his pipe from his mouth.

"Getting it back? You mean—the old government returned to power?" He stared at Donal. "Who'd give it back to us?"

"William for one, I'd imagine," said Donal. "This isn't *his* way of doing things—piecemeal. But you can bet as long as he's about returning it, he'll exact a price for it."

Galt shook his head.

"I don't follow you," he said.

"William finds himself working with the Venus group right now," Donal pointed out. "But he's hardly out to do them a kindness. His own aims are what concerns him—and it's those he'll be after in the long run. In fact, if you look, I'll bet you see two kinds of negotiations going on at this Conference. The short range, and the long range. The short range is likely to be this matter of an open market. The long range will be William's game."

Galt sucked on his pipe again.

"I don't know," he said, heavily. "I don't hold any more of a brief for William than you do—but you seem to lay everything at his doorstep. Are you sure you aren't a little overboard where the subject of him is concerned?"

"How can anyone be sure?" confessed Donal, wryly. "I think what I think about William, because—" he hesitated, "if I were in his shoes, I'd be doing these things I suspect him of." He paused. "William's weight on our side could swing the conference into putting enough pressure on New Earth to get the old government back in power, couldn't it?"

"Why—of course."

"Well, then." Donal shrugged. "What could be better than William setting forth a compromise solution that at one and the same time puts him in the opposite camp and conceals as well as requires a development in the situation he desires?"

"Well—I can follow that," said Galt, slowly. "But if that's the case, what's he after? What is it he'll want?"

Donal shook his head.

"I'm not sure," he said carefully. "I don't know."

On that rather inconclusive note, they ended their own private talk and Galt took Donal off to meet with some of the other delegates.

The meeting developed, as these things do, into a cocktail gathering in the lounges of the suite belonging to Project Blaine of Venus. Blaine himself, Donal was interested to discover, was a heavy, calm-looking white-haired man who showed no surface evidences of the character Galt had implied to him.

"Well, what do you think of him?" Galt murmured, as they left Blaine and his wife in the process of circulating around the other guests.

"Brilliant," said Donal. "But I hardly think someone to be afraid of." He met Galt's raised eyebrows with a smile. "He seems too immersed in his own point of view. I'd consider him predictable."

"As opposed to William?" asked Galt, in a low voice.

"As opposed to William," agreed Donal. "Who is not—or, not so much."

They had all this time been approaching William, who was seated facing them at one end of the lounge and talking to a tall slim woman whose back was to them. As Galt and Donal came up, William's gaze went past her.

"Well, Marshall!" he said, smiling. "Protector!" The woman turned around; and Donal found himself face to face with Anea.

If five years had made a difference in the outward form of Donal, they had made much more in that of Anea. She was in her early twenties now, and past the last stages of that delayed adolescence of hers. She had begun now to reveal that rare beauty that would deepen with age and experience and never completely leave her, even in extreme old age. She was more developed now, than the last time Donal had seen her, more fully woman-formed and more poised. Her green eyes met Donal's indeterminate ones across mere centimeters of distance.

"Honored to see you again," said Donal, inclining his head.

"The honor is mine." Her voice, like the rest of her, had matured. Donal looked past her to William. "Prince!" he said.

William stood up and shook hands, both with Donal and with Galt.

."Honored to have you with us, Protector," he said cheerfully to Donal. "I understand the marshal's proposing you for delegate. You can count on me."

"That's good of you," answered Donal.

"It's good for me," said William. "I like open minds around the Conference table and young minds—no offense, Hendrik—are generally open minds."

"I don't pretend to be anything but a soldier," growled Galt.

"And it's precisely that that makes you dangerous in negotiations," replied William. "Politicians and businessmen always feel more at home with someone who they know doesn't mean what he says. Honest men always have been a curse laid upon the sharpshooter."

"A pity," put in Anea, "that there aren't enough honest men, then, to curse them all." She was looking at Donal.

William laughed.

"The Select of Kultis could hardly be anything else but savage upon us underhanded characters, could you, Anea?" he said.

"You can ship me back to the Exotics, any time I wear too heavily on you," she retorted.

"No, no." William wagged his head, humorously. "Being the sort of man I am, I survive only by surrounding myself with good people like yourself. I'm enmeshed in the world of hard reality—it's my life and I wouldn't have it any other way—but for vacation, for a spiritual rest, I like to glance occasionally over the wall of a cloister to where the greatest tragedy is a blighted rose."

"One should not underestimate roses," said Donal. "Men have died over a difference in their color."

"Come now," said William turning on him. "The Wars of the Roses—ancient England? I can't believe such a statement from you, Donal. That conflict, like everything else, was over practical and property disputes. Wars never get fought for abstract reasons."

"On the contrary," Donal said. "Wars invariably get fought for abstract reasons. Wars may be instigated by the middle-aged and the elderly; but they're fought by youth. And youth needs more than a practical motive for tempting the tragedy of all tragedies —the end of the universe—which is dying, when you're young."

"What a refreshing attitude from a professional soldier!" laughed William. "Which reminds me—I may have some business to discuss with you. I understand you emphasize the importance of field troops over everything else in a world's armed forces—and I hear you've been achieving some remarkable things in the training of them. That's information right down my alley, of course, since Ceta's gone in for this leasing of troops. What's your secret, Protector? Do you permit observers?"

"No secret," said Donal. "And you're welcome to send observers to our training program any time, Prince. The reason behind our successful training methods is the man in charge—my uncle, Field Commander Ian Graeme."

"Ah—your uncle," said William. "I hardly imagine I could buy him away from you if he's a relative."

"I'm afraid not," answered Donal.

"Well, well—we'll have to talk, anyway. By heaven —my glass seems to have got itself empty. Anyone else care for another?"

"No thank you," said Anea.

"Nor I," said Donal.

"Well, I will," Galt said.

"Well, in that case, come along marshal," William turned to Galt. "You and I'll make our own way to the bar." They went off together across the lounge, Donal and Anea were left facing each other.

"So," said Donal, "you haven't changed your mind about me."

"No."

"So much for the fair-mindedness of a Select of Kultis," he said ironically.

"I'm not superhuman, you know!" she flashed, with a touch of her younger spirit. "No," she said, more calmly, "there's probably millions as bad as you—or worse—but you've got ability. And you're a self-seeker. It's that I can't forgive you."

"William's corrupted your point of view," he said.

"At least he makes no bones about being the kind of man he is!"

"Why should there be some sort of virtue always attributed to a frank admission of vice?" wondered Donal. "Besides, you're mistaken. William"—he lowered his voice—"sets himself up as a common sort of devil to blind you to the fact that he is what he actually is. Those who have anything to do with him recognize the fact that he's evil; and think that in recognizing this, they've plumbed the depths of the man."

"Oh?" Her voice was scornful. "What *are* his depths, then?"

"Something more than personal aggrandizement. You who are so close to him, miss what the general mass of people who see him from a distance recognize quite clearly. He lives like a monk—he gets no personal profit out of what he does and his long hours of work. And he does not care what's thought of him."

"Any more than you do."

"Me?" Caught by an unexpected amount of truth in this charge, Donal could still protest. "I care for the opinion of the people whose opinion I care for."

"Such as?" she said.

"Well you," he answered, "for one. Though I don't know why."

About to say something, and hardly waiting for him to finish so she could say it, she checked suddenly; and stared at him, her eyes widening.

"Oh," she gasped, "don't try to tell me that!"

"I hardly know why I try to tell you anything," he said, suddenly very bitter; and went off, leaving her where she stood.

He went directly out from the cocktail gathering and back to his own suite, where he immersed himself in work that kept him at his desk until the small hours of the morning. Even then, when he at last got to bed, he did not sleep well—a condition he laid to a walking hangover from the drinks at the cocktail gathering.

His mind would have examined this excuse further —but he would not let it.

PROTECTOR III

". . . A typical impasse," said William, Prince of Ceta. "Have some more of this Moselle."

"Thank you, no," answered Donal. The Conference was in its second week and he had accepted William's invitation to lunch with him in William's suite, following a morning session. The fish was excellent, the wine was imported—and Donal was curious, although so far they had spoken of nothing of real importance.

"You disappoint me," William said, replacing the decanter on the small table between them. "I'm not very strong in the food and drink department myself —but I do enjoy watching others enjoy them." He raised his eyebrows at Donal. "But your early training on the Dorsai is rather Spartan?"

"In some respects, yes," answered Donal. "Spartan and possibly a little provincial. I'm finding myself sliding into Hendrik Galt's impatience with the lack of progress in our talks."

"Well, there you have it," said William. "The soldier loves action, the politician the sound of his own voice. But there's a better explanation than that, of course. You've realized by now, no doubt, that the things that concern a Conference aren't settled at the Conference table"—he gestured with his hand at the food before him—"but at small tete-a-tetes like these."

"I'd guess then that the tete-a-tetes haven't been too productive of agreements so far." Donal sipped at the wine left in his glass.

"Quite right," said William cheerfully. "Nobody really wants to interfere in local affairs on a world; and nobody really wants to impose an institution on it from the outside, such as the open market, against the will of some of its people." He shook his head at Donal's smile. "No, no—I'm being quite truthful. Most of the delegates here would just as soon the problem of an open market had never come up at all on New Earth, so that they could tend to their own styles of knitting without being bothered."

"I'll still reserve my judgment on that," said Donal. "But in any case, now we're here, we've got to come to some decision. Either for or against the current government; and for or against the market."

"Do we?" asked William. "Why not a compromise solution?"

"What sort of compromise?"

"Well that, of course," said William, in a frank tone, "is why I asked you to lunch. I feel very humble about you, Donal—I really do. I was entirely wrong in my estimate of you, five years ago. I did you an injustice."

Donal lifted his right hand in a small gesture of deprecation.

"No . . . no," said William. "I insist on apologizing. I'm not a kind man, Donal. I'm interested only in buying what others have to sell—and if a man has ability, I'll buy it. If not—" He let the sentence hang significantly. "But you *have* ability. You had it five years ago, and I was too concerned with the situation to recognize it. The truth of the matter is, Hugh Killien was a fool."

"On that, I can agree with you," Donal said.

"Attempting to carry on with Anea under my nose —I don't blame the girl. She was still a child then, for all her size. That's the way these Exotic hothouse people are—slow growing. But I should have seen it and expected it. In fact, I'm grateful to you for what you did, when I think back on it."

"Thank you," murmured Donal.

"No, I mean that absolutely. Not that I'm talking to you now out of a sense of gratitude alone—I wouldn't insult your credulity with such a suggestion. But I am pleased to be able to find things working out in such a way that my own profit combines with the chance to pay you a small debt of gratitude."

"At any rate, I appreciate it," said Donal.

"Not at all. Now, the point is this," said William, leaning forward over the table, "personally, of course, I favor the open market. I'm a businessman, after all, and there's business advantages to perfectly free trading. But more than open markets, it's important to business to have peace between the stars; and peace comes only from a stable situation."

"Go on," said Donal.

"Well, there are after all only two ways of imposing peace on a community—from the inside or from the outside. We don't seen to be able to do it to ourselves from the inside; so why not try imposing it from the outside?"

"And how would you go about that?"

"Quite simply," said William, leaning back in his float. "Let *all* the worlds have open markets, but appoint a separate, individual supraplanetary authority to police the markets. Equip it with sufficient force to back up its authority against even individual governments if need be—and appoint a responsible individual in charge whom governments will think twice about tangling with." He raised his eyes calmly to Donal across the table and paused to let expectation build to its proper peak in this young man. "How would you like the job?" he asked.

"I?"

Donal stared at him. William's eyes were shrewd upon him. Donal hesitated; and the muscles of his throat worked, once.

"I?" he said. "Why, the man who commanded a force like that would be—" the word faltered and died, unspoken.

"He would, indeed," said William, softly. Across from him Donal seemed to come slowly back to himself. He turned narrowed eyes on William. "Why come to me with an offer like this?" he demanded. "There are older commanders. Men with bigger names."

"And that is just precisely why I come to you, Donal," replied William, without hesitation. "Their stars are fading. Yours is rising. Where will these older men be twenty years from now? On the other hand, you —" he waved a self-explanatory hand.

"I!" said Donal. He seemed to be dazzled. "Commander—"

"Call it Commander in Chief," said William. "The job will be there; and you're the man for the job. I'm prepared, in the name of Ceta, to set up a tax on interplanetary transactions which, because of our volume of trade, we will bear the most heavily. The tax would pay for your forces, and yourself. All we want in exchange is a place on a three-man commission which will act as final authority over you." He smiled. "We could hardly put such power in your hands and turn you loose under no authority."

"I suppose—" Donal was hesitant. "I'd have to give up my position around Procyon—"

"I'm afraid so," said William, frankly. "You'd have to remove any suspicion of conflicting interests."

"I don't know." Donal's voice was hesitant. "I might lose this new post at any time—"

"There's no need to worry about that," said William. "Ceta should effectively control the commission —since we will be paying the lion's share. Besides, a force like that, once established, isn't easy to disband. And if they're loyal to their commander—and your troops, I hear, usually are very much so—you would be in a position to defend your own position, if it came to that."

"Still—" Donal still demurred. "Taking a post like that I'd inevitably make enemies. If something *should* go wrong, I'd have no place to turn, no one would hire me—"

"Frankly," said William, sharply, "I'm disappointed in you, Donal. "Are you completely lacking in foresight?" His tone took on a little impatience. "Can't you see that we're inevitably trending toward a single government for all the worlds? It may not come tomorrow, or even in the next decade; but any supra-planetary organization must inevitably grow into the ultimate, central authority."

"In which case," said Donal, "I'd still be nothing but a hired hand. What I want"—his eyes burned a little more brightly—"is to own something. A world . . . . why not? I'm equipped to control a world; and defend it." He turned on William. "You'll have *your* position," he said.

William's eyes were hard and bright as two cut stones. He laughed shortly.

"You don't mince words," he said.

"I'm not that kind of man," said Donal, with a slight swagger in his tone. "You should have expected me to see through this scheme of yours. You want supreme authority. Very well. Give me one of the worlds—under you."

"And if I was to give you a world," said William. "Which one?"

"Any fair size world." Donal licked his lips. "Well, why not New Earth?"

William laughed. Donal stiffened.

"We're getting nowhere," said Donal. He stood up. "Thank you for the lunch." He turned and headed for the exit from the lounge.

"Wait!"

He turned to the sound of William's voice. The other man was also on his feet; and he came toward Donal.

"I've underestimated you again," said William. "Forgive me." He placed a detaining hand on Donal's arm. "The truth is, you've only anticipated me. Indeed, I'd intended you to be something more than a hired soldier. But . . . all this is in the future," he shrugged. "I can hardly do more than promise you what you want."

"Oh," said Donal. "Something more than a promise.

You could give me a contract, confirming me as the supreme authority on New Earth."

William stared at him and this time he did laugh, loudly and long.

"Donal!" he said. "Excuse me . . . but what good would a contract like that be?" He spread his arms wide. "Some day New Earth may be mine to write you a contact for. But now——?"

"Still, you could write it. It would serve as a guarantee that you mean what you say."

William stopped laughing. His eyes narrowed.

"Put my name to a piece of writing like that?" he said. "What kind of a fool to you take me for?"

Donal wilted a little under the angry contempt in the older man's voice.

"Well . . . at least draw up such a contract," he said. "I suppose I couldn't expect you to sign it. But . . . at least I'd have something."

"You have something that could possibly cause me some slight embarrassment," said William. "I hope you realize it'd do nothing more than that—in the face of my denial of ever having discussed the matter with you."

"I'd feel more secure if the terms were laid out ahead of time," said Donal, almost humbly. William shrugged, not without a touch of scorn.

"Come on then," he said; and led the way across the room to a desk. He pressed a stud on it and indicated a grille. "Dictate," he said.

Later, leaving William's suite of rooms with the unsigned contract in his pocket, Donal came out into the general hotel corridor outside so swiftly that he almost trod upon the heels of Anea, who seemed also to be leaving.

"Where away?" he said. She turned on him.

"None of your business!" she snapped; but an expression which the inescapable honesty of her face would not permit her to hide, aroused his sudden suspicions. He reached out swiftly and caught up her right hand, which was clenched into a fist. She struggled, but he lifted the fingers easily back. Tucked into the nest of her palm was a tiny contact snooper mike.

"You *will* continue to be a fool," he said, wearily, dropping her hand with the mike still in it. "How much did you hear?"

"Enough to confirm my opinion of *you!*" she hissed.

"Bring that opinion to the next session of the Conference, if you can get in," he said. And went off. She stared after him, shaken with a fury, and a sudden pain of betrayal for which she could find no ready or sensible explanation.

She had, she told herself through that afternoon and the evening that followed, no intention of watching the next session personally. Early the next morning, however, she found herself asking Galt if he would get her a visitor's pass to the Conference room.

The marshal was obliged to inform her that at William's request, this session of the Conference was to be a closed one. He promised, however, to bring her what news he could; and she was forced to rest uneasily content with that.

As for Galt, himself, he went on to the Conference, arriving some few minutes late and discovering that the session had already started. William himself had begun the proposal of a plan that made the Dorsai Marshal of Freiland stiffen to attention, even as he was sitting down on his float at the Conference table.

". . . To be established by a vote of this body," William was saying. "Naturally," he smiled, "our individual governments will have to ratify later, but we all know that to be pretty much a formality. A supraplanetary controlling body—having jurisdiction over trade and contracts, only—in conjunction with a general establishment of the open market, satisfies the requirements of all our members. Also, once this is out of the way, there should be no reason why we should not call upon the present insurgent government of New Earth to resign in favor of the previous, regular government. And I expect that if we call with a united voice, the present heads of state there will yield to our wishes." He smiled around the table. "I'm open for questions and objections, gentlemen."

"You said," spoke up Project Blaine, in his soft, precise voice, "something about a supranational armed force which would enforce the rulings of this controlling body. Such an armed force is, of course, contrary to our principles of individual world-rights. I would like to say right now that I hardly think we would care to support such a force and allow it such freedom if a commander inimical to our interests was at its head. In short—"

"We have no intention of subscribing to a commander other than one with a thorough understanding of our own principles and rights," interrupted Arjean, of St. Marie, all but glaring at the Venusian. Galt's shaggy brows shot together in a scowl.

There was something entirely too pat about the way these two had horned in. He started to look over at Donal for confirmation of this suspicion but William's voice drew his attention back to the Cetan.

"I understand, of course," said William. "However, I think I have the answer to all of your objections." He smiled impersonally at all of them. "The top commanders, as you know, are few. Each one has various associations which might make him objectionable to some one or more of the delegates here. In the main, I would say what we need is a professional soldier who is nothing more than a professional soldier. The prime examples of this, of course, are our Dorsai—"

The glances around the table swung quickly in on Galt, who scowled back to hide his astonishment.

". . . The Marshal of Freiland would, therefore, because of his position in his profession and between the stars, be our natural choice. But—" William barely got the word out in time to stifle objections that had begun to voice themselves from several points around the table, "Ceta recognizes that because of the marshal's long association with Freiland, some of you may not welcome him in such a position. We're therefore proposing another man entirely—equally a Dorsai, but one who is young enough and recently enough on the scene to be considered free of political prejudice—I refer to the Protector of Procyon, Donal Graeme."

He gestured at Donal and sat down.

A babble of voices broke out all at once, but Donal was on his feet, looking tall, and slim, and remarkably young amongst the group of them. He stood, waiting, and the voices finally died down.

"I won't keep you for more than a minute," said Donal, looking around at them. "I agree thoroughly with Prince William's compromise solution to the problem of this Conference; because I most heartily believe the worlds *do* need a watchdog over them to prevent what's just now taken place, from happening." He paused, and looked around the table again. "You see, honored as I am by Prince William's nomination, I can't accept because of something which just recently came into my hands. It names no names, but it promises things which will be a revelation to all of us. I also will name no names, but I would guess however that if this is a sample of what's going on, there are probably half a dozen other such writings being traded around."

He paused to let this sink in.

"So, I hereby refuse the nomination. And, further,

I'm now withdrawing as a Delegate from this Conference in protest against being approached in this manner. I could not accept such a post or such a responsibility except with perfectly clean hands and no strings attached. Good-by, gentlemen."

He nodded to them and stepped back from their stunned silence. About to turn toward the exit, he stopped and pulled from his pocket the unsigned and nameless contract he had received from William the previous day. "Oh, by the way," he said. "This is the matter I was talking about. Perhaps you'd all like to look it over."

He threw it onto the table in their midst and strode out. As he left the lounge behind him, a sudden eruption of voices reached to his ears.

He did not go directly back to his own suite, but turned instead to Galt's. The doorbot admitted him; and he made his way to the main lounge of the suite, striding in with the confidence of one who expects to find it empty.

It was not, however. He had made half a dozen long strides into the room before he discovered another person seated alone at a chess board on a little table, and looking up at his entrance with startled eyes.

It was Anea.

He checked and inclined his head to her.

"Excuse me," he said. "I was going to wait for Hendrik. I'll take one of the other lounges."

"No," she had risen to her feet. Her face was a little pale, but controlled. "I'm waiting for him, too. Is the session over?"

"Not yet," he replied.

"Then let's wait together." She sat down at the table again. She waved a hand at the pieces, presently set up in the form of a knights-castles problem. "You play?"

"Yes," he said.

"Then join me." It was almost an order the way she said it. Donal showed no reaction, however, but crossed the lounge and took a seat opposite her. She began to set out the pieces.

If she expected to win, she was mistaken. Donal won three swift games; but oddly without showing any particular flair or brilliance. Consistently he seemed able to take advantage of opportunities she had overlooked, but which had been there before her in perfect obviousness all the time. The games seemed more a tribute to her obtuseness, than his perception. She said as much. He shrugged.

"You were playing me," he said. "And you should rather have been playing my pieces."

She frowned; but before she had a chance to sort this answer out in her mind, there was the sound of steps outside the lounge, and Galt entered, striding along and excitedly.

Donal and she both rose.

"What happened?" she cried.

"Eh? What?" Galt's attention had been all for Donal. Now the older man swung on her. "Didn't he tell you what happened up to the time he left?"

"No!" She flashed a look at Donal, but his face was impassive.

Quickly, Galt told her. Her face paled and became shadowed by bewilderment. Again, she turned to Donal; but before she could frame the question in her mind, Donal was questioning Galt.

"And after I left?"

"You should have seen it!" the older man's voice held a fierce glee. "Each one was at the throat of everybody else in the room before you were out of sight. I swear the last forty years of behind-the-scenes deals, and the crosses and the double-crosses came home to roost in the next five minutes. Nobody trusted anybody, everybody suspected everybody else! What a bombshell to throw in their laps!" Galt chuckled. "I feel forty years younger just for seeing it. Who was it that actually approached you, boy? It was William, wasn't it?"

"I'd rather not say," said Donal.

"Well, well—never mind that. For all practical purposes it could have been any of them. But guess what happened! Guess how it all ended up—"

"They voted me in as commander in chief after all?" said Donal.

"They—" Galt checked suddenly, his face dropping into an expression of amazement. "How'd you know?"

Donal smiled a little mirthlessly. But before he could answer, a sharp intake of breath made both men turn their heads. Anea was standing off a little distance from them, her face white and stiff.

"I might have suspected," she said in a low, hard voice to Donal. "I might have known."

"Known? Known what?" demanded Galt, staring from one to the other. But her eyes did not waver from Donal.

"So this was what you meant when you told me to bring my opinion to today's session," she went on in the same low, hate-filled voice. "Did you think that this . . . this sort of double-dealing would change it?"

For a second pain shadowed Donal's normally enigmatic eyes.

"I should have known better, I suppose," he said, quietly. "I assumed you might look beyond the necessities of this present action to—"

"Thank you," she broke in icily. "Ankle deep into the mud is far enough." She turned on Galt. "I'll see you another time, Hendrik." And she stalked out of the room.

The two men watched her go in silence. Then Galt slowly turned back to look at the younger man.

"What's between you two, boy?" he asked.

Donal shook his head.

"Half of heaven and all of hell, I do believe," he said; and that was the most illuminating answer the marshal was able to get out of him.

COMMANDER IN CHIEF

Under the common market system, controlled by the United Planetary Forces under Commander in Chief Donal Graeme, the civilized worlds rested in a highly unusual state of almost perfect peace for two years, nine months, and three days absolute time. Early on the morning of the fourth day, however, Donal woke to find his shoulder being shaken.

"What?" he said, coming automatically awake.

"Sir—" It was the voice of Lee. "Special Courier here to see you. He says his message won't wait."

"Right." Groggily, but decisively, Donal swung his legs over the edge of his sleeping float and reached for his trunks on the ordinary float beside him. He gathered them in, brushing something to the floor as he did so.

"Light," he said to Lee. The light went on, revealing that what he had knocked down was his wrist appliance. He picked it up and stared at it with blurry eyes. "March ninth," he murmured. "That right, Lee?"

"That's right," responded the voice of Lee, from across the room. Donal chuckled, a little huskily.

"Not yet the ides of March," he murmured. "But close. Close."

"Sir?"

"Nothing. Where's the courier, Lee?"

"The garden lounge."

Donal pulled on the trunks and—on a second's impulse—followed them with trousers, tunic and jacket, complete outerwear. He followed Lee through the pre-dawn darkness of his suite on Tomblecity, Cassida, and into the garden lounge. The courier, a slim, small, middle-aged man in civilian clothes, was waiting for him.

"Commander—" the courier squinted at him. "I've got a message for you. I don't know what it means myself—"

"Never mind," interrupted Donal. "What is it?"

"I was to say to you 'the gray rat has come out of the black maze and pressed the white lever.'"

"I see," said Donal. "Thank you." The courier lingered.

"Any message or orders, commander?"

"None, thank you. Good morning," said Donal.

"Good morning, sir," said the courier; and went out, escorted by Lee. When Lee returned, he found Donel already joined by his uncle Ian Graeme, fully dressed and armed. Donal was securing a weapons belt around his own waist. In the new glare of the artificial light after the room's darkness, and beside his dark and giant uncle, the paring-down effect of the last months showed plainly on Donal. He was not so much thinned down as stretched drum-tight over the hard skeleton of his own body. He seemed all harsh angles and tense muscle. And his eyes were hollowed and dark with fatigue.

Looking at him, it would be hard not to assume that here was a man either on the verge of psychological and nervous breakdown, or someone of fanatic purpose who had already pushed himself beyond the bounds of ordinary human endurance. There was something of the fanatic's translucency about him—in which the light of the consuming will shows through the frailer vessel of the body. Except that Donal was not really translucent, but glowed, body and all, like one fine solid bar of tempered steel with the white, ashy heat of his consuming but all-unconsumable will.

"Arm yourself, Lee," he said, pointing to a weapons belt. "We've got two hours before sun-up and things begin to pop. After that, I'll be a proscribed criminal on any world but the Dorsai—and you two with me." It did not occur to him to ask either of the other men whether they wished to throw themselves into the holocaust that was about to kindle about him; and it did not occur to the others to wonder that he did not. "Ian, did you make a signal to Lludrow?"

"I did," said Ian. "He's in deep space with all units, and he'll hold them there a week if need be, he says —incommunicado."

"Good. Come on."

As they left the building for the platform awaiting them on the landing pad outside; and later, as the platform slipped them silently through the pre-dawn darkness to a landing field not far from the residence, Donal was silent, calculating what could be done in seven days time, absolute. On the eighth day, Lludrow would have to open his communication channels again, and the orders that would reach him when he did so would be far different from the sealed orders Donal had left him and which he would be opening right now. Seven days—

They landed at the field. The ship, a space-and-atmosphere courier N4J, was lying waiting for them, its ground lights gleaming dimly on steady-ready. The forward lock on the great shadowy cylinder swung open as they approached; and a scar-faced senior captain stepped out.

"Sir," he said, saluting Donal, and standing aside to let them enter. They went in and the lock closed behind them.

"Coby, captain," said Donal.

"Yes, sir." The captain stepped to a grille in the wall. "Control room. Coby," he said. He turned from the grille. "Can I show you to the lounge, commander?"

"For the time being," said Donal. "And get us some coffee."

They went on into the courier's lounge, which was fixed up like the main room on a private yacht. And presently coffee was forthcoming on a small autocart from the galley, which scooted in the door by itself and parked itself in the midst of their floats.

"Sit down with us, Cor," said Donal. "Lee, this is Captain Coruna El Man, Cor, my uncle Ian Graeme."

"Dorsai!" said Ian, shaking hands.

"Dorsai!" responded El Man. They smiled slightly at each other, two grimly-carved professional warriors.

"Right," said Donal. "Now that introductions are over—how long will it take us to make it to Coby?"

"We can make our first jump immediately we get outside atmosphere," answered El Man, in his rather harsh, grating voice. "We've been running a steady calculation on a standby basis. After the first jump, it'll take a minimum of four hours to calculate the next. We'll be within a light-year of Coby then, and each phase shift will take progressively less calculation as we zero in. Still—five more calculation periods at an average of two hours a period. Ten hours, plus the original four makes fourteen, straight drive and landing in on Coby another three to four hours. Call it eighteen hours—minimum."

"All right," said Donal. "I'll want ten of your men for an assault party. And a good officer."

"Myself," said El Man.

"Captain, I . . . very well," said Donal. "You and ten men. Now." He produced an architectural plan from inside his jacket. "If you'll all look here; this is the job we have to do."

The plan was that of an underground residence on Coby, that planet which had grown into a community from a collection of mines and never been properly terraformed. Indeed, there was a question whether even with modern methods, it could be. Vega, an AO type star, was too inhospitable to its planets, even though Coby was the fourth out from her, among seven.

The plan itself showed a residence of the middle size, comprising possibly eighteen rooms, surrounded by gardens and courtyards. The differences, which only began to appear as Donal proceeded to point them out, from an above-ground residence of the ordinary type on other planets, lay in the fakery involved. As far as appearances went, someone in the house, or in one of the gardens, would imagine he was surface-dwelling on at least a terraformed world. But eight-tenths of that impression would be sheer illusion. Actually, the person in question would have ultimate rock in all directions—rock ten meters overhead at the furthest, rock underfoot, and rock surrounding.

For the assault party, this situation effected certain drawbacks, but also certain definite advantages. A drawback was, that after securing their objective—who was a man Donal did not trouble himself to identify—withdrawal would not be managed as easily as it might on the surface, where it was simply a matter of bundling everyone into the nearby ship and jumping off. A great advantage, however, which all but offset the drawback mentioned, was the fact that in this type of residence, the rock walls surrounding were honeycombed with equipment rooms and tunnels which maintained the above-ground illusion—a situation allowing easy ingress and surprise.

As soon as the four with him had been briefed, Donal turned the plans over to El Man, who went off to inform his assault party, and suggested to Lee and Ian that they join him in getting what sleep they could. He took himself to his own cabin, undressed and fell into the bunk there. For a few minutes his mind, tight-tuned by exhaustion, threatened to wander off into speculations about what would be taking place on the various worlds while he slept. Unfortunately, no one had yet solved the problems involved in receiving a news broadcast in deep space. Which was why, of course, all interstellar messages were taped and sent by ship. It was the swiftest and, when you came right down to it, the only practical way to get them there.

However, twenty years of rigid training slowly gained control of Donal's nerves. He slept.

He woke some twelve hours later, feeling more rested than he had in over a year. After eating, he went down to the ship's gym; which, cramped and tiny as it was, was still a luxurious accessory on a deep-space vessel. He found Ian methodically working out in the Dorsai fashion—a procedure the large dark man went through every morning when conditions did not prohibit it, as conscientiously and as nearly without thought as most men shave and brush their teeth. For several minutes Donal watched Ian on the single bar, doing arm twists and stands; and when his uncle dropped to the mat, his wide torso gleaming with perspiration and the reek of it strong in Donal's nostrils, Donal took him on at grips-and-holds.

The results were a little shocking to Ian. That Ian was stronger than he was only to be expected. His uncle was the bigger man. But Donal should have had a clear edge in speed, both because of age and because of his own natural reflexes, which were unusually good. The past year's strain and physical idleness, however, had taken their toll. He broke three holds of his uncle's with barely a fraction of a second to spare; and when he did, at last, throw the older man, it was by the use of a feint he would have scorned to use his senior year at school back on the Dorsai, a feint that took sneaking advantage of a slight stiffness he knew to be the result of a old wound in his uncle's deep-scarred left arm.

Ian could hardly have failed to recognize the situation and the reason behind the slightly unfair maneuver that had downed him. But nothing seemed to matter to him these days. He said nothing, but showered and dressed with Donal; and they went in to the lounge.

Shortly after they sat down there, there was the medication warning, and—a few minutes later—the shock of a phase shift. On the heels of it, El Man came walking into the lounge.

"We're in range, commander," he said. "If you want the news—"

"Please," said Donal.

El Man touched one of the walls and it thinned into transparency through which they could see the three-dimensional image of a Cobyman seated at a desk.

". . . Has been spreading," came the voice of the

man at the desk, "following quickly upon the charges brought by the Commission for the Common Market System against Commander in Chief Graeme of the United Planetary Forces. The Com Chief himself has disappeared and most of his deep-space units appear presently to be out of communication and their whereabouts are presently unknown. This development has apparently sparked outbreaks of violence on most of the civilized worlds, in some cases amounting to open revolt against the established governments. The warring factions seem split by a fear of the open markets on the part of the general populaces, and a belief that the charges against Graeme are an attempt to remove what safeguards on the rights of the individual still remain in effect.

"As far as this office has been informed, fighting is going on on the present worlds—Venus, Mars, Cassida, New Earth, Freiland, Association, Harmony, and St. Marie; and the governments of the following worlds are known to be deposed, or in hiding—Cassida, New Earth, and Freiland. No outbreaks are reported on Old Earth, Dunnin's World, Mara, Kultis, or Ceta. And there is no present violence here on Coby at all. Prince William of Ceta has offered the use of his leased troops as a police force to end the disturbances; and levies of Cetan troops are either on, or en route to, all trouble spots at the present time. William has announced that his troops will be used to put down trouble wherever they find it, without respect to what faction this leaves in power. 'Our job is not to take sides,' he is reported as stating, 'but to bring some kind of order out of the present chaos and put out the flames of self-destruction.'

"A late signal received from Old Earth reports that a number of the insurgent factions are agitating for the appointment of William as World's Regent, with universal authority and strong-man powers to deal with the present emergency. A somewhat similar movement puts forward the name of Graeme, the missing Com Chief for a similar position."

"That's all for now," concluded the man at the desk, "watch for our next signal in fifteen minutes."

"Good," said Donal, and gestured to El Man to shut off the receiver, which the scarred Dorsai captain did. "How long until earthfall?"

"A couple of hours," replied El Man. "We're a bit ahead of schedule. That was the last phase shift. We're on our way in on straight drive now. Do you have co-ordinates on our landing point?"

Donal nodded; and stood up.

"I'll come up to control," he said.

The process of bringing the N4J into the spot on the surface of Coby, corresponding to the co-ordinates indicated by Donal, was a time-consuming but simple procedure—only mildly complicated by Donal's wish to make their visit undetected. Coby had nothing to defend in the sense a terraformed world might have; and they settled down without incident on its airless surface, directly over the freight lock to one of the subsurface transportation tunnels.

"All right," said Donal, five minutes later, to the armed contingent of men assembled in the lounge. "This is an entirely volunteer mission, and I'll give any of you one more chance to withdraw without prejudice if you want to." He waited. Nobody stirred. "Understand," said Donal, "I want nobody with me simply because he was shamed into volunteering, or because he didn't want to hesitate when his shipmates volunteered." Again he waited. There were no withdrawals. "Right, then. Here's what we'll be doing. You'll follow me down that freight lock and into a receiving room with a door into a tunnel. However, we won't be taking the door, but burning directly through one of the walls to the service section of an adjoining residence. You've all seen a drawing of our route. You're to follow me, or whoever remains in command; and anyone who can't keep up gets left behind. Everybody understand?" He looked around their faces.

"All right," he said. "Let's go."

He led out down the passageway of the ship, out through their lock and down into the freight lock into the receiving room. This turned out to be a large, gloomy chamber with fused rock walls. Donal measured off a section of one wall and set his torchmen to work. Three minutes later they were in the service section of a Coby residence.

The area in which they found themselves was a network of small tunnels wide enough for only one man at a time, and interspersed with little niches and crannies holding technical devices necessary to the maintenance and appearance of the residence. The walls were coated with a permanent illuminating layer; and, in this cold white light, they filed along one of the tunnels and emerged into a garden.

The cycle of the residence's system was apparently now set on night. Darkness held the garden and a fine imitation of the starry heavens glittered overhead. Ahead and to their right was the clump of main rooms, soft-lit with interior light.

"Two men to hold this exit," whispered Donal. "The rest of you follow me."

He led the way at a low crouching run through the garden and to the foot of some wide stairs. At their top, a solitary figure could be seen pacing back and forth on a terrace before an open wall.

"Captain—" said Donal. El Man slipped away into the bushes below the terrace. There was a little wait in the artificial night and then his dark shadow was seen to rise suddenly upon the terrace behind the pacing figure. They melted together, sagged, and only the shadow of El Man was left. He beckoned them up.

"Three men to hold this terrace," whispered Donal, as they all came together at the head of the stairs. El Man told off the necessary number of the assault party; and they continued on into the lighted interior of the house.

For several rooms it seemed almost as if they would achieve their objective without meeting anyone other than the man they had come to seek. Then, without anything in the way of warning at all, they were suddenly in the middle of a pitched battle.

As they emerged into the main hall, hand weapons opened up on them from three converging rooms at once. The shipmen, automatically responding to training, dropped to the floor, took cover and returned the fire. They were pinned down.

They were, but not the three Dorsai. Donal, Ian, and El Man, reacting in that particular way that was a product of genes, reflexes and their own special training, and that made the Dorsai so particularly valuable as professional soldiers—these three had responded automatically and in unison a split-second before the fire opened up on them. It was almost as if some small element of precognition had entered the picture. At any rate, with a reaction too quick for thought, these three swung about and rushed one of the enemy doorways, reached it and closed with their opponents within before that opposition could bring their fire to bear. The three found themselves in a darkened room and fighting hand to hand.

Here again, the particular character of the Dorsai soldier paid off. There were eight men in ambush within this particular room and they were all veteran soldiers. But no two of them were a match at hand-to-

hand fighting with any single Dorsai; and in addition
the Dorsai had the advantage of being able, almost by
instinct, to recognize each other in the dark and the
melee, and to join forces for a sudden common effort
without the need for discussion. The total effect of
these advantages made it almost a case of three men
who could see fighting eight who were blind.

In Donal's case, he plunged into the dark room
right on the heels of El Man and to El Man's left,
with Ian right behind *him*. Their charge split the defenders within into two groups and also carried them
farther back into obscurity—a movement which the
Dorsai, by common silent consent improved on for
the purpose of further separating the enemy. Donal
found himself pushing back four men. Abandoning
three of these to Ian behind him under the simple
common-sense precept that you fight best when you
fight only one man at a time, he dove in almost at the
level of his opponent's knees, tackled him, and they
went down and rolled over together, Donal taking advantage of the opportunity to break the other soldier's
back in the process.

He continued his roll and came up, pivoting and
instinctively side-stepping. A dark body flung past
him—but that instinct spoken of before warned him
that it was El Man, flinging himself clear across the
room to aid the general confusion. Donal reversed his
field and went back the way from which El Man had
come. He came up against an opponent plunging forward with a knife held low, slipped the knife,
chopped at the man's neck with the calloused edge
of his hand—but missed a clean killing stroke and
only broke the man's collar bone. Leaving that opponent however in the interests of keeping on the
move, Donal spun off to the right, cornered another
man against the wall and crushed this one's windpipe
with a stiff-fingered jab. Rebounding from the wall,

and spinning back into the center of the room, his ears told him that El Man was finishing off one opponent and Ian was engaged with the remaining two. Going to help him, Donal caught one of Ian's men from behind and paralyzed him with a kidney punch. Ian, surprisingly enough, was still engaged with the remaining enemy. Donal went forward and found out why. Ian had caught himself another Dorsai.

Donal closed with both men and they went down in a two-on-one pin, the opponent in a stretcher that held him helpless between Donal and his uncle.

"Shai Dorsai!" gasped Donal. "Surrender!"

"Who to?" grunted the other.

"Donal and Ian Graeme," said Ian. "Foralie."

"Honored," said the strange Dorsai. "Heard of you. Hord Van Tarsel, Snelbrich Canton. All right then, let me up. My right arm's broken, anyway."

Donal and Ian let go and assisted Van Tarsel to his feet. El Man had finished off what else remained, and now came up to them.

"Hord Van Tarsel—Coruna El Man," said Donal.

"Honored," said El Man.

"Honor's mine," replied Van Tarsel. "I'm your prisoner, gentlemen. Want my parole?"

"I'd appreciate it," said Donal. "We've got work to do here yet. What kind of contract are you under?"

"Straight duty. No loyalty clause. Why?"

"Any reason why I can't hire you on a prisoner's basis?" asked Donal.

"Not from this job." Van Tarsel sounded disgusted. "I've been sold twice on the open market because of a typo in my last contract. Besides," he added, "as I say, I've heard of you."

"You're hired, then. We're looking for the man you're guarding here. Can you tell us where we'll find him?"

"Follow me," said Van Tarsel; and led the way back through the darkness; and opened a door. They stepped through into a short corridor that led them up a ramp and to another door.

"Locked," said Van Tarsel. "The alarm's gone off." He looked at them. Further than this he could not in honor go, even on a hired prisoner's basis.

"Burn it down," said Donal.

He and Ian and El Man opened up on the door, which glowed stubbornly to a white heat, but finally melted. Ian threw a concussion bolt at it and knocked it open.

Within, a large man with a black hood over his head was crouched against the far wall of the room, a miner's heavy-duty ion gun in his hand pointing a little unsteadily at them and shifting from one to the other.

"Don't be a fool," said Ian. "We are all Dorsai."

The gun sagged in the hand of the hooded man. A choked, bitter exclamation came from behind the mask.

"Come on." Donal gestured him out. He dropped the gun and came, shoulders bowed. They headed back through the house.

The fire fight in the hall was still going on as they retraced their footsteps; but died out as they reached the center hall. Two of the five men they had left behind there were able to navigate on their own power and another one could make it back to the ship with assistance. The other two were dead. They returned swiftly to the terrace, through the garden, and back into the tunnel, picking up the rest of their complement as they went. Fifteen minutes later, they were all aboard and the N4J was falling into deep space.

In the lounge, Donal was standing before the hooded man, who sat slumped on a float.

"Gentlemen," said Donal, "take a look at William's social technician."

Ian and El Man, who were present, looked sharply over at Donal—not so much at the words as at the tone in which he had said them. He had spoken in a voice that was, for him, unexpectedly bitter.

"Here's the man who sowed the whirlwind the civilized worlds are reaping at this moment," went on Donal. He stretched out his hand to the black hood. The man shrank from him, but Donal caught the hood and jerked it off. A slow exhalation of breath slipped out between Donal's lips.

"So you sold out," he said.

The man before them was ArDell Montor.

COMMANDER IN CHIEF II

ArDell looked back at him out of a white face, but with eyes that did not bend before Donal's bleak glance.

"I had to have work," he said. "I was killing myself. I don't apologize."

"Was that all the reason?" asked Donal, ironically.

At that, ArDell's face did turn aside.

"No—" he said. Donal said nothing. "It was her," ArDell whispered. "He promised me her."

"*Her!*" The note in Donal's voice made the other two Dorsai take an instinctive step toward him. But Donal held himself without moving, under control. "Anea?"

"She might have taken pity on me—" ArDell whispered to the floor of the lounge. "You don't understand . . . living close to her all those years . . . and I was so miserable, and she . . . I couldn't help loving her—"

"No," said Donal. Slowly, the sudden lightning of his tension leaked out of him. "You couldn't help it." He turned away. "You fool," he said, with his back to ArDell. "Didn't you know him well enough to know when he was lying to you? He had her in mind for himself."

"William? *No!*" ArDell was suddenly on his feet. "Not him—with her! It can't be . . . such a thing!"

"It won't," said Donal, wearily. "But not because it depends on people like you to stop him." He turned back to face ArDell. "Lock him up, will you captain." El Man's hard hand closed on ArDell's shoulder and turned him toward the entrance to the lounge. "Oh . . . and captain—"

"Sir?" said El Man, turning to face him.

"We rendezvous with all units under Fleet Commander Lludrow as soon as possible."

"Yes, sir." El Man half-pushed, half-carried ArDell Montor out of the room; and, as if symbolically, out of the main current of the history of mankind which he had attempted to influence with his science for William, Prince of Ceta.

The N4J set out to make contact with Lludrow. It was not a thing to be quickly or easily accomplished. Even when it is known where it should be, it is far from easy to track down and pinpoint as small a thing as a fleet of human ships in the inconceivable vastnesses of interstellar space. For the very good reasons that there is always the chance of human error, that a safety margin must always be maintained—better to fall short of your target than to come out too close to it—and that there is, for practical purposes, no such thing as standing still in the universe. The N4J made a phase shift from where it calculated it was, to where it calculated the fleet to be, sent out a call signal and got no answer. It calculated again, signaled again—and so continued until it got first, a very faint signal in response, then a stronger one, and finally, one which permitted communication. Calculations were then matched between the flagship of the fleet and the N4J—and at last a meeting was effected.

By that time, better than three more days of the alloted week of incommunicado had passed. Donal went aboard the flagship with Ian, and took command.

"You've got the news?" was his first question of Lludrow when the two of them were together again.

"I have," said the Fleet commander. "I've had a ship secretly in shuttle constantly between here and Dunnin's World. We're right up to date."

Donal nodded. This was a different problem from the N4J's of finding Lludrow. A shuttle between a planet whose position and direction of movement was well known, and a fleet which knew it's own position and drift, could hop to within receiving distance of that same planet in one jump, and return as easily, provided the distance was not too great—as it sometimes was between the various planets themselves—for precise calculation.

"Want to see a digest—or shall I just brief you?" asked Lludrow.

"Brief me," said Donal.

Lludrow did. The hysteria that had followed on the charges of the Commission against Donal and Donal's disappearance had caused the existing governments, already shaky and torn by the open-market dissention, to crumble on all the worlds but those of the Exotics, The Dorsai, Old Earth, and the two small planets of Coby and Dunnin's World. Into the perfect power vacuum that remained, William, and the armed units of Ceta had moved swiftly and surely. Pro-tem governments in the name of the general populace, but operating directly under William's orders, had taken over New Earth, Freiland, Newton, Cassida, Venus, Mars, Harmony and Association and held them now in the iron grip of martial law. As William had cornered less sentient materials in the past, he had just prior to this cornered the field troops of the civilized world. Under the guise of training, reassignment, lease, stand-by—and a dozen other paper maneuvers, William had had under Cetan contract actual armies on each of the worlds that had fallen into disorder. All that had been necessary for him, was the landing of small contingents, plus officers for the units already present, with the proper orders.

"Staff meeting," said Donal.

His staff congregated in the executive room of the flagship. Lludrow, Fleet Commander, Ian, Field Commander—and half a dozen senior officers under each.

"Gentlemen," said Donal, when they were seated around the table. "I'm sure all of you know the situation. Any suggestions?"

There was a pause. Donal ran his eye around the table.

"Contact Freiland, New Earth—or some place where we have support," said Ian. "Land a small contingent and start a counteraction against the Cetan command." He looked at his nephew. "They know your name—the professionals on all sides. We might even pick up support out of the enemy forces."

"No good," said Lludrow, from the other side of the table. "It's too slow. Once we were committed to a certain planet, William could concentrate his forces there." He turned to Donal. "Ship for ship, we over-match him—but his ships would have ground support from whatever world we were fighting on; and our ground forces would have their hands full trying to establish themselves."

"True enough," Donal said. "What's your suggestion, then?"

"Withdraw to one of the untouched worlds—the Exotics, Coby, Dunnin's World. Or even the Dorsai, if they'll take us. We'll be safe there, in a position of strength, and we can take our time then about looking for a chance to strike back."

Ian shook his head.

"Every day—every hour," he said, "William grows stronger on those worlds he's taken over. The longer we wait, the greater the odds against us. And finally, he'll have the strength to come after us—and take us."

"Well, what do you want us to do, then?" demanded Lludrow. "A fleet without a home base is no striking weapon. And how many of our men will want to stick their necks out with us? These are professional soldiers, man—not patriots fighting on their home ground!"

"You use your field troops now or never!" said Ian shaking his head. "We've got forty thousand battle-ready men aboard these ships. They're my responsibility and I know them. Set them down on some backwater planet and they'll fall apart in two months."

"I still say—"

"All right. All right!" Donal was rapping with his knuckles on the table to call them back to order. Lludrow and Ian sat back on their floats again; and they all turned to look at Donal.

"I wanted you all to have a chance to speak up," he said, "because I wanted you to feel that we had explored every possibility. The truth of the matter is that both you gentlemen are right in your objections

—just as there is some merit in each of your plans. However, both your plans are gambles; long gambles —desperate gambles."

He paused to look around the table.

"I would like to remind you right now that when you fight a man hand-to-hand, the last place you hit him is where he expects to be hit. The essence of successful combat is to catch your enemy unawares in an unprotected spot—one where he is not expecting to be caught."

Donal stood up at the head of the table.

"William," he said, "has for the last few years put his emphasis on the training of ground troops—field troops. I have been doing the same thing, but for an entirely different purpose."

He placed his finger over a stud on the table before him and half-turned to the large wall behind him.

"No doubt all you gentlemen have heard the military truism that goes—you can't conquer a civilized planet. This happens to be one of the ancient saws I personally have found very irritating; since it ought to be obvious to any thinking person that in theory you can conquer anything—given the necessary wherewithal. The case for conquering a civilized world, becomes then a thing of perfect possibility. The only problem is to provide that which is necessary to the action."

They were all listening to him—some a little puzzled, others doubtfully, as if they expected all of what he was saying to turn suddenly into some joke to relieve the tension. Only Ian was phlegmatic and aborbing.

"Over the past few years, this force, which we officer, has developed the wherewithal—some of it carried over from previous forces, some of recent development. Your men know the techniques, although they have never been told in what way they were going to apply them. Ian, here, has produced through rigorous training the highly specialized small unit of the field forces—the Group, which under ordinary battle conditions numbers fifty men, but which we have streamlined to a number of thirty men. These Groups have been trained to take entirely independent action and survive by themselves for considerable periods of time. This same streamlining has gone up through the ranks—extending even to your fleet exercises, which have also been ordered, with a particular sort of action in mind."

He paused.

"What all this boils down to, gentlemen," he said, "is that we are all about to prove that old truism wrong—and take a civilized world, lock, stock, and barrel. We will do it with the men and ships we have at hand right here, and who have been picked and trained for this specific job—as the planet we are about to take has been picked and thoroughly intelligenced." He smiled at them. They were all sitting on the edges of their floats now.

"That world,"—he pressed the stud that had been under his finger all this time; the wall behind him vanished to reveal the three-dimensional representation of a large, green planet—"is the heart of our enemy's power and strength. His home base—Ceta!"

It was too much—even for senior officers. A babble of voice burst out around the table all at once. Donal paid no attention. He had opened a drawer at his end of the table and produced a thick sheaf of documents, which he tossed on the table before him.

"We will take over Ceta, gentlemen," he said. "By, in a twenty-four hour period, replacing *all* her local troops, *all* her police, *all* her garrisons and militia and law enforcement bodies and arms, with our own men."

He pointed to the sheaf of documents.

"We will take them over piecemeal, independently, and simultaneously. So that when the populace wakes up the following morning they will find themselves guarded, policed and held, not by their own authorities, but by us. The details as to targets and assignments are in this stack, gentlemen. Shall we go to work?"

They went to work. Ceta, large, low-gravity planet that it was, had huge virgin areas. Its civilized part could be broken down into thirty-eight major cities, and intervening agricultural and residential areas. There were so many military installations, so many police stations, so many armories, so many garrisons of troops—the details fell apart like the parts of a well-engineered mechanism, and were fitted together again with corresponding units of the military force under Donal's command. It was a masterpiece of combat preplanning.

"Now," said Donal, when they were done. "Go out and brief your troops."

He watched them all leave the conference room— all, with the exception of Ian, whom he had detained; and Lee, for whom he had just rung. When the others were gone, he turned to the two still with him.

"Lee," he said, "in six hours every man in the fleet will know what we intend to do. I want you to go out and find a man—not one of the officers—who doesn't think it'll work. Ian"—he looked over at his uncle— "when Lee finds such a man and reports to you, I want you to see that the man is sent up to see me, right away. Is that clear?"

The other two nodded; and went out, to do each his own job in his own fashion. So it was that a disgruntled Groupman from a particular landing force had a surprising meeting and surprisingly cordial chat with his commander in chief, and that they went out together, half an hour later, arm-in-arm, to the control room of the flagship, where Donal requested, and got, a voice-and-picture hookup to all ships.

"All of you," Donal said, smiling at them out of their screens after he had been connected, "have by this time been informed about the impending action. It's the result of a number of years of top-level planning and the best intelligence service we have been lucky enough to have. However, one of you has come to me with the natural fear that we may be biting off more than we can chew. Therefore, since this is an entirely new type of operation and because I believe firmly in the rights of the individual professional soldier not to be mishandled, I'm taking the unprecedented step of putting the coming assault on Ceta to a vote. You will vote as ships, and the results will be forwarded by your captain, as for or against, to the Flagship here. Gentlemen"—Donal reached out an arm and brought the man Lee had discovered into the screen area with him—"I want you to meet Groupman Theiss, who had the courage to stand up like a free man and ask questions."

Caught unawares, and dazzled by the sudden limelight into which he had been thrust, the Groupman licked his lips and grinned a little foolishly.

"I leave the decision to all of you," added Donal, and signaled for the viewing eyes to be cut off.

Three hours later, Groupman Theiss was back on his own ship, astounding his fellow soldiers with an account of what had happened to him; and the votes were in.

"Almost unanimous," reported Lludrow, "in favor of the attack. Only three ships—none of the first line, and none troop carriers—voting against."

"I want those three ships held out of the attack," said Donal. "And a note made of their names and captains. Remind me about that after this is over. All right." He got up from the float where he had been sitting in the Flagship Lounge. "Give the necessary orders, commander. We're going in."

They went in. Ceta had never taken the thought of enemy attack too seriously. Isolated in her position as the single inhabitable planet, as yet largely unexplored and unexploited, that circled her KO type sun of Tau Ceti; and secure in the midst of an interstellar maze of commitments that made every other planetary government to some extent dependent upon her good will, she had only a few ships in permanent defensive orbit about her.

These ships, their position and movement fully scouted by Donal's intelligence service, were boxed and destroyed by Donal's emerging fleet almost before they could give warning. And what warning they did give fell on flabbergasted and hardly-believing ears.

But by that time the assault troops were falling planetward, dropping down on city and military installation and police station behind the curtain of night as it swung around the big, but swiftly-turning world.

They came down in most cases almost on top of their targets, for the ships that had sowed them in the sky above had not been hampered in that action by enemy harassment. And the reaction of those on the ground was largely what might have been expected, when veteran troops, fully armed and armored, move in on local police, untried soldiers in training, and men relaxed in garrison. Here and there, there was sharp and bitter fighting where an assault unit found itself opposed to leased troops as trained in war as they. But in that case, reinforcements were speedily brought in to end the action.

Donal himself went down with the fourth wave;

and when the sun rose the following morning large and yellow on the horizon, the planet was secured. Two hours later, an orderly brought him word that William himself had been located—in his own residence outside the city of Whitetown, some fifteen hundred kilometers distance.

"I'll go there," said Donal. He glanced around him. His officers were busy, and Ian was off somewhere with an arm of his field troops. He turned to Lee. "Come on, Lee," he said.

They took a four-man platform and made the trip, with the orderly as guide. Coming down in the garden of the residence, Donal left the orderly with the platform, motioned Lee to accompany him, and entered the house.

He walked through silent rooms, inhabited only by furniture. All the residents of the house seemed to have vanished. After some little time, he began to think that perhaps the report had been in error; and that William was gone, too. And then he passed through an archway into a little anteroom and found himself facing Anea.

She met his gaze with a pale but composed face.

"Where is he?" asked Donal.

She turned and indicated a door on the far side of the room.

"It's locked," she said. "He was in there when your men started to land; and he's never come out. Nobody else would stay here with him. I . . . I couldn't leave."

"Yes," said Donal, somberly. He examined the locked door from across the room. "It wouldn't have been easy—for him."

"You care about him?" Her voice brought his head up sharply. He looked at her, seeking some note of mockery in her expression. But there was none. She was honestly questioning.

"I care somewhat for every man," he said. He walked

across the room to the door and laid his hand upon it on a sudden impulse, he put his thumb into the finger-lock—and the door swung open.

A sudden coldness blossomed inside him.

"Stay with her," he threw over his shoulder to Lee. He pushed open the door, found himself faced by another, heavier door—but one which also opened to his touch—and went in.

At the end of a long room William sat behind a desk occupied by a mass of papers. He stood up as Donal entered.

"So you're finally here," he said, calmly. "Well, well."

Going closer, Donal examined the man's face and eyes. There was nothing there to evoke such a notion; but Donal had the sudden suspicion that William was not as he should be.

"It was a very good landing. Very good," said William tiredly. "It was a clever trick. I acknowledge the fact, you see. I underestimated you from the first day I met you. I freely admit it. I'm quite conquered—am I not?"

Donal approached to the other side of the desk. He looked into William's calm exhausted face.

"Ceta is in my control," said Donal. "Your expeditionary forces on the other worlds are cut off—and their contracts aren't worth the paper they're written on. Without you to give the orders, it's all over with."

"Yes . . . yes, I thought as much," said William, with the hint of a sigh. "You're my doom, you know—my weird. I should have recognized it earlier. A force like mine among men must be balanced. I thought it would be balanced with numbers; but it wasn't." He looked at Donal with such a strange, searching expression that Donal's eyes narrowed.

"You're not well," said Donal.

"No, I'm not well." William rubbed his eyes, wearily. "I've been working too hard lately—and to no purpose. Montor's calculations were foolproof; but the more perfect my plan, the more perfectly it always went awry. I hate you, you know," said William, emotionlessly, dropping his hand and looking up at Donal again. "No one in all the history of man has ever hated the way I hate you."

"Come along," said Donal, going around the desk toward him. "I'll take you to someone who can help you—"

"No. Wait—" William held up his hand and backed away from Donal. Donal stopped. "I've got something to show you first. I saw the end the minute I got reports your men were landing. I've been waiting nearly ten hours now." He shivered, suddenly. "A long wait. I had to have something to keep myself occupied." He turned about and walked briskly back to a set of double doors set in a far wall. "Have a look," he invited; and pressed a button.

The doors slid back.

Donal looked. Hanging in the little close area revealed there was something only barely recognizable by what was left of its face. It was, or had been, his brother Mor.

SECRETARY FOR DEFENSE

Flashes of clarity began to return.

For some time, now and again, they had been calling him from the dark corridors down which he walked. But he had been busy, too busy to respond until now. But now—slowly—he let himself listen to the voices, which were sometimes those of Anea, and Sayona, and Ian, and sometimes the voices of those he did not know.

He rose to them reluctantly, slow to abandon the halls of darkness where he traveled. Here was the great ocean he had always hesitated to enter; but now that he was in it, it held him warm, and would have possessed him except for their little voices calling him back to petty things. Yet, duty lay to them, and not to it—that duty that had been impressed on him from his earliest years. The things undone, the things ill-done—and what he had done to William.

"Donal?" said the voice of Sayona.

"I'm here," he said. He opened his eyes; and they took in a white hospital room and the bed in which he lay, with Sayona and Anea and Galt standing beside it—along with a short man with a mustache in the long pink jacket of one of the Exotic psychiatric physicians.

Donal swung his legs over the edge of the bed and

stood up. His body was weak from long idleness, but he put the weakness aside the way a man puts aside any irritating, but small and unimportant thing.

"You should rest," said the physician.

Donal looked at him casually. The physician looked away; and Donal smiled, to ease the man.

"Thanks for curing me, doctor," he said.

"I didn't cure you," said the physician, a little bitterly, his head still averted.

Donal turned his glance on the other three; and a sadness touched him. In themselves, they had not changed, and the hospital room was like similar rooms had always been. But yet, in some way, all had dwindled—the people and the place. Now there was something small and drab about them, something tawdry and limited. And yet, it was not their fault.

"Donal" began Sayona, on a strangely eager, questioning note. Donal looked at the older man; and he, like the physician, looked automatically away. Donal shifted his glance to Galt, who also dropped his eyes. Only Anea, when he gazed at her, returned his glance with a child's pure stare.

"Not now, Sayona," said Donal. "We'll talk about it later. Where's William?"

"One floor down . . . Donal—" the words broke suddenly from Sayona's lips in a rush. "What did you do to him?"

"I told him to suffer," said Donal, simply. "I was wrong. Take me to him."

They went slowly—and, on Donal's part, a little unsteadily—out the door and down to a room on the floor below. A man there lay rigid on a bed like the one Donal had occupied—and it was hard to recognize that man as William. For all the asepsis of the hospital, a faint animal smell pervaded the room; and the face of the man was stretched into a shape of inhumanity by all known pain. The skin of the face was tautened over the flesh and bones like cloth of thinnest transparency over a mask of clay; and the eyes recognized no one.

"William—" said Donal, approaching the bed. The glazed eyes moved toward the sound of his voice. "Mor's trouble is over."

A little understanding flickered behind the Pavlovian focusing of the eyes. The rigid jaws parted and a hoarse sound came from the straining throat. Donal put his hand on the drum-tight brow.

"It'll be all right," he said. "It'll be all right, now."

Slowly, like invisible bonds melting away, the rigidity began to melt out of the man before them. Gradually he softened back into the shape of humanity again. His eyes, now comprehending, went to Donal as if Donal's tall form was one light in a cavern of lightlessness.

"There'll be work for you to do," said Donal. "Good work. All you ever wanted to do. I promise you."

William sighed deeply. Donal took his hand from the brow. The eyes dropped closed; and William slept.

"Not your fault," said Donal, absently, looking down at him. "Not your fault, but your nature. I should have known." He turned a little unsteadily, to the others who were staring at him with new eyes. "He'll be all right. Now, I want to get to my headquarters on Cassida. I can rest on the way. There's a great deal to do."

The trip from the Maran hospital where both Donal and William had been under observation, to Tomblecity on Cassida, passed like a dream for Donal. Waking or dreaming, he was still half in that ocean into which at Mor's death he had finally stepped, and the dark waters of which would never entirely leave him now. It was to become finally a matter of living with it—this sea of understanding along the margin of which he had wandered all the young years of his life, and which no other human mind would be able to comprehend, no matter how long his explanation. He understood now why he understood—this much had the shock of Mor's death brought him. He had been like any young animal, hesitant on the edge of the unknown, before his own uncertain desires and the sharp nudge of circumstance combined to tumble him headlong into it.

He had had to learn first to admit, then to live with, and finally to embrace his difference.

It had been necessary that what was uniquely Donal be threatened—first by the psychic shocks of the phase shift during the attack on Newton; and second by the manner of Mor's dying, for which only he knew how truly he was responsible—in order that he be forced to fight for survival; and fighting, discover fang and use of claw. In that final battle he had seen himself at last, full-imaged in the unplumbed depths; and recognized himself at last for what he was—a recognition no one else would ever be able to make. Anea, alone, would know without needing to understand, what he was; it is Woman's ancient heritage to appreciate without the need to know. Sayona, William, and a few such would half-recognize, but never understand. The rest of the race would never know.

And he—he himself, knowing and understanding, was like a man who could read, lifting the first small book from a library the shelves of which stretched off and away to infinity. A child in a taller land.

Anea, Sayona, Galt and the others came with him back to Tomblecity. He did not have to ask them to come with him. Now, they followed instinctively.

DONAL

The man was different.

Already, a few people were beginning to say it. And in this fact lay the seeds of a possible difficulty. It was necessary, considered Donal, that a means be taken to lightning-rod such a recognition, and render it harmless.

He stood in that position which was becoming very common with him of late, alone on a balcony of his residence outside Tomblecity, hands clasped behind his back like a soldier at parade rest, gazing out toward the Milky Way and the unknown stars. He heard Anea come up behind him.

"Sayona's here," she said.

He did not turn. And after a moment she spoke again.

"Do you want me to talk to him by myself?" she asked.

"For a little while," answered Donal, still without moving. He heard her footsteps move away from him into the bigness of the lounge behind him. He lost himself in the stars again; and, after a moment, there was the sound of a man's voice and a murmur of conversation between it and Anea's. At this distance, their words were indistinguishable; but Donal did not have to hear the words to know what they were saying.

Eight months had gone by since he had opened his

eyes onto the full universe that was exposed to his view alone. *Eight months,* thought Donal to himself. And in that short time, order had been returned to the civilized worlds. A parliament of peoples had been formed with an interiorly elected council of thirty-two Senior Representatives, two for each world. Today, here on Cassida, that parliament had voted on it's choice for a permanent Secretary for Defense—

Donal's mind reached out and enclosed the problem of what Sayona would, this moment, be saying to Anea.

". . . And then he went around the room, a little before the voting." Sayona's voice was now murmuring in the lounge behind him. "He said a word here, and a word there—nothing important. But when he was done, he had them in the palm of his hand. It was just as it was last month when he mingled with the delegates to the full parliament."

"Yes," replied Anea, "I can see it how it was."

"Do you understand?" asked Sayona, looking at her keenly.

"No," she said, serenely. "But I've seen it. He blazes —*blazes*—like an atomic flare among a field full of little campfires. Their small lights fade when they get too close to him. And he hoods his light, when he's amongst them, to keep from blinding them."

"Then you're not sorry—?"

"Sorry!" Her happy laugh tore his question to foolish ribbons.

"I know," said Sayona, soberly, "what effect he has on men. And I can guess his effect on other women. Are you sure you've got no regrets?"

"How could I?" But she looked at him suddenly, questioningly. "What do you mean?"

"That's why I've come tonight," said Sayona. "I've got something to tell you . . . if I can ask you a question after I'm through?"

"What kind of question?" she queried sharply.

"Let me tell you first," he said. "Then you can answer or not, whichever you like. It's nothing that can touch you—now. Only I should have told you before. I'm afraid I've put it off, until . . . well, until there was no more putting off possible. What do you know about your own gene history, Anea?"

"Why," she looked at him, "I know all about it."

"Not this part," said Sayona. "You know you were bred for certain things—" He put one old, slim hand on the edge of her float in a gesture that begged for understanding.

"Yes. Mind and body," she answered, watching him.

"And more," said Sayona. "It's hard to explain in a moment. But you know what was behind Montor's science, don't you? It treated the human race as a whole, as a single social entity, self-repairing in the sense that as its individual components die off they are replaced by the birth of new components. Such an entity is manipulable under statistical pressures, in somewhat the same manner that a human being may be manipulated by physical and emotional pressures. Increase the temperature of a room in which a man stands, and he will take off his jacket. This was William's key to power."

"But—" she stared at him. "*I'm* an individual—"

"No, no. Wait," Sayona held up his hand. "That was *Montor's* science. Ours on the Exotics had somewhat the same basis, but a differing viewpoint. We regarded the race as manipulable through its individuals, as an entity in a constant state of growth and evolution by reason of the birth of improved individuals among the mass that constituted it. Gene-selection, we believed, was the key to this—both natural or accidental, and controlled."

"But it is!" said Anea.

"No," Sayona shook his head slowly. "We were wrong. Manipulation by that approach is not truly possible; only analysis and explanation. It is adequate for an historian, for the meditative philosopher. And such, Anea, have we of the Exotics been, wherefore it seemed not only valid, but complete, to us.

"But manipulation by that means is possible only in small measure—very small. The race is not controllable from within the race; such gene-selection as we did could use only those characteristics which we *already* knew and understood. And it repelled us from those genes which we detected, and could not understand, and, of course, we could not work with ones we did not know existed, or could exist.

"We were, without seeing the fact, crippled both at the beginning and the end; we had only the middle. We could not conceive of characteristics to breed toward—goals—which were not already presented to us, and already understood by us. That was the proper end, however—truly new characteristics. And the beginning was, necessarily, truly new genes, and gene-combinations.

"The problem was stated long ago; we deceived ourselves that the statement was not meaningful. Simply, it is this; could a congress of gorillas, gathered to plan the breeding of the supergorilla, plan a human being? Discard the line of development of mightier muscles, stronger and longer teeth, greater specialization to master their tropical environment?

"Manipulation of the race from within the race is a circular process. What we can do, the valuable thing we can do, is to stabilize, conserve, and spread the valuable genetic gifts that come to us from outside our own domain.

"William—and you must have known this better than any one else, Anea—belongs to that small and select group of men who have been the conquerors of history. There's a name, you know, for this rare and freakish individual—but a name means nothing by itself. It's only a tag hung on something we never completely understood. Such men are unopposable—they can do great good. But also, usually, an equally great deal of harm, because they are uncontrolled. I'm trying to make you understand something rather complex. We, on the Exotics, spotted William for what he was when he was still in his early twenties. At that time the decision was taken to select the genes that would result in you."

"*Me!*" She stiffened suddenly, staring at him.

"You." Sayona bent his head to her briefly. "Didn't you ever wonder that you were so instinctively opposed to William in everything he did? Or why he was so perversely insistent on possessing your contract? Or why we, back on Kultis, allowed such an apparently unhappy relationship to continue?"

Anea shook her head slowly. "I . . . I must have. But I don't remember—"

"You were intended as William's complement, in a psychological sense." Sayona sighed. "Where his instincts were for control for the sake of controlling, yours were toward goals, purposes, and you did not care who controlled so long as the control was directed toward that purpose. Your eventual marriage —which we aimed for—would have, we hoped, blended the two natures. You would have acted as the governor William's personality needed. The result would have beneficial . . . we thought."

She shuddered.

"I'd never have married him."

"Yes," said Sayona with a sigh, "you would have. You were designed—if you'll forgive the harsh word —to react at full maturity to whatever man in the galaxy stood out above all others." A little of Sayona's gravity lifted for a moment, and a twinkle crept into his eyes. "That, my dear, was by no means difficult to provide for; it would have been near impossible to prevent it! Surely you see that the oldest and greatest of the female instincts is to find and conserve the strength of the strongest male she can discover. And the ultimate conservation is to bear his children."

"But—there was Donal!" she said, her face lighting up.

"Quite so," Sayona chuckled. "If the strongest male in the galaxy were wrongly directed, misusing his great strength—still, for the sake of the great value of that strength, you would have sought him out. Strength, abilities, are tools; these are important. How they are used is a separate matter.

"But with Donal on the scene . . . Well, he was the ruin of all our theories, all our plans. The product of one of those natural accidents, outside our domain, a chance combining of genes even superior to William's. The blending of a truly great line of thinkers, with an equally great line of doers.

"I failed to realize this, even when we tested him." Sayona shook his head as though to clear it. "Or . . . perhaps our tests were just not capable of measuring the really important characteristics in him. We . . . well, we don't know. It's that that worries me. If we've failed to discover a true mutation—someone with a great new talent that could benefit the race, then we have failed badly."

"Why, what would it have to do with you?" she asked.

"It would be in the area where we are supposed to have knowledge. If a cyberneticist fails to recognize that his companion has a broken bone, he is not culpable; if a physician makes the same mistake, he merits severe punishment.

"It would be our duty to recognize the new talent, isolate it, and understand it, we on the Exotics. It may be that Donal has something he does not recognize himself." He looked at her. "And that is the question I must ask you. You are closer to him than anyone else; do *you* think Donal may have something—something markedly different about him? I don't mean simply his superior genius; that would be simply more of the same kind of thing other men have had; I mean some true ability over and above that of the normal human."

Anea became very still for a long moment, looking beyond rather than at Sayona. Then she looked at Sayona again, and said, "Do you want me to guess? Why don't you ask him?"

It was not that she did not know the answer; she did not know how, or what she knew, nor did she know how to convey it, nor whether it was wise to convey it. But the knowing within her was quietly and completely certain that Donal knew, and would know what should and should not be said.

Sayona shrugged wryly. "I am a fool; I do not believe what all my own knowledge assures me. It was perfectly certain that the Select of Kultis would make such an answer. I am afraid to ask him; knowing that makes the fear no less. But you are right, my dear. I . . . will ask him."

She lifted her hand.

"Donal!" she called.

Out on the balcony he heard her voice. He did not move his eyes from the stars.

"Yes," he answered.

There were footsteps behind him, and then the voice of Sayona. "Donal—"

"You'll have to forgive me," said Donal, without

turning. "I didn't mean to make you wait. But I had something on my mind."

"Quite all right," said Sayona. "I hate to disturb you —I know how busy you've been lately. But there was a question I wanted to ask."

"Am I a superman?" asked Donal.

"Yes, that's essentially it," Sayona chuckled. "Has somebody else been asking you the same question?"

"No," Donal was smiling himself. "But I imagine there's some would like to."

"Well, you mustn't blame them," said Sayona, seriously. "In a certain sense, you actually are, you know."

"In a sense?"

"Oh," Sayona made a little dismissing gesture with his hand. "In your general abilities, compared to the ordinary man. But that wasn't my question—"

"I believe you have said that a name is without meaning in itself. What do you mean by 'Superman'? Can your question be answered, if that tag has no meaning, no definition?

"And who would want to be a Superman?" asked Donal in a tone halfway between irony and sadness, his eyes going to the depth beyond depth of starspace. "What man would want sixty billion children to raise? What man would cope with so many? How would he like to make the necessitous choices between them, when he loved them all equally? Think of the responsibility involved in refusing them candy when they shouldn't—but could—have it, and seeing that they went to the dentist against their wills! And if 'Superman' means a unique individual—think of having sixty billion children to raise, and no friend to relax with, complain to, to blow off steam to, so that the next day's chores would be more bearable.

"And if your 'Superman' were so super, who could force him to spend his energies wiping sixty billion

noses, and cleaning up the messes sixty billion petu-
lant bratlings made? Surely a Superman could find
some more satisfying use for his great talents?"

"Yes, yes," said Sayona. "But of course, I wasn't
thinking of anything so far-fetched. He looked at
Donal's back with mild annoyance. We know enough
about genetics now to realize that we could not have,
suddenly, a completely new version of the human
being. Any change would have to come in the shape
of one new, experimental talent at a time."

"But what if it were an undiscoverable talent?"

"Undiscoverable?"

"Suppose," said Donal, "I have the ability to see a
strange new color? How would I describe it to you—
who cannot see it?"

"Oh, we'd locate it all right," replied Sayona. "We'd
try all possible forms of radiation until we found one
you could identify as the color you were seeing."

"But still you wouldn't be able to see it, yourselves."

"Well, no," said Sayona. "But that would be hardly
important, if we knew what it was."

"Are you sure?" persisted Donal, not turning. "Suppose there was someone with a new way of thinking,
someone who in childhood forced himself to do his
thinking within the framework of logic—because that
was the only way those around him thought. Gradually, however, as he grows older he discovers that
there are relationships for him that do not exist for
other minds. He knows, for example, that if I cut
down that tree just below us out here in my garden,
some years in time, and some light-years in distance
away, another man's life will be changed. But in logical terms he cannot explain his knowledge. What
good would it do you then, to know what his talent
was?"

"No good at all, of course," said Sayona, good-humoredly, "but on the other hand it would do him no good at all, either, since he lives in, and is part of a logical society. In fact, it would do him so little good, he would undoubtedly never discover his talent at all; and the mutation, being a failure, would die aborning."

"I disagree with you," said Donal. "Because I, myself, am an intuitional superman. I have a conscious intuitive process. I use intuition consciously, as you use logic, to reach a conclusion. I can cross-check, one intuition against the other, to find out which is correct; and I can build an intuitive structure to an intuitive conclusion. This is one, single talent—but it multiplies the meaning and the power of all the old, while adding things of its own."

Sayona burst out laughing.

"And since, according to my own argument, this ability would do you so little good that you wouldn't even be able to discover it, it therefore stands that you wouldn't be able to answer my question about being a superman in the affirmative, when I ask it! Very good, Donal. It's been so long since I've had the Socratic method used in argument against me I didn't even recognize it when I came face to face with it."

"Or perhaps you instinctively would prefer not to recognize my talent," said Donal.

"No, no. That's enough," said Sayona, still laughing. "You win, Donal. Anyway, thank you for setting my mind at rest. If we had overlooked a real possibility, I would have held myself personally responsible. They would have taken *my* word for it and—I would have been negligent." He smiled. "Care to tell me what the real secret of your success has been, if it's not a wild talent?"

"I *am* intuitive," said Donal.

"Indeed you are," said Sayona. "Indeed you are. But to be merely intuitive—" he chuckled. "Well,

thank you, Donal. You don't know how you've relieved my mind on this particular score. I won't keep
you any longer." He hesitated, but Donal did not turn
around. "Good night."

"Good night," said Donal. He heard the older man's
footsteps turn and move away from him.

"Good night," came Sayona's voice from the lounge
behind him.

"Good night," answered Anea.

Sayona's steps moved off into silence. Still Donal
did not turn. He was aware of the presence of Anea
in the room behind him, waiting.

"Merely intuitive," he echoed to himself, in a whisper. *"Merely—"*

He lifted his face once more to the unknown stars,
the way a man lifts his face from the still heat of
the valley to the coolness of the hills, in the early part
of the long work day when the evening's freedom is
yet far off. And the look on his face was one which
no living person—not even Anea—had seen. Slowly,
he lowered his eyes, and slowly turned; and, as he
turned, the expression faded from him. As Anea had
said, carefully he hooded the brilliance of his light
that he might not blind them; and, turning full
around at last, entered once more, and for a little
while again, into the habitation of Man.

THE END

DAW=sf BOOKS

GREAT NOVELS OF HEROIC ADVENTURE ON EXOTIC WORLDS

☐ **THE TIDES OF KREGEN** by Alan Burt Akers.
(#UY1247—$1.25)

☐ **RENEGADE OF KREGEN** by Alan Burt Akers.
(#UY1271—$1.25)

☐ **KROZAIR OF KREGEN** by Alan Burt Akers.
(#UW1288—$1.50)

☐ **KIOGA OF THE WILDERNESS** by William L. Chester.
(#UW1253—$1.50)

☐ **ONE AGAINST A WILDERNESS** by William L. Chester.
(#UW1280—$1.50)

☐ **ALDAIR IN ALBION** by Neal Barrett, Jr.
(#UY1235—$1.25)

☐ **ALDAIR, MASTER OF SHIPS** by Neal Barrett, Jr.
(#UW1326—$1.50)

☐ **HADON OF ANCIENT OPAR** by Philip José Farmer.
(#UW1241—$1.50)

☐ **FLIGHT TO OPAR** by Philip José Farmer.
(#UW1238—$1.50)

☐ **BUNDUKI** by J. T. Edson.
(#UW1243—$1.50)

☐ **THE NAPOLEONS OF ERIDANUS** by Pierre Barbet.
(#UY1240—$1.25)

☐ **HUNTERS OF THE RED MOON** by Marion Zimmer Bradley.
(#UY1230—$1.25)

☐ **DIADEM FROM THE STARS** by Jo Clayton.
(#UW1293—$1.50)

☐ **A WORLD CALLED CAMELOT** by Arthur H. Landis.
(#UY1244—$1.25)

☐ **THE BARBARIAN OF WORLD'S END** by Lin Carter.
(#UW1300—$1.50)

DAW BOOKS are represented by the publishers of Signet and Mentor Books, THE NEW AMERICAN LIBRARY, INC.

DAW BOOKS

☐ **THE 1977 ANNUAL WORLD'S BEST SF.** Featuring Asimov, Tiptree, Aldiss, Coney, and a galaxy of great ones. An SFBC Selection. (#UE1297—$1.75)

☐ **THE 1976 ANNUAL WORLD'S BEST SF.** A winner with Fritz Leiber, Brunner, Cowper, Vinge, and more. An SFBC Selection. (#UW1232—$1.50)

☐ **THE 1975 ANNUAL WORLD'S BEST SF.** The authentic "World's Best" featuring Bester, Dickson, Martin, Asimov, etc. (#UW1170—$1.50)

☐ **THE DAW SCIENCE FICTION READER.** The unique anthology with a full novel by Andre Norton and tales by Akers, Dickson, Bradley, Stableford, and Tanith Lee. (#UW1242—$1.50)

☐ **THE YEAR'S BEST FANTASY STORIES: 2.** The only annual of its kind, edited by Lin Carter, and starring DeCamp, Davidson, Swann, Leiber, and many more. (#UY1248—$1.25)

☐ **THE YEAR'S BEST HORROR STORIES: SERIES IV.** Another great DAW service volume, this one has Hal Clement, Lafferty, Lumley, Leiber, and other favorites. (#UY1263—$1.25)

DAW BOOKS are represented by the publishers of Signet and Mentor Books, THE NEW AMERICAN LIBRARY, INC.

Presenting JOHN NORMAN in DAW editions . . .